1 of

Brought up in Ayrshire, Alice Renton worked at various jobs in London before moving, after her marriage, to Canada. On returning to the UK two years later, she settled in Sussex with her husband, Tim Renton, who became an MP in the '70s. They have five adult children. She divides her time between London, Sussex and Scotland and runs a tree nursery and consultancy business.

Alice Renton has written two non-fiction books, *VICTORIA, The Biography of a Pigeon* and *TYRANT OR VICTIM? A History of the British Governess*. *Winter Butterfly* is her first novel.

Winter Butterfly

Alice Renton

First published in 1996
by HEADLINE BOOK PUBLISHING

First published in paperback in 1996
by HEADLINE BOOK PUBLISHING

A HEADLINE REVIEW paperback

10 9 8 7 6 5 4 3 2 1

ISBN 0 7472 5479 6

Printed and bound in Great Britain by
Cox & Wyman Ltd, Reading, Berks

HEADLINE BOOK PUBLISHING
A division of Hodder Headline PLC
338 Euston Road
London NW1 3BH

For my dear family,
whose behaviour so far
has been very encouraging

Chapter One

'I hope I can do it.' The voice on the telephone was hesitant.

'If anyone can, you can.'

'It's very risky, you realise?'

'And it's my last chance.' The second voice was pleading. 'I'll make it worth your while.'

'You'll be sharing the risks, don't worry. Right. We'll give it a go. I need a lot more detail.'

'You shall have it, Terry. Meet me here at one.'

The day began as it meant to go on, raining in the steady, listless way that it had rained all week.

Mrs Robert Rokeby-Jones eased herself on to her back and studied, as she had studied every morning for so many years, the ceiling above her bed.

A light-brown patch had appeared some ten years earlier in the corner nearest to her bedside table, just above the end of the curtain rail that spanned the wide window. For a time this patch had been vague in its growth, expanding spasmodically in a shapeless sort of way, as if uncertain what to make of itself. Then, slowly, it had taken form, and the unmistakable shape of a knight in armour had emerged, just from the waist upwards, with the visored helmet looking towards the arched rise of his horse's neck, which ended in a suggestion

1

of pricked ears. The lower parts of both knight and horse remained a slowly spreading, amorphous stain, but the upper sections were clearly defined, occupying and giving a special interest to that corner of the ceiling.

On this wet morning, however, there was a new development. A pale but hefty lance was taking shape, rising at a forty-five-degree angle from the pommel of the saddle. If it occurred for a second to Mrs Rokeby-Jones that it might be seen as a monstrous phallus she discarded the thought at once. She knew that if she allowed herself to see it as a phallus, a phallus it would be for ever, and she preferred her courtly friend to be armed in a fashion more in keeping with the romantic image of knight errantry.

Another thought was less easily disposed of. The damp patch on the ceiling had recently taken on a more active life. She ought really to mention it to someone. She analysed her reluctance to do this. Last time Mrs Rokeby-Jones had mentioned damp to her son, Patrick, he had said:

'It's hardly worth mending the roof, since you're the only person sleeping in that part of the house. I suggest you move downstairs, where it's warmer and drier. You can't enjoy going up and down all the time, anyway. You'll fall, one of these days.'

She didn't want to leave this room. It had been her bedroom as a child and for the last forty-odd years, and she was used to it. And she was particularly fond of the damp patch. It was friendly and familiar, and she would miss it. Nor did she fancy sleeping on the ground floor. Faces at the window, perhaps. And she did not object to going up and down stairs. It was exercise, after all, even though she no longer took them at a run as she once had, a long time ago.

But Patrick would persuade her, given half a chance. He always seemed to be able to persuade her to do things she didn't want to do.

So she decided to keep the damp patch to herself, until someone else noticed its spread. Then, she supposed, someone, probably her son-in-law Lionel, would be cross, and she would feel guilty. Then there would be the fuss of builders banging about the house. And there would be expense, which would lead to more discussions about money, and that would all lead again to another subject that was always in their minds, and that she did not want to think about.

She groped awkwardly for the watch which lay on the table beside her. Her searching hand knocked over a glass of water and a spreading pool dripped steadily on to the carpet.

She sighed. Looking upward, she located the button at the end of a wire wound round the mahogany bedhead, and pressed it.

In the kitchen, at the end of a narrow passage leading from the main hall, a buzzer rasped. A few minutes later it stuttered again, for longer. And again a few minutes after that.

Then Mrs Rokeby-Jones rolled on her side and slid her long legs over the side of the bed.

From the wall telephone in the kitchen she rang her middle daughter, Louise, who did not answer. Then she rang her youngest, Flora.

'I think she must have gone.'

'Gone? The woman? You've got to be joking. She was there yesterday. I spoke to her.'

'I don't know what you said, Flora, but she was in a mood last night, when she gave me my supper. It might be more sensible if you let me speak to my own employee, since it I who have to . . .'

'Oh, Mother, you know you are putty in their hands. I'll come down, I suppose.'

3

'Really, there's no need. It is very sweet of you, but . . .'

There was no point in going on, since the line had gone dead, leaving Mrs Rokeby-Jones staring at the handset. She shrugged.

Flora did come, arriving mid-morning from London, her car wheels digging a hole in the gravel as she slid to a halt. A sure sign of temper, thought Mrs Rokeby-Jones.

She had gathered her courage together, and planned to speak while it lasted. She began in the front hall, as Flora pulled off her jacket and dumped it with her shoulder bag on a chair.

'Flora, I think I shall ring the agency myself. I can cope with this and I . . .'

'Mother, let's not have this argument again, please. You know you're not any good at negotiating with these people. You just end up paying them too much and getting the ones that don't work, or they steal, or whatever. I am trained at this kind of thing, and you must just leave it to me.'

The courage was slipping, but Mrs Rokeby-Jones took a tug on it.

'I don't really think that redundancy counselling is necessarily a . . .'

'Give me the phone,' said Flora, pushing past her mother to where it stood on a small fruit-wood table in the drawing room. 'Where's the number? I don't only do redundancy counselling. You could spend some time getting your address book in order, Mother. You're not exactly busy. Is this it?'

She dialled, and Mrs Rokeby-Jones looked out of the window at the dripping trees.

With her hand over the mouthpiece Flora fired questions and answered most of them herself.

'Did she take all her stuff? Yes? What's her room like

– in a mess I suppose. Was her money up to date? Yes, of course, it was banker's order. I think that is a mistake, don't you? A definite mistake.'

She glared at the receiver. 'Oh, come on, answer. I suppose she caught the early bus, unless someone picked her up. They are so devious, these women. It really is a bit rough. Poor you.'

She put the receiver down hard on the telephone.

'No answer. Damn. They're probably doing their wretched Christmas shopping. I hope their business crashes. Look, Mother, I've got to get back to London. I have a pig of a day. I'll leave something in the oven for your lunch, and I've brought some stuff from my fridge to keep you going. I'll ring Beatrice from the office – she's got time to cope'

A short time later, Flora left again, digging up more gravel.

'Look, she can't stay on her own alone in that house. And we will never get another woman before Christmas.'

The desk on whose edge Flora was resting her elbow was tidy to the point of bleakness. As she spoke she doodled with her left hand on a blank pad. Her right hand held a cordless telephone to her ear.

'Flora, *we* had her for Christmas last year,' wailed her sister Beatrice down the line, 'and I do think someone else should have a turn. Anyway, I am *so* busy. I have a mass of meetings, and I am absolutely up to my eyes right up to Christmas Day.'

'All right, Bea, calm down. Well, perhaps she can go to Patrick, do you think? Can you imagine Mother in that place? And what on earth do gays do at Christmas, anyway? Bugger all. Joke. Oh little town of Gomorrah.'

'Look.' Flora got the squeak of protest that she expected, and half-smiled as Beatrice's voice rose. 'I really don't like you talking about Patrick like that, and I don't want the children hearing this sort of thing about their uncle. For goodness' sake, he's your brother, our brother.'

'You've always been overprotective about your children,' said Flora. 'They certainly know a lot more about real life than you do. For goodness' sake, they're not infants. I remember the fuss you made when I kindly disillusioned them about Father Christmas. You'd have gone on until they'd been the laughing stock of the neighbourhood.'

'It was cruel, and you know it. They were tiny, and you spoiled all their fun.'

'Your fun, you mean,' said her sister. 'Dressing Henry up like a freak in a red hat and cotton wool and making him stand outside in the cold.'

Beatrice had always, in Flora's opinion, carried the 'Christmas is for the children' ethos far too far. Adults sharing the festive house had been expected uncomplainingly to put up with lack of sleep, of privacy, and of most other comforts, even the gastronomic ones, so that the children could have them all on demand. Her young had been monstrously spoilt.

'You're just jealous, Flora, because you haven't got any.'

'If I had children like yours, Bea, I'd have drowned them at birth.'

'Flora, you are odious. I really h . . .' Beatrice was spluttering with annoyance. 'I'm ringing off. You can ring me back later if you want to, but only to talk about Mother. I am *not* having her here for Christmas. I am far too busy. What's more, Henry is writing every day, he is at a *crucial* stage in his book and he must not be disturbed. So you can bloody well sort it out.'

And she rang off.

Flora sat for a minute looking at the telephone, chewing her lower lip. It might have been wiser on this occasion to resist baiting her sister. She looked at the pad and her drawing of Beatrice's face on the body of a spider, her legs encircling her brood. Another spider lay on its back beside her, with its legs in the air and a stream of 'z's issuing from its open mouth.

She took the pencil up again, and extended one of the spider's legs, so that it ended in a hand with outstretched fingers. Each of the fingers she embedded in a small container marked 'pie'.

Flora had inherited her ability to draw from her mother. There had been a time, as a girl, when she had longed to go to art school. Her mother, she thought wryly, would have let her. It would have led, she assumed, to quite a different life: Flora Jones, artist, rather than Flora Jones, counsellor. She had long ago dropped the Rokeby. Not only did she feel it was too florid for her job, but, more importantly, it linked her too much with things no longer relevant. She was free of all that.

She leant back in her chair and shut her eyes for a minute, emptying her mind and trying to calm her thoughts. Her next client was waiting, and deserved her full attention.

Meanwhile, not far from Winchester, Beatrice put down the telephone and turned to her husband.

'Here we go again. I don't know what Mother *does* with those women. Just when we thought we had got her one who would last. It's enough to drive you demented. I shall have to ring Patrick.'

Henry Fordham, sitting at the lunch table and crumbling some cheese on his plate, watched his wife with interest as she jabbed the buttons of the handset. As she started to talk, his eyes followed the plastic-covered telephone wire from the handset to the wall, and then in his mind he saw it emerging from the outside wall of the house and up on to a telegraph pole, the sharp fragments of Beatrice's voice skittering along inside it. He saw the telephone line swooping from pole to pole, down the valley and up over the Hampshire hills, joining other wires in a massive cable as it swept towards London, with the high-pitched tones still clearly distinguishable amid the burble of others, the words hopping jaggedly along, not fading, but getting ever more piercing as they neared Pimlico. Finally, diving like little darts through the wall of the house in Cambridge Street, up to the first floor, out through the white-on-white wildly contemporary sponged paintwork, up the wire and into the handset which he could see his brother-in-law tucking under his chin. He would be sitting in a black-and-white-triangle-upholstered armchair, dressed in a white silk dressing gown piped in black . . . A cigarette? Probably, although he was unlikely to have breakfasted yet. No, that was uncharitable. It was nearly two o'clock. Was he alone? Perhaps. Perhaps not. In any case, he was there, and apparently listening to his sister.

'She just walked out, evidently, with no warning at all,' said Beatrice. 'Yes . . . She woke up this morning and rang for her, and nothing happened. She got herself down to the kitchen and found a mad note on the table. What? . . . Well, it said that the bus service was inadequate, and so was the television reception. Oh yes, and she'd seen a mouse, so she was leaving. Mad. I think they're *all* mad, these women, but then you'd have to be, to do it in the first place. It's probably how they deal with unemployment in lunatic asylums. Perhaps we should word the next ad we put in "Wanted, someone mad enough to want to deal with an elderly, vague, hopeless lady in her own home" . . . I'm *not* being facetious. You make me interview them, and then blame me when it goes wrong – how can I *tell*? Anyhow, Mother would drive anyone mad even if I did find a sane one in the first place. I mean, you have at least to tell staff what you want. They expect it. Mother just smiles sweetly and lets them do what *they* want, so of course they take advantage . . . I *did* get references – I always do. They sounded all right, but you can't tell who's written them. In fact, I spoke to someone on the telephone who said she was reliable but unimaginative. That sounded all right, didn't it? . . . Well, she had enough imagination to leave an old woman alone in an enormous house . . . well, it's large, but the size of the house is not important, Patrick . . . bloody woman . . . This week of all weeks, when everything is such a rush. I have got to do a big dinner . . . well, a charity do actually, on Wednesday. How the *hell* am I going to get down there to sort Mother out? And we'll have to get some kind of woman right away to cover Christmas, and that costs a fortune. If only Flora would do something sometimes. It's *always* me. I know you're too busy, but I could do with a bit of help occasionally . . . Well, so you say, but Flora has just been saying the most horrible things to me, and she thinks that just because she has a full-time job she . . . Well, I'm not ringing her back, thank you very much, but perhaps *you* could ring Loopy and get *her* to suggest something, or do something . . . Yes, all right, when you've spoken to her . . . right . . . Yes. Bye.'

She sat down opposite her husband, who had lowered his eyes to his newspaper, and went on in the same tone, while pulling the dirty lunch plates towards her and stacking them noisily.

'I'm just fed up with Mother, Patrick, Flora, the whole business. No one ever thinks of me, *my* needs, *my* time. And you don't care either. You don't know how lucky you are, Henry, that your parents are dead . . . Are you listening?'

'I hear you.'

'I said, you don't know . . .'

'I heard what you said, my love. My ears, as you well know, are in a state of permanent loan. Actually, I am rather fond of my honoured mother-in-law.'

'Because you don't have to cope with her,' said Beatrice, turning in the doorway to the kitchen. 'Bring the glasses, will you? You must have finished by now. And the water jug. You only see her at Christmas, or whatever, and you pour her drinks and flirt with her. If you had to deal with her on a day-to-day basis, like I do . . .'

Henry stretched across the table.

'Is there any more coffee? You surprise me, beloved – I would have thought that the odd day, even the odd month goes by without your having any communication with your mother at all . . .'

Beatrice could be heard putting the plates down with a crash on the kitchen sideboard. She reappeared in the doorway, her eyes blazing. Beatrice's storms blew up with Hebridean speed.

'Henry, for God's sake, how can you be so ungrateful? *All* the family problems I cope with and you don't do a thing to help, and now you accuse me of neglecting my mother . . . It's . . . it's . . . un*believable*! Get your own beastly coffee . . .'

As the door slammed, Henry sighed and raised his newspaper again, only slightly more disturbed than he appeared.

An hour and a half later, Flora too was ringing her brother. There had been no answer from his flat, but his work number found him.

'Rokeby Antiques hold on a minute please I have a call on another line.'

'Patrick? Stop the rubbish, it's Flora. Thank God you're in, and obviously not busy. Look, we have got to do something about Mother at Christmas . . . No, she can't stay with me, because of my lodgers, and she can't stay at home, because her latest woman has walked out. You heard? Good . . . Well, it would be inhuman for her to stay at Bloomfield alone. I can't get Loopy or the Member on the telephone. They'll be at some wretched conference or coffee morning or something. You've got to find them, and explain that they've got to have her, because Beatrice is sticking her toes in, mean bitch. She says they had her last year, which I'd forgotten. They only had her for two days, anyway, so it can't exactly have exhausted them. But Bea is up to her eyes bossing some wretched charity about, and as usual her precious Henry is deep into some fearfully important part of his book and mustn't have his blessed tranquillity disturbed.'

She paused suspiciously.

'Are you listening?'

'Yes,' Patrick lied, putting down the *Daily Telegraph* and taking his feet off his desk. 'Every word. What a problem, darling. Now tell me, what do you suggest?'

'I just said,' said Flora. 'You've got to get Loopy and Lionel to have her. It's their turn, and Loopy can't say Lionel is too busy, because even he has to admit Parliament stops at Christmas, and he can do a hand's turn for the family for a change.'

'Excellent,' said Patrick. 'You're quite right. Loopy and Lionel . . .'

'I can't hear you. What are you doing?'

'Lighting a fag.' She heard a long exhalation. 'Yes. That's it. Loopy and Lionel.'

'Well, will you ring them?'

'Sorry,' said Patrick. 'No can do, darling. Telephone's buggered up.'

'But you're speaking on it now!' Flora's patience was going.

'Yep. Incoming calls only. Isn't it hell? Wrecking my life.'

'Oh, damn,' said Flora. 'You always have an excuse. Patrick, you've got to help me. I am always having to deal with Mother and her problems, and you never do a bloody thing, even when you go down there.'

'Come, darling, I did all that investigation last year about a home for her. It wasn't my fault she got better and decided to stay where she is. I wasted days and days. Exhausting. It's driving me mad, always at her beck and call. What did you say she was becking about this time?'

'I told you, Patrick, and so did Beatrice.' Flora's exasperation grew audibly. 'Listen. Her wretched woman has walked out.'

'Well,' said her brother languidly, 'tell her to find another one herself, instead of bothering us.'

'She can't. She's no good at it. She just takes the first one on offer, because she says you can't tell anyway till you get to know them. She has a point, actually. Hang on a minute.'

A head had appeared round the door of Flora's office and said, 'Your two o'clock appointment's here.'

'Say I'll be five minutes,' said Flora, 'and give him something intriguing to read. Patrick? You there? You know Father always did everything like that. And anyway, she'd never get one now, before Christmas. If you can't get Loopy to have her, you'd just better have her yourself.'

'Me? Darling, you're joking. Anyway, I've lent my spare room to a friend of a friend. He's an awful bore, between you and me, but there you are. Can't let him down over Christmas. I don't think she'd fancy him, actually, or vice versa.' He giggled.

Flora opened her mouth wide and looked at the ceiling.

'Flora,' Patrick went on, 'you always seem to think you know more about Mother's needs than anyone else, so since you're so good at it, why don't you have her up to London? You can go to the pantomime together. And you can bring her round here for a drink,' he added generously.

'Patrick, I told you, both my spare rooms are full. You know I take lodgers.'

'I thought one of them always went away over Christmas.'

'No,' said Flora. 'You thought wrong.'

She did not hesitate in lying to her brother. For one thing, he had been lying to her. But also she had been in the habit in recent years of spending the three days of Christmas helping in a centre for homeless people, 'palliating her conscience', and she had no wish to allow her family to know this or to start analysing her motives. In any case, the idea of being alone with her mother at Christmas, of all times, appalled her, and she guessed that it would secretly appal her mother too. Christmas being an emotive time, in the best of circumstances, there was always a danger of reminiscence bubbling up without warning. Reminiscence was something Flora did not need.

'Right, then,' she said. 'The ball's in your court. If you can't have her you are going to have to persuade Loopy, or we will all end up having to go to Mother at Bloomfield.'

'Oh, God.' She could hear Patrick sitting up, both mentally and in his chair.

'Exactly, oh God,' she said. 'But if we can't agree on who's going to have her, we'll all have to share her, and Bloomfield is the only house that is big enough, and we will have to take turns with the cooking, and that means you too. So you had better ring Loopy and persuade her, or else.'

Flora was not for a second seriously considering staying in her mother's house at Christmas or any other time, but that was another story, which she had no intention of discussing with her brother. In any case, this suggestion of a family party would, she knew, be effective.

'Oh God,' said Patrick again. 'All right. I'll try. I mean, I'll go and borrow someone's phone.'

There was a faint snore.

Louise Leetham turned to look at her husband, the Honourable Member for Surrey Downs, in the passenger seat beside her, and sighed as she saw that his head had already flopped forward and slightly to one side, his mouth gaping. She had counted on half an hour on the way home to talk about things, but if he was asleep already there was little chance of getting any sense out of him tonight.

Louise almost always drove when they were in his Surrey constituency, and she invariably took the wheel if they had been at a dinner or a fund-raising event and had been drinking. That is, if Lionel had been drinking. She had to refuse anything stronger than orange juice so as to be ready for when he said, squeezing her affectionately round the waist as he made his goodbyes, 'Meet my chauffeur – a little noisy on the gears, but worth every penny of her salary.' It always made them laugh. His speciality with his constituents was keeping them smiling. He started his speeches with a few jokes to 'soften them up', as he called it, followed by anecdotes of

14

events all happening at two or three a.m. 'in the House', demonstrating without actually stating it what late hours he had to keep to perform his duty to his constituents. Another ploy was 'Last Saturday I had spent an hour or two opening my mail when, suddenly . . .' It all added to the image of hard work and devotion. It was, in fact, Louise who opened his mail at weekends, justifying her small cut from his secretarial allowance, and the tiny number of letters that came to his ex-directory home address never took her more than five minutes to open unless there was an anti-abortion or an animal rights lobby on.

Lionel's little titbits of 'life of an MP' were always accompanied by hilarious stories which, if true, had usually happened to one of his colleagues. He kept a notebook full of second-hand jokes.

The audiences loved them.

'He's wonderful, your hubby. He works so hard, but he always sees the funny side. He must keep you in stitches.'

'Yes,' said Louise mechanically. 'He has some very funny stories.'

She might have added, 'and absolutely no sense of humour at all. His habit of telling funny stories gives a false impression of him. Life with Lionel is no joke.'

But she never did. She enormously enjoyed playing the role of the MP's devoted and supportive wife, and having people say how lucky he was to have her.

If Lionel knew he had little to say in a speech, he used more jokes. His speech tonight had been almost a parody of his own style: little more than a string of funny stories interspersed with generalisms on government policy that could have been read in any newspaper that week. Though she sat always with her head cocked upwards towards him, her eyes never leaving his face, and an expression of rapt interest on hers, it was rare that Louise heard anything in a speech of Lionel's that she had not already heard better expressed elsewhere.

She drove down the narrow lanes that made a short cut between the market town at the centre of the constituency and the rented house that was their base at weekends, 'where my constituents can find me weeding at their leisure'. As they neared it, Louise made up her mind. Lionel would be leaving early in the morning. He was flying from Heathrow at eight a.m. as a member of a parliamentary delegation to Kenya. She must speak to him now.

She pulled up in a farm gateway.

'Are we here?' Lionel yawned and stretched.

'No, I must talk to you.'

He peered out into the night.

'What the hell have you stopped here for?'

'I thought it was a nice picnic spot.'

'Louise, don't try to be funny. I have an early start. Go on.'

Louise restarted the engine and pulled into the road.

'Lionel, don't go to sleep again. I shan't see you for a week and there are some things we must talk about.'

'Well?' He slid back down in his seat, and shut his eyes.

'Lionel, please,' she said. 'I can't cope with it on my own. There are problems with Mother. Her woman walked out, and Patrick rang. I didn't tell you earlier because I knew you were concentrating on your speech. Beatrice is trying to get another, but she has to interview them, and meanwhile Mother is on her own. It is hopeless trying to get someone quickly at this time of year, so Patrick wondered could we possibly have her for Christmas?'

Lionel had been dropping off again but the last words roused him.

'No,' he said.

'Lionel, please, it wouldn't hurt, just once. It is only for a few days, perhaps a week, or till just after the New Year. She hasn't been for ages, and she is my mother.'

Lionel sat up in his seat.

'Now listen to me, Louise,' he said.

This is going to be a long one, she thought.

'I sometimes think that you have no idea of the strains of an MP's life. These breaks in the parliamentary sessions are for recuperation and to catch up on the work that one hasn't had time to finish. I would be letting my constituents down, and myself, and ultimately you and the children, too, if I didn't remember this. I am in no position to act as host to itinerant in-laws. You have a brother, and two sisters, one of whom has a good-sized house, all of whom have the time and leisure to entertain their mother. I have none of these, and I have a duty to sixty-three thousand voters, who do not expect me to return to work after a well-earned break as mentally and physically exhausted as I go into it. Just think a bit, in future, before you come up with suggestions that affect me as well as you.'

'Lionel,' said Louise, 'you need hardly see her. I will do everything. I tell you what, I will get a girl to do the meals, so that will free me to look after Mother and take her out for long drives and keep her out of your way, and . . .'

'And who would pay for that?' said Lionel explosively. 'You seem to think that a parliamentary salary is limitless. Do you know that a long-distance lorry driver earns the same salary as I do?'

Louise groped for the relevance of this interesting fact to Lionel's argument, but failed to find it.

'And imagine the extra heating bills,' Lionel continued. 'Old women are always cold. It would mean heating night and day, and yet another room to heat if you got a girl, probably a foreigner, and they're always cold too. I sometimes wonder whether you think at all.'

'I do think, quite a lot,' said Louise bravely. 'And I think we have a duty to Mother too.'

But she was beaten, to her considerable relief, and her conscience was entirely clear as to how hard she had tried. So that settled that. She could have anticipated word for word the rest of Lionel's argument.

'Your duty to your mother is to bring her to her senses, and to point out that she has a duty too. What has she ever done for us? She sits there in that huge house, gobbling electricity, waited on night and day by those women . . .'

And on it went, through the years of his mother-in-law's luxurious life, through his own struggle to care for her daughter despite the burdens of his career, to the inevitable end.

'There are places for people like her, where she will be properly cared for, and where she can – er – live out her life in dignity. What do you think we pay our taxes for? No, I don't mean a state home – don't squirm like that – you could find a perfectly decent private place, and it would cost a fraction of what it costs to keep that house going.'

You would think, thought Louise sourly, that he was paying to keep Mother in Bloomfield, that it was all coming out of his own pocket. But there was no point in saying this. It would mean listening to him covering up the real reason for his resentment. What he could not stand was the unrealised value of Bloomfield, the fact that the housing market was stronger and that he could not get his hands on the share of that value that would one day, presumably, come to Louise.

'I just can't quite see Mother in a home . . .' she said, with a residual pang of conscience, rubbing her hands up and down the sides of the steering wheel.

'She would be far happier, and you wouldn't be scratching around for somewhere for her to go every Christmas,' said Lionel conclusively.

'I think I had better go over there, to Bloomfield, during your week in Kenya.'

'You do that – it will do you good to have a break.'

The thought of his trip to Kenya cheered him, and so did the reminder that Louise believed it to be two days longer than was actually planned. It made him feel quite beneficent towards his wife.

He reached up and squeezed her hand, pinching her ring finger painfully against the wheel. She winced, but managed a smile.

'Anyhow, poppet, I'd much rather have a cosy Christmas with just the two of us, and the boys, of course, wouldn't you? Here we are, Loopy. Home Sweet Home.'

They drove between the tightly packed rhododendron hedges that lined the short driveway.

'What time do you want to be woken?' Louise asked, switching off the engine.

'Oh, about five thirty, I suppose. No breakfast, though. I'll get something on the aeroplane. Just a cup of coffee, and some toast and marmalade.'

This was Lionel being considerate.

Louise pictured herself as she would be the following morning, standing shivering on the doorstep in her dressing gown, watching the rear lights of Lionel's car until it was out of sight, knowing that his mind was already far beyond Heathrow. Then she would wonder if it was worth going back to bed.

Lionel walked into the house, followed by Louise. The telephone was ringing. She took it in the kitchen. It was her brother Patrick.

'Loopy?' he said. 'Me again. It's about Mother, and Christmas.'

'I can't handle this,' said Louise. 'I'll get Lionel.'

'Lionel, old chap,' said Patrick, as soon as his brother-in-law was on the line, 'we need your help. The mother-figure is all alone, her companion woman has walked out, she's alone in the house, Christmas is coming, Beatrice and Henry have got problems of some kind, Flora hasn't got a spare room, I'm booked, and we all think you should have her for Christmas. Care in the Community and all that. Set a good example to the voters. We know you'll do the right thing and give her a good time. And – no, don't say anything yet. If you have her, I promise you I will tackle her again about going into a home.'

Lionel Leetham swallowed his rising protest.

'How?'

'You leave that to me. I can persuade her into anything, given a bit of time. I'll tell her she owes it to us, Father would have wanted it, that sort of thing. I can do it.'

'Well, I hope you can, and high time too. But we can't have her here for Christmas, that's for sure. Much as I should like to help,' he added as an afterthought.

'Why not?' said Patrick. 'You've got oodles of space there in that house. You would hardly notice her.'

'Unfortunately,' said Lionel, leaning comfortably against the worktop and tucking his spare thumb into the sleeve hole of his waistcoat, 'what you refer to as my oodles of space is reserved for a constituency event on Christmas Eve, and the builders are moving in on the twenty-seventh to repair the roof well which is leaking into all the bedrooms. The house is virtually uninhabitable. We can't possibly have your mother here. You'll have to excuse me now, Patrick. I have an important call on the other line. Let us know what you decide.'

He put down the receiver.

'What a lot of fibs!' said his wife. 'Who'd ever have a constituency party on Christmas Eve?'

'One has to be firm with your brother. His own life is so given over to idleness that he has no concept of how busy others can be. He really cannot imagine that I can simply drop everything for days just to entertain your mother. I have a responsibility to my constituents. The correspondence piles up whatever the season. Fibs you may call it, but I shall have to go up to my office in the House most days, to sign letters and work on my report to the Cabinet.'

Louise wiped some crumbs from the worktop into her hand and dropped them into the waste bin. She had maintained and nurtured her ignorance of her husband's extramarital relationships for so long that she had almost come to believe herself that they had no irregularities in their marriage. But talk of going into the London office over Christmas was stretching even her capacity for appearing to be unsuspicious.

'Well, I expect Flora will think of something,' she said blandly. 'Only two days till the children come home. Will you have time to finish the Christmas shopping with me?'

Her tone became a little wistful. 'I've made a list.'

'Loops, you just don't seem to understand,' said Lionel, patting her bottom as he moved towards the staircase. 'I do actually lead a very busy life.'

He only called her Loops when he was in a good mood. She smiled gratefully.

'I'll manage then, darling,' she said.

At such times she had to remind herself consolingly that nothing in his life, his parliamentary affairs, his money affairs, his dreary little sexual escapades and even his relationship with his children, would hold together without her acquiescence and support. He was far too stupid to know it, but he was totally dependent on Louise, and this was her little secret that kept her going.

In any case, it was worth it. Louise was a snob, and she knew it. She loved and needed the tiny eminence that her position as an MP's spouse gave her, loved the interest that people at dinner parties expressed in her life. 'And do tell, have you often met the Prime Minister? What's he really like? And could you live in Number Ten, if you had to? What's it like inside?' She loved the annual Royal Garden Party, despite being adrift with her new hat in a crowd of three thousand people of whom she knew about ten. She even loved the way people in shops locally looked up when she wrote a cheque, and said, 'Any relation to the MP?'

She would never do anything to jeopardise it all.

Chapter Two

Bloomfield was a medium-sized Elizabethan manor house near the South Downs. It was close enough to their rising slopes to be sheltered from the prevailing south-west wind, far enough from them not to lose the light of the setting sun until well into the evening. It was surrounded by some fifteen acres of pastureland that had never been ploughed, but grazed by many generations of sheep. The fields in summer were rich with wild flowers, and good mature chestnuts and lime trees stood comfortably among them. A small stream surfaced from beneath the Downs and linked the fields to the garden. Bloomfield was within reach, but not within sight, of an attractive small town, with a regular seventy-minute train service to London. The tiny estate was itself surrounded by more private land, which was part of the South Downs Environmentally Sensitive Area, designated as being of Outstanding Natural Beauty and Special Scientific Interest. In other words, no one could build so much as a henhouse nearby without planning permission, which was as hard to obtain as a ticket to the moon.

Not to put too fine a point on it, Bloomfield was worth a bomb. That it had not been properly maintained for a decade and a half, hardly, indeed, since Lieutenant-Colonel Rokeby-Jones had had a terminal heart attack while berating his gardener, would not affect its selling price.

In the drawing room, which was full of good furniture and outdated decoration, Beatrice was looking disapprovingly at the shredded material on the arms of the sofa on which she was perched. Beatrice seldom relaxed in the depths of a chair, but always sat in a position from which she could leap to her feet and be useful.

'You would have thought that one of those women could occasionally have wielded a needle,' she said. 'I can't think what they think they are paid for.'

Then she returned to her theme. She was haranguing her sisters, who both lay sprawled on a sofa opposite.

'I still don't understand why you two couldn't have let me know you were coming. You *know* I am up to my eyes at home, and have had to drop *everything* to get here and cope. Henry can hardly boil an egg himself, and I had to rush out and get convenience things he can deal with, which costs a *fortune*. If you had told me you would be here I could have done some proper cooking for him.'

'He was not exactly going to starve in twenty-four hours,' said Flora.

'And I promised Jinny I would organise her flat for her this week,' Beatrice went on, 'and I have had to let her down *again*, which seems *so* unfair. It is too inconsiderate of you, but I suppose I am used to it.'

Flora surveyed her eldest sister with interest. It intrigued her that Beatrice could pretend that two grown-up children could take so much of a mother's time when they were self-supporting and living away from home. But she knew that Beatrice's need to be needed was an essential part of her, and she would happily run any kind of errand for her relatively unnoticing children. It hurt her that they now needed her so little, and the pretence that they relied on her was important to her self-esteem.

At the same time she was not naturally energetic, and her talk of ceaseless activity was a substitute for the real thing. The lack of appreciation, in which she wallowed so happily, was an inevitable result of this. What Beatrice really needed, reflected Flora unsympathetically, was a genuine problem to occupy her time and kick her into reality.

'Why on earth can't Jinny do her own flat?' she said, yawning.

'For goodness' sake, Flora,' said Beatrice, forgetting in her irritation to adopt her usual 'you couldn't possibly understand' tone to her youngest sister, 'Jinny has a very responsible job at Sotheby's, and gets home *exhausted* every evening – how can she possibly arrange to meet painters at her flat? It is hard enough for her to find time to choose the papers and curtain materials. And of course she likes to have my advice on that.'

'I should let her get on with it, idle kid. She just uses you.'

'Don't be silly, dear.' Beatrice had got the tone right now. 'She needs my help, and families don't let each other down. You wouldn't understand, not being married. You can just come and go at will. But you really *could* have telephoned and said you were going to be here, and then I needn't have come all this way.'

The habitual whine had returned to her voice. 'It's so unfair. I had to cancel a committee meeting as well.'

'How do you mean, cancel?' said Louise. 'You mean send your apologies?'

'Well, of course,' said Beatrice, 'and it looks very bad at the last minute like that, when one should be pulling one's weight.'

'It only gives other people a chance to pull their weight. Committees shouldn't depend on individuals.'

'I know that very well, Loopy. You can't teach me

about committees, thank you very much. I spend my *life* slaving away on committees. But I know all sorts of decisions will be taken which will simply mean more work for me when I get home, on top of everything I do already.'

The myth of Beatrice's frenetic activity and multiplicity of voluntary jobs had long been one only believed in by herself. It gave her an illusion of importance in the community which she fondly believed impressed her relations. It also helped to explain why she was so often away from home, and hid from them, she believed, the fact that in order to make ends meet she had a somewhat menial part-time catering job in a local golf club. It was not, she felt, deceitful to give this impression of being the mainstay of every local charity, because one day it would all be true. As soon as Henry had completed his great literary work she would take her proper place in society.

'Well, I tried to ring you yesterday evening,' said Flora, 'but you were never off the line, so I couldn't let you know. You're always gassing away on the telephone.'

'Well, I wasn't, so there,' said Beatrice. 'It was out of order. And I can't tell you what it has been like trying to get everything organised without a telephone. And I can't ring Henry now with it not working.'

'I expect he will enjoy the peace and quiet while you are away. With the telephone not ringing, I mean,' Flora added, just too late. 'He can get on with the deathless prose. How's the great book going?'

Beatrice ignored her, and spoke to Louise.

'Where has Lionel gone, anyway?'

'To Kenya.'

'Has he? What for?'

'It's a rather important parliamentary delegation, actually,' said Louise.

'What do they *do* on parliamentary delegations?' asked Beatrice.

'Especially rather important ones?' added Flora.

'Well,' said Louise, examining her nails, 'it's rather sensitive, so I can't tell you very much. He flew to Nairobi.'

This was the full extent of her knowledge of her husband's trip, but Beatrice was impressed into temporary silence.

Flora walked over to the window and wiped a hole in the condensation, the better to see the greyness of the day. The swelling folds of the Downs, which normally dominated the view, were swathed in low cloud, and invisible. There was nothing to be seen except dripping leaves, dripping bare branches and wet flagstones.

'I hate December,' she said venomously. 'And if there is going to be frost tonight, as they say, I don't see where it is going to come from. It looks like more rain to me.'

'Well, I didn't come all the way here to chat about the weather,' said Beatrice. 'I suppose I must put an advertisement together and post it, and then do some lunch, unless anyone else is feeling helpful. Heavens, it's nearly midday.'

She got to her feet.

'Why not repeat the old advertisement?' said Louise. 'Nothing has changed.'

'Because last time we only had one answer, which was the woman who just left.'

'Do we know why she left?'

'I expect Mother was tiresome, as usual, in some way,' said Beatrice. 'You can ask her. She's out somewhere with that awful dog, down by the stream, I think. That dog may be one reason the woman left – it really is quite disgusting now, and the whole house smells of pee. There is a place at the end of the bedroom passage that is full of its droppings, all hard. It's been going there for months, and the carpet is ruined.'

'It is a hideous carpet. And that dog means a lot to her,' said Flora.

'No, but Flora, it is filthy – you *know* it is. You always defend Mother. That dog is a real health hazard. And she feeds it from the table, on the same plates as people have to eat from. And its *disgusting* leaky eyes . . . It's time it was put down. *And* it sleeps in her bedroom. No wonder the women leave.'

'I thought you said they left because Mother was so tiresome,' said Louise. 'Actually, I always think of her as rather amenable.'

'Well, I don't actually mean tiresome, at least not with them, but she is so unrealistic. I mean, one has a good idea, *entirely* for her benefit, and she just vaguely wanders away from the subject. I was telling her this morning that it would only make sense for her to have her bedroom on the ground floor. When you are that age the *one* thing you don't do is strain yourself, and all the stairs make even *me* tired, running up and down them.'

'You could walk,' said Flora.

Beatrice went on.

'How can you keep a woman and expect her constantly to be going up and down stairs?'

'Well,' said Flora, 'she doesn't have to. Mother's not bedridden, or anywhere near it. I don't see why she shouldn't have any bedroom she wants. The woman only has to do a bit of dusting upstairs.'

Beatrice ignored her, addressing herself to Louise.

'And suppose Mother has a heart attack climbing up there. I mean, at her age you have to be rational. Seventy is seventy. I mean, Father was seventy-one when he died. Father's study would make a *perfectly* reasonable bedroom, and it's not far from the kitchen or from the woman's flat. It simply makes sense. Anyway, she wouldn't discuss it properly at all. She said there's an owl's nest in that big ash tree outside her bedroom window, and she has to keep an eye on it, for goodness' sake. I told her . . . well, in fact, we had a bit of a spat. I mean, I got a bit upset. That was when she went out with the dog, just before you arrived.'

'I thought something had happened,' said Flora. 'You had your pink look on. I suspect you have been trying to bully her.'

'Well, *you* would look pink if Mother had practically told you not to interfere,' said Beatrice, subsiding on to the window seat, her eyes filling with angry tears. 'I mean, it is *so* unfair, with all I do for her, slaving away, and when I am so busy. I *never* let her down when she needs me – I drop *everything* and come *rushing* over to cope. I only suggested . . . and she behaves as if . . .'

The rest was lost in a gush of sobs.

Her sisters watched impassively.

'Poor Mother,' said Flora.

'Oh, you beast, how *can* you? You beastly bitch. You always side with Mother, and you just pander to her. You never do anything really to help her. And Patrick says you both refused outright to have her for Christmas, which is so selfish. It's so *unfair*. I think you are *odious*.'

With her tear-streaked pink face and her fair crinkly hair sticking up where her anguished fingers had left it, she reminded her sisters of Beatrice at thirteen. Even her voice seemed to have gone back in years and assumed the old whining tone – 'it's so unfair'. To Beatrice, everything had always been so unfair.

'You look awful,' said Flora. 'For goodness' sake go and wash your face and calm down before Mother comes back. When you behave like this I honestly can't blame her for not wanting to discuss things with you. You get so worked up that . . . that . . .'

Flora's voice faded. Beatrice had stopped sobbing and was staring with her mouth open over Flora's shoulder. Louise gasped and Flora turned and saw the figure of her mother standing in the open doorway. Then her mouth fell open as well.

Mrs Rokeby-Jones had in youth been tall for a girl, and rather slim. She was still slim, and age had altered her basic framework very little. Her head and neck no longer rose quite as proudly and gracefully from her shoulders, and she walked a little stiffly now, and with a heavier tread. But she wore her clothes with style, old-fashioned though they were, and was still as tall as any of her daughters.

Today she was dressed in a heavy knitted cardigan, dark purple over a paler, thinner sweater on which lay a short string of pearls. Her lower half was clad in elderly brown box-pleated tweed and the still slender legs were encased in thick brown tights. Earlier she had been wearing a pair of flat-heeled brown slip-on shoes. Now she was wearing only one. This was not the only surprise. The discoloration in the tweed skirt, a darkening that extended almost to Mrs Rokeby-Jones' waist, showed that it had very recently been immersed in extremely dirty water. The dripping arms of the cardigan made it clear that they too were soaked, almost to the shoulders. The remaining shoe and both legs were covered in mud, as were her hands.

But the most striking thing of all was not the streaks of mud on Mrs Rokeby-Jones' face, but her expression of utter despair and desolation.

'Mother!' Louise was the first who managed to speak. 'What on earth . . .?'

Mrs Rokeby-Jones shook her head slowly from side

to side. She raised her hands slightly, and dropped them again.

'Sherry. Sherry.'

'What's happened? A drink? I'll get you some. Sit down.'

Beatrice was bustling about.

'No, it's the dog, you fool,' said Flora. 'What's happened, Mother?'

'Oh, Flora, it's you.' Mrs Rokeby-Jones looked at her youngest daughter without curiosity. 'It's Sherry. I think he's drowned. I couldn't find him under the water. What shall I do? Help me.'

'Where was this? What happened?' asked Louise, leading her mother to a chair.

'The flooding. There's been so much rain. He thought he could walk across the little weir, as usual, but it was much deeper, and he slipped off. He just disappeared.'

'Mother, honestly,' said Beatrice. 'It's a merciful release. He was so old.'

Mrs Rokeby-Jones stared at her.

'He just disappeared and didn't come up again,' she said.

'He probably knew nothing about it,' said Louise. 'You're soaking wet, Mother. You'd better come upstairs.'

Her mother shook her head in disbelief.

'You just have no idea, do you, any of you.'

Flora put an arm awkwardly round her shoulders.

'Come upstairs, Mother. I am so sorry about it, but I don't see what we can do.'

'You mean you won't help me look for him?'

'Well, what's the point?' said Louise. 'If you couldn't find him, how can we? And it's raining again. Mother, look, it's all for the best, really.'

'Mother, where did you say he went in?' said Flora.

At that moment a bell rang, long and loud.

'That's the front door,' said Louise. 'Who on earth has to come just at this moment? Get Mother upstairs and clean her up.'

But Mrs Rokeby-Jones was already on her feet and moving towards the hall. She opened the door, and cried out.

On the step stood a woman in a shapeless woollen hat and a raincoat that was tied at the waist with a piece of rope. In her arms she carried the sodden body of a hairy dog.

'Sherry – oh, you found him. My poor Sherry.'

'He's not dead,' said the woman.

'Not?'

'Not quite.'

'What shall we do?'

'Heat. A stove?'

Wordlessly Mrs Rokeby-Jones led the woman towards the kitchen.

'Where on earth did she come from?' said Flora, back in the drawing room some minutes later.

'I have no idea. Who is she, anyway? I thought we'd got rid of that disgusting dog at last,' said Beatrice.

'God knows. She's clearly a tramp.' Louise's instinctive urge to ring the police had been suspended in deference to her mother.

'Where did she appear from, for goodness' sake?' said Flora again. 'And how did she know where the dog was? How did she know the dog was drowning?'

'She must have been in the garden. Probably waiting to burgle the house,' Louise said, with some satisfaction.

'You'd better get along to the kitchen, Bea,' said Flora, 'and get the silver out of the dishwasher.'

'Why don't you? The kitchen stinks of wet dog. They've actually got it lying on the Aga wrapped in a blanket. The whole place will have to be fumigated. I'm not going to cook on it after that. How are we going to have lunch?'

'Oh, come on Bea,' said Louise, 'even you can eat a sandwich for once. We don't all need three-course lunches, like Henry, to sustain our creative urges.'

'Shut up, Loopy, or she'll blub again,' said Flora.

'You beast, Loopy, you know Henry is the least demanding person in the . . . Anyway, who's talking? We all know Lionel and the way he messes you around. Yes, he does, he does!' Beatrice's voice rose triumphantly. 'Patrick told me that . . . Oh, you bitch.'

A hard push laid her back in her chair, but she managed to kick Louise's shin as she went, causing a cry of pain.

'Children, children, calm down,' said Flora. 'Remember we have sickness in the house. Poor Sherry needs quiet in his period of convalescence.'

She was enjoying herself. She had always had a gift for starting quarrels between her sisters, from which she then kept well clear.

Then she saw the woman standing in the doorway, watching them. The front of her ancient raincoat was streaked with mud. Wan wispy strands of wet hair strayed from under a tea-cosy hat and stuck against her cheeks. The narrow face was expressionless.

Flora stood up.

'Thank you for your help,' she said. 'I know my mother is very grateful. We will look after everything now. We don't want to hold you up any more, and I expect you will be wanting to get on your way.'

'No,' said the woman, 'not as long as I am needed here.'

For a moment Flora was taken aback.

'I don't think you understand,' she said. 'You are not

needed any more. We are very grateful to you for saving my mother's dog, but you can go now. I will come with you to the door.'

'No,' said the woman again.

Louise and Beatrice listened in fascination, aware that Flora was for once at a loss.

'I beg your pardon, but . . .'

At this moment their mother appeared.

'Please,' she said to the woman, 'will you come quickly?'

As they disappeared, Beatrice said, 'Well!' in a tone so full of meaning that Flora said, 'Shut up, you cow,' and Beatrice knew that she had scored.

Before she lost her advantage, she said:

'I am going home. I'd like to get back before dark, and I think between the two of you you can deal with things here. I suggest you ring the local agency first. Good luck.'

She left the room.

'Good riddance,' said Flora. 'Can you stay the night, Loopy? I'll come down again first thing in the morning and perhaps we can get something fixed temporarily.'

'I must say,' said Louise, 'today's exhibition has made me even more determined not to be here for Christmas. Anything but that. And I know I couldn't get Lionel to come here. I say, Flora, perhaps we can persuade her to give one of those retirement homes a try over the festive season. We could probably get her in somewhere.'

'That's a bit drastic, isn't it?' said Flora.

'No,' said Louise, 'it's not. It really *is* a thought. She actually might agree to that, as it's only for a short time. We can put the dog into some kennels, or something. And then, you never know, she might find she enjoyed it. After all, she must get pretty lonely here with only one of those women to talk to. She'd have company, wouldn't she? Companionship. That place near Horsham has short-stay rooms as well as permanent accommodation. Patrick sussed it all out last year. It is a very attractive house, in private grounds. And they probably have some kind of Christmas festivities, they usually do, I'm sure, in that sort of place.'

Louise noticed as she spoke that Flora was watching her with a wondering smile on her face. As soon as she stopped she wished she hadn't started.

'Atta girl, Loopy! Lionel's been working on you, hasn't he? "Let's put the old girl away, have her properly looked after, where she won't be a burden on her family, she'd be much happier, what?" I can just hear him, though I never thought I'd hear *you* talking like that.'

'No!' Louise burst out furiously, then, 'Well, yes, I suppose. Flora, if I tell you something, you won't tell anyone, promise?'

Flora shook her head slowly, wide-eyed with innocence.

'You see, things have not been so good between me and Lionel for a while.'

'*Really?*' said Flora. 'I would never have known.'

'No, of course not,' said Louise, serious and gazing into the grate. 'He is, you know, a very remarkable man, incredibly hard-working and devoted. They have their eye on him, you know, for high office. But the strain of it all tells on him, and he has so many commitments. It is beginning to come between us, in certain ways, and I know that if I had some extra money it would take some of the pressure off. Do you see what I mean? It's for the sake of the children, too. You know?'

'You mean,' said Flora, 'that if we could get Mother to move out of Bloomfield, we could sell it and you could use your cut to buy Lionel's ongoing devotion. Why on earth don't you just say so? It's perfectly understandable, Lionel being what he is.'

'Flora, how can you? You put everything in the worst possible light. It's not at all like that . . .'

'Of course it is,' said Flora, lighting a cigarette. 'Want one? Let's face it, we all feel the same about Bloomfield being sold, whatever our reasons. Patrick told me ages ago that he can't manage on the income from that shop of his. In fact, I have promised to go with him to the lawyers. He wants to make them show us Mother's father's will, in which he left Bloomfield to her. He thinks we may be able to find out from it just how and when we can get Mother out of the place.'

'Do you think they'll show it to you?' said Louise eagerly. 'Can I come? You won't tell Lionel, will you?'

'No, you can't come. We don't need a delegation. And don't you tell Beatrice. She'd probably blurt it out to Mother in one of her rages. I imagine we must have a right to see the will. I mean, we are the ultimate beneficiaries, presumably.'

'That's just what I want to find out,' said Louise. 'Do we have to wait till Mother dies, or do we have the right to get her out of the house at any time? I must say, I don't feel very happy, talking about her like this.'

'Well,' said Flora, unimpressed, 'you shouldn't be so squeamish, if it's what you're thinking. Patrick is a bit chicken, too. But not all the time. The thing is, we may have to get the trustees to agree before the lawyers will come clean. Anyhow, we'll bloody well have a go. If there were more sense in life Patrick and I would be the trustees, and then we could have done anything we want.'

Flora spoke with unusual passion, which attracted Louise's attention.

'Do you need the money too?' she asked curiously.

'What for? I always thought you earned a lot more than . . .'

'You think too much,' said Flora furiously. 'What I earn is none of your business. Just understand that I will back you all the way in getting rid of Bloomfield.'

'All right, keep your hair on. I was only . . . What's that?' Louise said suddenly. She had been sitting crouched forward, her face between her hands, gazing at Flora, who stood in front of the fireplace with her hands in the pockets of her jeans. Now she lifted her head and looked towards the door. 'I think something's happened.'

'Oh God, what next?' said Flora, as she turned to follow her sister towards the kitchen.

'He never really woke up,' said Mrs Rokeby-Jones. 'But I am sure he knew I was beside him, and he was warm and dry. Oh Sherry, my poor little chap.'

Her eyes were shining, but she was not crying. She kept stroking the shaggy body that lay curled on a pile of blanket on the warm plate of the Aga.

'I'll lift him down into his basket now, I think. I brought it down earlier from my bedroom when I thought he . . .' Her voice broke, but she restrained herself.

Her two daughters suddenly became aware that the woman was standing in a dark corner of the kitchen, watching them, her arms folded across the string that tied her coat together.

'Mother, she can go now, can't she?' whispered Flora.

Mrs Rokeby-Jones looked at her daughter for a long moment, and then turned to the woman. 'You'll stay, won't you, for a while? You don't have to rush away? I would like your help tomorrow.'

The woman nodded. Her face showed nothing. Only

her eyes moved behind her pale plastic-rimmed glasses, watching the three other women.

'Mother!' Louise hissed.

'Please will you get a room ready for our guest, Louise,' said her mother. 'She is going to help me bury Sherry tomorrow, when I hope it will not be so wet. I don't want to bother you two, because you never liked him anyway. And he didn't like you much, either, if you don't mind me saying so.'

'Mother,' said Flora, quietly but firmly, 'what has come over you? Will you come to the drawing room for a moment? We would like to talk to you.'

To their relief, Mrs Rokeby-Jones followed her daughters meekly along the passage, and sat in an armchair facing them.

'I must put on some dry clothes,' she said absently. And then:

'I know what you are going to say, and I don't quite know what has come over me either. But I ask you both, I plead with you both, please let that woman stay until I have buried Sherry, and then you can say what you want.'

In the kitchen passage the woman was standing in silence. She was straining her ears to hear the response to this plea. The urgency in the tone interested her.

'For God's sake, Mother, we can help you bury that wret . . . Sherry,' said Louise. 'Of course we will, and put a bloody great cross on his grave if you want. But you cannot have a completely unknown tramp to sleep in the house. Use your sense!'

'Please, Mother,' said Flora more gently. 'Of course you are upset, we quite understand. But there are some risks one cannot take. We will say goodbye to her now, and if she wants to come back in the morning when the rain has stopped and help bury Sherry, of course she

can. Is that all right? I'll tell her, so you don't have to.
All right?'

'Oh, all right,' said Mrs Rokeby-Jones limply. 'I knew
you would do this. All right. But you will be very polite
to her? Oh dear.'

'I'll deal with it. Loopy, run Mother a hot bath,' said
Flora. 'I'm off. I'll be down tomorrow, Mother, early.'

And Mrs Rokeby-Jones lay back in the armchair and
turned her head to look at the dismal sky through
the window, her eyes very wide and staring. It was
a technique she had used often in the past. She had
felt tears coming, and she did not want her daughters
to see them. She could hear her husband's voice, *Are you
crying, Cecilia? Are you crying?*

Chapter Three

It appeared in the morning, much to Mrs Rokeby-Jones'
relief and to Louise's irritation, that the woman had spent
the night in the log shed.

When Flora arrived, she said she wasn't surprised, the
way their mother had encouraged her.

'Well, let's get it all done quickly anyway,' she said,
'and then we can get rid of her. I don't like the idea of
her hanging around here.'

'She must have something to eat. She was really very
kind,' said Mrs Rokeby-Jones.

'She has,' said Louise. 'I took her a mug of tea
and a toasted sandwich in the front porch. She looked
quite surprised, but she didn't say thank you or anything.'

Mrs Rokeby-Jones led a small procession down to a
spot in the garden where, she said, Sherry had often
curled up in the sun. The woman carried the blanket-
wrapped body, and Louise carried the spade. The rain
had stopped early in the night, and there had been the
predicted frost, not heavy, but enough to dry the surface
of the soil. The sky was clear and blue, and the Downs
reclined benignly in the sun. The gloom of the previous
day was totally dispelled.

On reaching the chosen spot, just in front of a large
forsythia bush, the woman silently took the spade from

Louise and gave it to Flora, who said, 'Well, really,' and started digging.

After a few minutes, panting, and with her unsuitable London shoes caked with mud, she glared up at Louise.

'You can stop smirking, Loopy, and lift those bits of flint out.'

'No,' interrupted the woman. 'Wire netting. This size.' She held her hands some way apart.

Walking away, Louise thought, why do we all seem to do what she says?

When the body was laid in the grave, the wire was placed over it.

'Stops foxes,' said the woman.

'Oh, Sherry,' said Mrs Rokeby-Jones, and accepted a handful of soil from the woman, which she sprinkled into the hole.

'This is ridiculous,' said Flora. 'Are we going to say a prayer now?'

'You want to?' said the woman, looking at her.

'No, I do not,' said Flora, and turned furiously towards the house, leaving one of her shoes in the mud where she had stood. 'Oh, f . . . ff . . . flip.'

The woman picked up the spade and quickly filled the hole, replacing the turf carefully and treading it in with small steps. Her feet were protected by elderly and cracked rubber boots.

'Flat stone,' she said.

'There's a bit of broken paving beneath the window by the front door,' said Mrs Rokeby-Jones. 'Louise, dear, will you get it?'

Her daughters out of sight, she stood for a moment gazing sadly at the little mound.

'He was old, and a bit smelly, I know, but he was . . .'

'A friend,' said the woman.

'Yes, my friend. I had a friend.'

The woman made no comment.

'The thing about dogs,' said Mrs Rokeby-Jones,' is that they let you be yourself.'

Flora left again for London, and Louise left for the local town to talk to the employment agency. She took the woman with her, and dropped her by the bus station, since she expressed no opinion as to where she would like to go.

Louise returned in triumph an hour and a half later.

'Perfect, Mother. They had a cancellation, a woman with all the right references, cooks, light cleaning, middle-aged, companion/housekeeper. She sounds charming, just what you need. She's free for three weeks, which solves the immediate problem.'

'Thank you, Louise,' said her mother. 'It is very kind of you to take so much trouble. I am very grateful, and it means that I can stay comfortably here for Christmas without any of you worrying. I *am* sorry to have been such a nuisance.'

'Nonsense, Mother dear,' said Louise brightly, cheered by her own competence. 'You're never a nuisance. I am delighted to have got you fixed up. She's called Mrs Rainer, and she will be here by six this evening. She has her own car, which is a blessing. I'll be getting off, then. I can't be over again before Christmas, I'm afraid. There's so much to do, with Lionel away and the children coming home. But we'll telephone on the day, of course, and wish you a happy Christmas. And I've left you a little present – on the mantelpiece in the hall. Not to be opened before Christmas – don't forget!'

'Thank you, dear. You're very good to me. Have a happy Christmas.'

An hour later, the bell rang. Mrs Rokeby-Jones opened the front door, and saw the raincoat tied with a string, and the wisps of hair emerging from under the knitted hat.

'Oh, it's you!'

'Yes,' said the woman.

'You've come back.'

'Yes.'

'Did you walk?'

'Yes.'

'Er . . . my daughters have gone.'

'Yes.'

The conversation was not getting anywhere, and Mrs Rokeby-Jones was at a loss as to how it should continue. Although the day was now quite mild, they could not stand on the doorstep like this indefinitely.

'Er . . . would you like to come in?'

'Yes.'

After slight hesitation, Mrs Rokeby-Jones walked towards the kitchen.

'It's nicer in here,' she said, and wondered why.

The woman untied the string from round her waist, and hung the battered raincoat behind the kitchen door. Under it she wore an equally shapeless dress of some sludge-coloured artificial fibre, and a sagging cardigan. She was of medium height, but seemed to be about two sizes smaller than her clothes. The hat stayed on.

Mrs Rokeby-Jones watched as she lifted the kettle from the Aga and filled it under the tap.

'Tea or coffee?' said the woman.

'Coffee, please,' said Mrs Rokeby-Jones.

Neither of them spoke while the kettle came to the boil, then the woman filled the cups while Mrs Rokeby-Jones put the milk and sugar on the table.

'Now,' said the woman, as she sat down opposite Mrs Rokeby-Jones, 'tell me.'

'Tell you what?'

'Anything you like.'

'I beg your pardon? Why should I tell you anything?
I have simply asked you in to thank you for certain kindnesses, and I really am most grateful. But
that is all.'

'Never mind. You will.'

'Will what?'

'Tell me. In time.'

Mrs Rokeby-Jones frowned.

'You mean . . . you're staying?'

'Do you need me?'

'Well, I . . . I need someone, it's true. But I think I have
already . . .'

'Do you need me?'

'Perhaps I do. But this is most irregular.'

'Ask me.'

'Ask you?'

A nod.

'Ask you to stay?'

'Go on.'

'Will you stay, please?'

The woman nodded again and sipped her coffee.

Christmas came and went, and on Boxing Day evening,
home, weary and depressed, Flora said, 'Oh Lord, I never
rang Mother.'

Guiltily, she reached for the telephone. She imagined
it ringing in the hall of Bloomfield. There were only two
telephones there, and the other was in her mother's
bedroom. After the bell had rung sixteen times she
wondered if she had dialled a wrong number. But then
a voice said, 'Hello?' It was not her mother.

'Hello, this is Flora Jones. Rokeby-Jones. Can I speak
to my mother, please?' A long pause. 'Hello? Mother? I
rang to wish you a happy Christmas.'

'Oh, thank you, dear. I hope you have enjoyed yours.'

'Yes, I suppose so. Some parties, friends to dinner. Back to work tomorrow. Thanks for the book, and yes, that was the right one. It's very good. Did you like the Floris?'

'Yes, delicious, dear. My bathroom smells like a brothel.'

'Mother! Are you drunk? That doesn't sound like you.'

'Well, we were having a drink, but I don't think I am drunk, really.'

'You mean you and your . . . your companion?' asked Flora. 'I don't think I know her name.'

'Er . . . no . . . neither do I.' This was said with a suggestion of a giggle.

'You mean you haven't asked her? How extraordinary. Is she all right?'

Flora's heart sank at the thought of the whole boring round of agencies and advertisements starting again, quite apart from the family arguments that would be generated. But her mother's voice came back quickly.

'Yes. Yes, quite all right.'

'Didn't the agency tell you her name? They *must* have, Mother.'

'Well, it wasn't exactly the agency,' said Mrs Rokeby-Jones. 'Look, dear, I sent the agency woman away when she came. I told her I was suited.'

'What the hell . . .? How are you suited? Who have you got?'

'Now, calm down, Flora. I have got a very nice woman. You have met her. She helped with Sherry.'

'*What?* You don't mean that old tramp woman? I don't believe this. Have you gone absolutely mad? You're off your head!'

'If you are going to talk like that, dear, you had better

46

ring off. It's not nice. I am quite capable of engaging my own staff.'

Mrs Rokeby-Jones' voice now sounded more like itself, if rather firmer than usual.

'Mother, I am going to ring Patrick and I suppose we'd better come down.'

'No, thank you, dear.' The firmness was still there. 'I am rather busy, and don't want any visitors at the moment. Happy New Year.'

And she rang off.

The woman was looking at her, leaning against the doorway into the kitchen passage, arms folded.

'Did you hear me?' asked Mrs Rokeby-Jones, aghast.

'Yes,' said the woman approvingly.

'I *must* be drunk, as she said. But I don't think I am.'

'No.'

'I have never done that before. You egged me on, you know. You said . . . What did you say?'

'Nothing,' said the woman.

'What *is* your name, actually?'

It was odd, thought Mrs Rokeby-Jones, how they had managed without any effort at all to live together for several days in perfect harmony without using any names.

'Do you need it?'

'Well, it would be a help, when people ask.'

'Ruth,' said the woman.

'Ruth. Just Ruth?'

'It'll do.'

Beatrice and Flora were talking. Flora had failed to get either Patrick or Louise on the telephone the night before, so had now rung her elder sister as a last resort. Beatrice was predictably irate.

'What on earth was that *idiot* Loopy up to? She

was getting a woman from the agency, wasn't she, Flora?'

'Loopy is a waste of space, we all know that. We should have known better than to leave her to deal with it. She got a woman, and Mother appears to have sent her away again.'

'Sent her away?' Beatrice's voice rose in excitement at the prospect of having two people to blame. 'That's ridiculous! Honestly, Flora, is this senility or just determination not to be co-operative? I just don't know what to think . . . You know, Mother never gave me a *hint* of this when I rang her on Christmas Day. How typically irresponsible. *Now* say she is not tiresome! But it is really *unforgivable* of Loopy not to have seen the agency woman in and got her settled with Mother.'

'Shut up, Bea,' said Flora. 'I know all that. The thing is, we've somehow got to get rid of that tramp. Mother appears to have gone off her head, temporarily. She spoke quite strangely, and I have a suspicion they have been hitting the bottle together. She actually told me she didn't want me to come down – told me not to. I wonder what that woman has been saying to her? I thought she was more than a mere bag lady. You've no idea how she took control.'

'Got the best of you, I hear, Flora. Louise told me it was quite a giggle . . .'

Beatrice giggled too, enjoying the thought.

'She'll giggle all right,' said Flora sharply, 'when I tell her she's responsible for the agency cancellation fee and any loss we all suffer from her letting that woman into the house. I will make sure Lionel knows whose fault it was.'

Beatrice knew better than to annoy Flora further.

'Oh Lord,' she said, 'the woman's probably cleared the house by now, and got Mother to sign a will or something. She's probably got accomplices. Have you spoken to Patrick?' she said.

'Can't get him, the rat,' said Flora. 'I think he must be away. I'll try him again this evening.'

'Well, when you get him, he'd better go down. He can always handle Mother. I'll ring her, though. Oh God, just when I'm *so* busy. I really cannot take *anything* else on my plate at the moment.'

Flora noted that Beatrice was already putting markers down in case she was asked to help in a possible crisis.

'Got a bed to make, have we?' said Flora, and rang off.

Mrs Rokeby-Jones had got into the habit of going into the kitchen in the evening and sitting at the table with a gin and tonic in her hand. She found it soothing to watch the woman as she worked, and even to talk to her, though the conversation was always fairly one-sided. It was a reversal of the usual situation with her housekeepers. She normally found herself retreating from their incessant bright chat, and then feeling guilty about it. But this one was an unobtrusive and sympathetic listener, and Mrs Rokeby-Jones found herself talking freely, almost compulsively.

'I am afraid I am not very good at housework,' she confessed. 'It's odd, I know, nowadays, but I never really learned. My mother never had me taught to cook or anything. And my husband always insisted on having people who had been trained to do jobs – it was the army, I think, that made him very personnel-minded. So he dealt with the staff himself. When he was alive, the house was very different from the way it is now. Everything ran like clockwork. He was a wonderful organiser.'

'Yes?' said the woman, without looking up from her ironing.

'Oh, yes. He liked everything to be kept in order, looking nice. Flowers everywhere – they had to be fresh every two days. I am quite good at arranging flowers. And tapestry. I did all the cushions. And the rug in the drawing room. That took me some years. I wasn't idle. He didn't like me to be idle.'

'Cooking?'

'We had a very good cook. Several, really. One after the other. He ordered the meals, of course. He knew a lot about that sort of thing.'

The telephone rang, and the call was taken by the small white appliance by the telephone. They could hear Beatrice's voice clacking away. 'Mother, please ring me back. I am so busy, and I can't keep ringing you like this. This machine is so tiresome. Ring me, will you?'

Mrs Rokeby-Jones had bought the machine two days earlier, while on a shopping expedition with Ruth. It had seemed to be her own idea, but she supposed that the woman had somehow suggested it. Ruth had wired it up, anyway, and it was proving worth its weight in gold. Telephone calls so often seemed to bring trouble of some kind, and this meant that one could be entirely selective about which calls one answered. As the machine switched off, she said:

'I have a feeling that my family may arrive soon, I'm afraid. One or other of them. Oh dear, that sounds very ungrateful. Of course, they are very good, really, the way they look after me.'

'Yes?'

There was a long pause, while Mrs Rokeby-Jones watched the iron slide rhythmically to and fro across a folded sheet. Then she said:

'You see, it must be quite difficult having an elderly mother to worry about, when they are all so very busy, with their own families, and their work.'

'At what?'

'What do they do? Oh, all sorts of things. Their lives have taken them in different directions. Beatrice, my eldest, you've met, of course. That was her on the telephone just now. She was born in 1945. She was lovely, with golden curls and those beautiful blue eyes. She does a huge amount of charity work – on all sorts of committees. She is always busy, immensely hard-working. A tremendous organiser. Her husband, Henry, was a civil servant, but never really happy in that. I think he had some disagreement with his department. Anyhow, he gave it up. He is a writer now. He used to dabble in it before. Very talented, of course. Actually, I am very fond of Henry.'

A different note came into her voice as she thought of her son-in-law, as if her mind had switched into another gear.

'He is very thoughtful. He watches people, and he is very careful about their feelings. He hides his own, though. There is an uncertainty about him, too, that I find attractive. But, oh well . . . He has been working on some mammoth biographical work for some time now. A positive saga, I would say.'

'First?' asked the woman.

'Er . . . yes. His first book, I believe.'

'Publisher?'

'Oh, I don't know that he has a publisher yet. He's not really got to that stage. Beatrice says he is keeping it under wraps, because there will probably be a tremendous rush when the time comes.'

Mrs Rokeby-Jones thought about this for a minute, before going on.

'They have two lovely children, a boy and a girl. I don't see them much, of course, because he is abroad, in America I think, and she has a very high-powered job in Sotheby's, the auctioneers. She has her own flat in London. But I used to be very fond of them, Peter and Jinny.'

The woman prompted her. She went on ironing all the time, but she appeared to be listening very closely to what Mrs Rokeby-Jones was saying.

'After her?'

'Well, Louise,' said Mrs Rokeby-Jones, 'that's number two. She made a rather interesting marriage, to a young MP. Not so young now, of course. Lionel Leetham, you will have heard of him, I expect. She was his secretary, his right hand. He couldn't do without her, so they got married. At least, I suppose there was more to it than that, but one doesn't hear much, as a parent.'

'No?' said the woman, with interest.

'Well . . . They have two boys, one in the theatre, Rupert, doing awfully well, and the other, Matthew, is still at college. Dear little boys, they were. Grown up, of course, now. Perhaps they will come, then you will meet them.'

'Perhaps.'

Mrs Rokeby-Jones sighed, and drained her coffee mug. She went on.

'Then comes Patrick, whom you haven't met, and then Flora, whom you have. Flora was my youngest, my baby. She was born four years after Patrick. She is quite a remarkable young woman. A very good brain, they used to say in her reports. Not that she used it to the full, but great potential, I know. A strange child, very sullen, but it covered a deep sensitivity. It often does, I think, in children. She does a sort of social work, counselling, brilliantly, I believe.'

'She married?'

'No, not exactly. She has, well, relationships, I believe

they call them nowadays. That's what these young people seem to prefer. Well, not so young. She is over forty – I can hardly believe it. But I am sure she is very good at her job.'

'Why?'

'Well, she is very sharp, and intelligent, and quick . . . and all that sort of thing.'

Another long pause, while Mrs Rokeby-Jones gazed towards the Aga, seeing nothing of its squat, reassuring enamelled shape. The woman's eyes were on her as her hands stacked the ironed linen.

'She could have difficulty in being totally sympathetic in her counselling, perhaps, but I am sure she is very professional. As I say, they all worry about me, quite unnecessarily, most of the time, but it is so good of them.'

'Time we left,' said the woman, unplugging the iron.

'Left? What do you mean?' Mrs Rokeby-Jones stared.

'Left. Went away.'

'Why should we leave?'

'Before they come.'

'But this is my home! I can't leave!'

Mrs Rokeby-Jones sat up straight in her chair. The woman folded the ironing board, smiling as she shook her head and said:

'Your prison.'

'How dare you? This is insulting.'

Mrs Rokeby-Jones, bristling impressively, rose to her feet and left the kitchen.

Some minutes later, she came back.

'Go on,' she said. 'What you were saying.'

'Tonight.'

'Leave tonight?'

The woman nodded.

'Go away? Just go? Together? Where to?'

The woman smiled, and shrugged her shoulders, but she made no reply.

'All right, if you really think so. I don't see why not,' said Mrs Rokeby-Jones. She felt as if she were in a dream. 'I think there's petrol in the car.'

'No car.'

'No car? But . . .'

'No car.'

'You've locked the back of the house?' said Mrs Rokeby-Jones, as they went through the front door. The woman nodded. 'Perhaps I should leave this key under the stone.' She looked around.

'Why?' said the woman.

'Well, in case the children come and want to get in. Or, well, shouldn't we?'

'Don't,' said the woman firmly.

'No?'

'No.'

Mrs Rokeby-Jones put the key in her purse.

It was a mild evening, and as they waited at the roadside, Mrs Rokeby-Jones said:

'I haven't been on a bus for years.'

Flora had no difficulty in persuading Patrick to drop in at her flat in Battersea after work. His first reaction had been that he was too busy, but as soon as she mentioned their grandfather's will he had found a forgotten slot in his schedule, and joined her half an hour later. He used her telephone.

'All right, Flora, that's fixed,' he said, lying back on her rather over firm sofa. 'We go to Asprey, Asprey and Walton next Thursday – that's January the fourth. The senior partner only comes in on Tuesdays and Thursdays, and he is the only trustee left. Old Mr Asprey, that is,

Mr Wilfred, they call him. I hope he's not too old to make sense. Do you think he will look like Wilfred Hyde-White?'

'He will certainly be a mysogynist,' said Flora. She was sitting on the floor opposite her brother, with her arms round her knees. 'Most male lawyers are. So you'll have to do the talking. We have got to insist on seeing our grandfather's will, and we must persuade him that Mother is senile, or has dizzy fits, or whatever, and that he has got to help us get her out of that house before she falls down the stairs or something. We may have to exaggerate a bit.'

'We can but try,' said Patrick. 'There certainly won't be any money coming until she's out of the house. There's no great hurry, though, is there? I wonder if Loopy will be difficult? She's such a snob. Do you remember that awful interview she gave in the *Telegraph*, about MPs' wives – "our family estate in Sussex" and all that?' Flora snorted. 'She may object to being deprived of her ancestral-home forelock-tugging background. By the way, Flora, why are *you* so keen to get Bloomfield sold? You're not short of dosh, are you?'

'Loopy is a social-climbing fool,' snapped Flora, ignoring the question, 'and so obsessed with her philandering pig's bladder of a husband that she can't see an inch beyond her nose. All you have to do is remind her that she needs the money from the house sale to hang on to Lionel. She knows that, just as she knows that her other way to keep him is to let him carry on with his women and pretend not to notice. Or else to threaten to divorce him. He might lose his precious little majority, and he isn't going to risk that. No, we can keep Louise under control. She may pretend to get all soppy about Mother, salving her conscience, but she won't foul it up.'

'Beatrice?'

'Oh, Bea's no problem. She's obsessed with herself and with how wonderfully she manages through all the vicissitudes of life. Poor Henry. She's as idle as hell, and she won't stir herself to stop us shifting Mother. She might say "over my dead body" at the start, but you need only suggest that the obvious answer is for her to house Mother in her own home and you will be surprised how quickly she will lie down and die, whimpering as she goes, "Oh, it's so unfair."'

Patrick laughed as Flora rolled over on her back and lay like a dog, her paws bent and begging. His volatile sister always made him feel slightly nervous, and he preferred her in this mocking mode.

'What about me?' he said. 'Mother trusts me, and she begged me not to go on about a home last year.'

'You're right, she does seem to trust you. I can't think why. That's why you are going to be so useful. You, Patrick, thank God, have got your head screwed on, and you need money. I know I can count on you. And if not, I know too much about you that you wouldn't want made public.'

Patrick gasped. It was like a kick in the stomach.

'I don't believe it. Flora, you wouldn't!'

'Well, I hope you won't have to find out. All right, then, Thursday. Then we will have to go down to Bloomfield and be firm with Mother.'

Three days after this conversation, on the evening of New Year's Day, Mrs Rokeby-Jones was sitting on a stool in the public bar of a small roadside hotel near Stratford-upon-Avon. She had never sat on a bar stool in her life before, having, on the two previous evenings, chosen the safety of a chair with a table in front of it. They had just moved through from the lounge bar, because, as she had said, the public seemed to be having more fun.

A darts match was in progress. Mrs Rokeby-Jones watched in fascination, not so much at the fall of the darts as at the beer bellies and intense concentration of the players. Her gin and tonic glass was empty, and she wished she had had the courage to order beer, but she had been fairly sure she would not enjoy it. The memory of the taste had gone. It was so long since she had sat in a pub garden drinking lager, watching young men in boats colouring a sunlit river with their laughter.

'I gave Patrick a darts board,' she said, 'when he was small. He needed a game to be good at. Poor Patrick. He was a little weak as a child. Chesty, you know. Which stopped him excelling at school. He is *very* artistic, of course, and has wonderful taste. He inherited that from his father. My husband had a remarkable eye for antique furniture, you see. He bought everything, all the good things, that is, in Bloomfield. I believe Patrick's shop is a great draw for those who know. Did I tell you he had an antiques business? It is in the Pimlico Road.'

'Married?' asked the woman.

Ruth was drinking beer. She was nearer than her companion to the beer-drinking generation. It was hard, really, to guess how old she was. Forty, perhaps? Sometimes she looked older, sometimes younger. It depended, rather, on whether or not she wore the woolly hat. She was not wearing it now, and looked almost girlish. She also looked much cleaner than when they had first met.

'No, not married. Not Patrick. There's time yet, but I think he may enjoy the bachelor life, you know. Freedom, no ties.'

'Gay?'

'Gay? You mean . . .? Oh no. Of course not. Well, I don't know. I suppose nowadays it doesn't matter. Though my husband would have . . . I suppose Patrick *is* gay, as they say. Yes, of course. Gay. And I am afraid rather promiscuous. I hope he's careful.'

She sat in silence for some minutes.

'Fond of him?' asked Ruth.

'I adore him. Oh dear. Yes, in a way. He was a dear little boy, but a compulsive liar. What *am* I saying? I shouldn't have had a second drink. He was, though. And, I suppose I have to admit it, he still is. Well, it's a skill of a kind, if you can get away with it. And he usually does. Probably his greatest skill, actually. Apart from diverting his problems on to others. I find Patrick very persuasive. He has a way of talking one into things, even things one knows are not right, or not wise, at any rate. But I do believe he means well. At least, I think he does. But . . . Oh dear. You make me doubt things, rather . . . things I have . . . I have not had trouble with before.'

The darts board was abandoned as the party of men who had been using it left.

'Play?' said the woman.

'Oh, can we? What fun. I won't be any good.'

'Ten minutes.'

'So soon?' asked Mrs Rokeby-Jones. 'Are we moving on again?'

The woman nodded, and handed her three darts.

Chapter Four

What news on the Rialto?' asked Henry as Beatrice put down the receiver. He had come down from his study at the top of the house and found her seated with her elbows on the kitchen table, her chin on her folded hands.

'The worst,' said Beatrice. 'Unbelievable. I told you Mother engaged the tramp who barged in the other day to work for her. If that weren't enough! Well, that idiot Loopy not only let it happen but now I find that she has not even been over there to throw her out. And she lives practically next door! Well, much closer than us. I only rang to ask her how she'd got on. She was too busy, she said, clearing up after the family had left. Busy! Her! She never did a hand's turn, except wait on that prig Lionel and those awful boys. Where are you going? Can't you at least listen for a moment? You're not having a drink now? It's only eleven o'clock.'

'"That which most doth take my Muse and me, Is a pure cup of rich Canary wine." No, of course not.'

Henry Fordham put an arm round his wife's plump shoulders.

'Are you working?' she asked.

'I am not sitting up there in my mountain fastness counting the birds in the trees, my fair Beatrice.'

Mollified, Beatrice went on.

'You realise that I may have to go over there again?

59

Mother seems to have put in an answering machine. It's so tiresome. I can't think where she got such an idea. It's not as if she needed it, when you think how little she goes out. In any case, she doesn't seem to know how to work it, because she never returns my messages.'

Henry smiled and quickly straightened his face again.

'I have been trying to get through to her for days,' his wife went on. 'Someone is going to *have* to go and deal with this ridiculous situation, and I suppose it will be me, as usual. If only you would come with me, for once. It's so unfair. Louise really *is* a bitch. And they are short-handed at the club, what with two off with flu, or pretending to have it, I shouldn't be surprised. I can't possibly go before the beginning of the week. Perhaps I can persuade Patrick to go before then. I don't really want to ring Flora again. She manages to say something nasty every time.'

'It is in the nature of the beast,' said Henry. 'Call me when lunch is ready.'

'Henry, couldn't you discuss it with me for once, instead of running away upstairs?' whined Beatrice.

'Your family has long been a mystery to me, my dear Beatrice, and it is my suspicion that one has to be of the blood even to attempt to fathom its depths. Still, if you desire it, I might come with you to visit the matriarch. But now, farewell. The Muse calls.'

He kissed his wife on the top of her head, and turned towards the door. Not for the first time Henry likened the wooden back staircase to his own personal stairway to the stars. It was an unwritten family rule that Henry should not be disturbed when he was at work.

Louise and Lionel were still at the Surrey house.

Lionel's return from Nairobi had not been followed by a period of peace and tranquillity, the normal result of his being away from home for a period. As a rule he behaved like a cream-sated cat for several days, and he would be especially nice to Louise, allowing to pass unnoticed conduct which would normally have released a stream of criticism. He might even bring her a small present. But not this time.

Something had gone wrong, clearly, with his plans, and the fact that he had not once gone up to London between Christmas and New Year gave Louise a good idea of what it was. He had given her for Christmas quite an expensive, if unattractive, mock-leopard coat. That had presumably been bought while he was feeling mildly guilty about the prospective aftermath of his jaunt to Kenya. If the aftermath had been a flop, he would now be resenting the waste of money. She had found out about his true return date when opening his mail, and had known that he would not join her at the Surrey house till two days later. She had not demeaned herself by ringing their house in London to confirm all this, but she guessed, rightly, that he was there, and not alone. He was so bad at disguising his tracks, she thought, but was not sure if this added to the insult to herself or whether it showed an almost endearing naïvety. In the Christmas spirit she decided on the latter, but did not feel particularly endeared.

When she opened the parcel under the Christmas tree she had nevertheless exclaimed with feigned delight, determined to create a happier atmosphere. But he said, when she put the coat on:

'I don't know; it looked different on the girl in the shop. Couldn't you put on high heels or something?'

By Boxing Day lunchtime both their sons had left, one claiming a party in London, the other saying, 'I only said I was coming for Christmas.'

Since then each day had been gloomier than the last. At lunch on New Year's Eve Lionel had said:

'For how much longer am I to be faced with recycled turkey?'

Louise had replied, 'It seems sensible to finish it up. And economical.'

'I can't think why you buy a huge, expensive turkey when you know the thing's only a gesture. You never think ahead, do you? It's typical of your total lack of organisation.'

The turkey could drag on for days, Louise knew, not just in its physical form but as a source of discord. She would have to get rid of it.

'Lionel, my mind hasn't perhaps really been on planning. I've been so worried about Mother. I think I may have to go over there again, because it seems she has taken on a quite unsuitable woman to look after her, and she may need help in getting rid of her.'

'What sort of unsuitable? Expensive, do you mean?' Lionel put down his knife and fork.

'Well, I don't know what she is paying her,' said Louise, 'but it is more a question of references, I think.'

'What do you mean?' Sensing bungling of some kind, Lionel seized on the chance to be angry with someone other than himself.

'Well, she didn't really have any.'

'For Christ's sake, who was in charge? That poncey brother of yours?' Lionel was getting pink.

'Oh dear. No. I think she did it herself.'

If she had to change the subject, thought Louise with irritation, why on earth had she chosen this one?

Slowly the story had been dragged out of her, and after Lionel had reduced her to a state of exhausted abjection he cheered up and said:

'We'll go over there. I'm not going to trust you on your

own, poor Loops, because you'll just make a balls-up again. Someone who knows a bit about the world is needed at this stage, and who can talk some sense into your mother. It is amazing to me that someone who was married for so long to a person in a senior position like your father can be so totally devoid of any knowledge of how life is managed or of their duty to their fellow beings. She needs a lesson in family solidarity, and if none of your siblings is prepared to give it to her, I am.

'Where are those brochures for retirement homes?' he went on, looking round. 'Dig them out, Louise. Don't tell me you've got rid of them? Do you *ever* think? This total organisational inability seems to run in your family. I shall have to get my secretary to . . . Well. In any case, I'll look into it. I'll do something about this.'

Lionel's face had clouded over with anger again at the thought of his secretary.

In a large, darkly panelled room in a handsome building not far from Charing Cross, a big partners' desk hung about with brass drawer-handles separated a tall, silver-haired man from his two visitors. He sat comfortably in a high-backed leather swivel chair. Behind him, a bookcase full from floor to ceiling with paper-bound tomes, tatty with use, stood between two long windows. The pair facing him were in low chairs whose leather-covered seats and arms gleamed from the sitting of generations of clients. They would have been more comfortable if they had sat deeply, but neither felt sufficiently relaxed to do so.

Mr Wilfred Asprey, senior partner of Asprey, Asprey & Walton, Solicitors, surveyed Patrick and Flora over his rimless spectacles. He cleared his throat.

'I have to say, and I am sure that you will not read anything untoward in to my saying it, that your request is not a very usual one. Obviously your late grandfather's will was cleared of probate very many years ago. Now, if you had been direct beneficiaries of that will there would be no reason to withhold from your gaze the copy which we do, of course, still retain in our files, if you had mislaid your own. But since your mother, Mrs Robert Rokeby-Jones—'

'We know who our mother is,' mouthed Flora, for whom ten minutes spent in this office had already been ten minutes too long.

'—was the sole beneficiary of the will, the document in our possession is now, technically speaking, her property. It would be normal to ask her permission before allowing any other person to view it. May I ask if you have her permission?'

'Yes, of cour . . .' said Flora.

'No,' said Patrick. 'We didn't realise it was necessary, and as she is very elderly and vague, and easily upset, we weren't going to bother her. But she would give her permission, I am sure,' he added.

'Your mother is now – let me see – only seventy, I believe?' said Mr Asprey, who looked not far off seventy himself. 'I talked to her quite recently, and she did not seem changed from the lady whom I have known for so many years. I am sorry to hear of this deterioration in her condition. Very sorry indeed. However, I am quite happy to make a telephone call to her again and put this question to her, while you wait. Perhaps that is the best solution.'

As Patrick and Flora looked at each other, he dialled a number that he apparently knew by heart.

'Hmm,' he said. 'A telephone answering machine. Very modern. I have to confess that I do not like them. Leaving a message on one engenders a sense of irredeemable commitment.'

He put the receiver down again. Then he put his elbows very deliberately on the edge of the desk and placed his fingertips together while he appeared to think deeply. Then, coming to a conclusion, he interlaced his fingers and looked first at the brother, then at the sister, and spoke again.

'You see, as the sole remaining trustee for the estate *and* your mother's solicitor I have a double responsibility that I am constrained to take very seriously. You may feel that I am being unnecessarily careful, but I have never regretted caution in the past. So I am afraid that, in the circumstances, without instructions from my client I do not feel I can divulge the information you require. Should you return with permission, in writing, of course, from Mrs Rokeby-Jones, to the effect that you should be given a copy of your late grandfather's will, I shall be only too happy to arrange for that to be done. Of course these are mere formalities, I would be the first to agree with you, but I believe that I should be doing less than my duty if I were to dispense with them on these occasions.'

'I see,' said Patrick. 'Well, that is really rather trying, but we will be in touch again about it. There is another matter that my sister may like to discuss with you, however, regarding Bloomfield and our mother's future plans.'

'Not today,' hissed Flora, and Mr Asprey looked unsurreptitiously at his watch.

'You will have to forgive me,' he said. 'I am running a little late, and I have a round of golf booked after lunch. The joys of semi-retirement, you know. But I look forward to welcoming you and your mother here at any time, by appointment, of course.'

A door opened silently, as if at a prearranged signal, and Patrick and Flora's coats were brought. Their hands were shaken, the wish that the fine weather might continue was expressed and they were in the street almost before they knew it.

'Bastard. Stupid, pompous, geriatric prat,' said Flora as they turned towards the Strand. 'He's brainwashed. He's atrophied. He's totally incapable of movement or change. You were a fool even to think we could talk to him about getting her out of Bloomfield. I can just imagine him banging on about her full and unqualified agreement to the proposed change in her circumstances, blah blah blah. By the way, I noticed that you were going to duck that one and make me do it, you weed. In any case, we'll never get him to help us over moving her. We've got to do it ourselves.'

'Wasn't he divine, though?' said Patrick. 'Straight out of *Bleak House*! It was hardly real. And he didn't look at all like Wilfred Hyde-White, more like an older version of that rather dishy lawyer in that film with . . .'

'Patrick!' said Flora, stopping in mid-pavement. 'For God's sake concentrate.'

'All right, all right, but give me time to get my breath back. Let's face it, darling, if we want to see the will we're going to have to go down there and get her to give us a note for him. And I suppose we can have a go at persuading her to think of moving out at the same time. I think it will have to be voluntary, though. But there's no great urgency actually to sell Bloomfield, really, is there?'

'Yes there is,' said Flora firmly. 'We have somehow got to make her life there untenable, then she will actually want to move.'

'We can easily get the old bat she's employed to give notice,' said Patrick. 'That could be quite fun. I'll goose her while she's doing the washing-up, or else do my Seth Starkadder act at her bedroom window. Leave her to me.'

'I suspect, from what I've seen of the tramp woman, that she's met your kind before, and she'll probably goose you back.'

'Don't be unkind, darling. You're going to need me to deal with Mother. She never can resist my blandishments.'

As they walked towards Trafalgar Square Flora was thinking hard.

'We are going to have to do more than blandish,' she said. 'We are going to have to get the others properly on side, no sentimentality. Once we have got rid of the woman, we are going to have to persuade Mother that we simply can't get another one. We may have to bribe the agencies to go along with it. That won't be a problem. Then, when she's faced with the rest of the winter alone in Bloomfield – we can talk about burglars, rapists, etcetera – I guess she'll soften up pretty quickly.'

She wished she felt as confident as she sounded.

They parted at the entrance to the Underground.

'Don't say anything to the others yet. Leave them to me, right?' said Flora, as she went down the steps.

'It's Terry. Can you hear me? I've got to be quick.'

'Thank God you've called. What's happening? Where are you?'

'You'll never guess.'

'You got in? That was quick. How did you get in?'

'I had a lucky break. Look, I can't talk. Just touching base.'

'When can you . . . Hello?'

The line went dead.

By Friday night, Mrs Rokeby-Jones and the woman had reached Carlisle, and were eating in a Chinese restaurant. A bottle of wine was nearly empty in front of them.

'I always thought spring rolls were something they did in aerobics classes,' said Mrs Rokeby-Jones.

Getting no reaction from her companion, she said:

'That was meant to be a joke.'

'Yes.'

'My husband always said I should never make jokes, because I always got them wrong.' She shrugged and smiled.

'Your husband?' asked the woman.

'Yes. Lieutenant-Colonel Robert Rokeby-Jones, his name was. I was married to him for forty years. Of course, he was a little older than me.'

'How much?'

'Well, more than a little, really. Fifteen years older. I was married when I was nineteen.'

'Why?'

'This is really delicious, you know,' Mrs Rokeby-Jones said, helping herself to something unidentifiable with sweet and sour sauce. 'You should try this soy sauce stuff on it.'

The woman accepted the bottle, and said again, 'Why?'

'Well, it has a pleasant, sharp taste. Oh. Why was I married, or why was I nineteen?'

'Both,' said the woman, smiling. She looked very pleasant when she smiled, thought Mrs Rokeby-Jones. It was a pity she took so little trouble with herself, as she could have been rather nice-looking, with that narrow, intelligent face. But she wore no make-up, and her hair was shambolic. The tea-cosy hat and those hideous glasses didn't help.

'Well?' said Ruth.

'Well, I was married because ... Well, he was a most remarkable man, a splendid soldier and a great gentleman. He had had a wonderful war record, and he had been decorated too. This was in 1943.'

68

'Brave?'

'Well, of course he was brave. He was wounded, you see, in 1942. He lost the sight in one eye, and had been in hospital for six months. But it didn't stop him being marvellously handsome. My mother said he could have swept her off her feet any day. Quite a catch, she said. That's what she said.'

The focus of Mrs Rokeby-Jones' eyes widened as she looked out through the long white paintings of smoky black prawns and angular crane-like birds that hung on the unpainted stone walls. Her gaze went far beyond the walls themselves, back deep into time.

'Your father?' prompted the woman, after a minute.

'My father. What?'

'He wanted you married?'

'Oh, my father. Well, he thought I should do a spell in a munitions factory, or in the Land Army, or something like that, first. Actually, I quite wanted to. But Mother said I would lose my chance, or that the Colonel might not wait. Someone else would catch him, she said. She said it for my own good, of course. She was very fond of me.'

'Was she?'

'Was she what?' Suddenly the distant look had gone and Mrs Rokeby-Jones' full attention was on the woman.

'Fond of you.'

'Well, of course she was. She was my mother. I think you are being rather overcurious.'

'Worries you?' asked the woman.

'Please, shall we talk about something else? Let us finish this bottle. It was not bad at all. I must get some more money tomorrow, before we go to the bus station. I saw a bank just down the road, with a cashpoint. We mustn't run out of money.'

'Well spent.'

'I think so. I really do. I don't think I have ever enjoyed myself so much in my life. Ever.'

'Your life?'

Mrs Rokeby-Jones divided the last drops of wine between herself and the woman, and then drained her glass.

'Let's go,' she said.

The bell rang again bleakly and distantly through the depths of the house. It had the desolate sound of a bell that is unheard.

The group on the doorstep looked at each other. Beatrice bent down to the letter box, but the Bloomfield box was not made to be peered through. Flora rang the bell once again, and waited.

'No answer. Not a sound,' said Beatrice.

'"Not a drum was heard, not a funeral note . . ."'

'Oh, do shut up, Henry. You are a pain beyond description.'

'My dear Flora,' said Henry reproachfully, 'I never thought to hear words of such harsh tone escape your rosy . . .'

'Henry, if you don't shut your mouth I will break your teeth.'

'Flora, leave Henry alone. This is serious,' said her brother.

Flora and Patrick had arrived together at Bloomfield and had been sitting discussing tactics in their car on the gravel in front of the house when Henry and Beatrice had pulled up beside them. After expressions of mutual surprise and irritation they had moved together on to the front doorstep.

'They must be out,' said Beatrice.

'Oh, well done, Bea,' said Flora.

'Where the hell would they go out to?' said Patrick. 'And both of them? Is the car there?'

Henry, who had moved away, said, 'I'll look in the garage.'

He was back shortly, and watched the back views of his in-laws as they moved from flowerbed to flowerbed, peering through the lower windows. He waited till they had all moved back on to the gravel and were wiping the mud from their shoes on the grass verge.

'Hell, my tights. Those bloody roses,' said Flora.

'The car's there,' said Henry.

'It can't be!' said Beatrice.

'I think I know a car when I see one.'

'They can't have gone for a walk?' said Patrick. 'Not both of them?'

'We've got to get into the house,' said Beatrice. 'They may be lying there . . . Anything could have happened.'

'There is always a key outside. Look under the stones. There used to be a broken one . . .' said Patrick.

'There's no key anywhere. I've looked,' said Flora.

'Smash a window, then. The kitchen window would be best, then you can reach the back-door lock.'

When they were in the house, there was a cold stillness that told them clearly that it had no living occupants. The dining room and the drawing room were empty, and in the small library the fireplace was full of dead, scattered ash.

'That woman,' said Beatrice. 'She may have murdered Mother in her bed.'

'Why are people always murdered in their beds?' said Flora.

'Let's check the silver,' said Patrick.

There was a loud knocking at the front door.

'Oh heavens,' said Bea, clutching Henry's arm. 'It must be the police.'

It was, in fact, Lionel and Louise.

'What are you doing here?' Lionel said aggressively to Patrick, who opened the door. Lionel's appearance in a check overcoat and a trilby caused his brother-in-law instant giggles.

'What do you think, sunshine? Looking for Mother.'

'Looking for her?' said Louise, peering past Lionel's shoulder. 'Isn't she here?'

'No, dear, she's not here, or if she is she's hiding. Hide and seek, you know? Party games?'

'Pull yourself together, Patrick,' said Lionel, striding forward. 'I can see someone needs to take charge here. Have you . . .'

He cracked his head with a resounding thud against a low beam, and cursed impressively.

'Lionel,' said Patrick urgently, 'would you mind doing that again, because I think Flora missed it.'

'You bloody little queer,' snarled Lionel. 'I'll smash your filthy face in if you . . .' He put his hand to his forehead and looked at it. 'God, I'm bleeding. Louise . . .'

'Children, children,' gasped Flora, semi-convulsed with laughter, 'have some respect fo . . . for Mother. We have got to find her.'

Lionel and Louise went to the cloakroom off the hall, while the others followed each other upstairs and from room to room. The MP and his wife rejoined them as they went into Mrs Rokeby-Jones' bedroom at the end of the wing. It was not one of the larger rooms, certainly not the 'master' bedroom of estate agents' parlance. But, though rather far from the centre of the house, it was pleasant enough, with its shabby chintz and full bookshelves.

Beatrice held Henry's hand as they stood looking round, and tried to pull him on when he picked up a book from his mother-in-law's bedside table.

'I never thought she would read Conrad,' he murmured in explanation.

'Good Lord, look at that,' said Lionel.

They all followed his gaze upwards to the ceiling between the window and the bed.

'Look at what?' said Louise.

'Are you blind? The water is clearly pouring in through the roof. This house is totally neglected.'

'Pouring in!' said Flora. 'That's just a dry stain. It's been there for years, anyway. Though it may be growing a bit, I admit.'

'If she must live in this unnecessarily large house, she should at least take some responsibility for it,' grumbled Lionel.

'I'll get someone in to look at the roof, I suppose,' said Patrick, fingering a walnut armoire.

'I would have thought,' said Flora, 'that finding out where Mother is would rate a higher priority than fussing about a bit of damp.'

Downstairs again, they stood looking at each other in the centre of the hall.

'What do we do?' said Louise.

'We ring the police, of course,' said Lionel, reasserting himself. The plaster on his forehead gave him a curious cock-eyed look which afforded Patrick much pleasure. 'We tell them that we have reason to believe . . . er . . . that there are suspicious circumstances, giving rise to a . . .'

'Don't talk twaddle, Lionel,' said Patrick. 'We are not your constituents. There are no suspicious circumstances, and the police will simply think you've gone round the twist. An old woman, two old women possibly, have left the house, locked it up, and haven't yet come back. What's suspicious about that? There are no bodies, no burglary, nothing at all to interest the police. They might be interested in how we got in, though. I can see the headlines, and the photographs, "MP injured in housebreaking brawl". They won't like that in Surrey Downs. How about "MP hits the roof"?'

'Patrick, you are clearly unfit to deal with this situation,' Lionel said. 'The first thing we do is find out where they have gone.'

'Or else we could simply wait till they come back?' suggested Louise, sitting down on one of the window seats.

'I'm not sitting around here all day,' said Flora. 'You can. I happen to have a job.'

'The answerphone is flashing like anything,' Beatrice called from the kitchen. 'That may give us a clue.'

'Miss Marples rides again,' said Flora, and followed the others down the passage.

They all listened as Beatrice ran the tape back and the machine went through its paces. Several times they heard Beatrice's high-pitched voice, becoming increasingly petulant, imploring her mother to ring her back. Flora's voice twice, 'God, are you still out?' and 'Hell. I'll ring again.' Two calls with no message, followed by a man's voice leaving simply, 'Number sixteen, ring me, will you?' ('Who the hell's that?' said Flora) and finally Lionel, surprised to find a machine, very pompous, 'Er . . . er . . . This is Lionel Leetham, calling on Wednesday at twelve oh five p.m., to say that Louise and I are on our way to you. We would like a serious talk, and hope this will be convenient. End of . . . er . . . message. From Lionel Leetham.'

'Foxtrot, Bravo, over and out,' said Flora.

'Christ, she never wiped any of them off,' said Patrick. 'When did you first call, Bea?'

'*Days* ago. Last week. When was it, Henry?'

'I don't make a practice of keeping track of your telephonic life, but I would say over a week ago.'

'More than a week ago! Do you think she has really been gone for more than a *week*? Has anyone here spoken to her since Wednesday of last week?'

They all shook their heads. 'No,' and 'I don't think so,' and 'You said you would,' and 'Well, I was busy.'

'Heavens,' said Beatrice. 'That was two days after Christmas. That's eleven days ago.'

'It's that woman, you know,' said Louise. 'I know it. It's her. She has done something to Mother.'

'Yes,' said Flora thoughtfully. 'And I wonder what?'

She had opened the hall cupboard and was examining the coats inside. She knew pretty well what should have been there.

'Surely we should ring the police?'

'For goodness' sake,' said Flora, 'don't get so panicky, Bea. You always overreact. Mother's a grown woman, and she has a right to come and go as she likes. She's merely showing a bit of independence. I'm rather impressed. How do you know how long she has been gone for? I know she is not returning our telephone calls, but she may have just gone out for the afternoon. We will simply make fools of ourselves if we go rushing hysterically to the police at this stage. We will just have to be patient, and wait till she rings us. We can telephone every day. I am going back to London, and I advise the rest of you to go home too.'

She opened the front door and looked at them over her shoulder.

Patrick shrugged, and looked at Louise, who looked at Lionel.

He said sullenly, 'We are certainly not going to find her by standing about here.'

'Well, if you really all think so,' said Beatrice weakly. 'What do you think, Henry?'

'I think Flora's right,' said Henry.

'And someone put a bit of cardboard in that window, where you broke the pane,' said Flora as she went out.

Chapter Five

'He called me "hen". Twice. What on earth did he mean by that?' said Mrs Rokeby-Jones as she and the woman stepped off a bus in Dumfries twenty-four hours later. The driver had handed them down two plastic bags full of their possessions, one inscribed 'Sainsbury's' and the other 'Mary Jane, Newbury'. Before the door closed he had called, 'Seven oh five is the last bus back the night, mind,' and given them a cheery wave.

The woman shrugged.

'Scottish. Friendly,' she said.

'To call someone a hen? Is it a term of endearment? Is it like "dear"?'

'Less patronising.'

'More like "love"?'

The woman nodded.

'Hen. I felt like going "Too-ook, took, took, tuk, tk tk tk tk . . ."' Mrs Rokeby-Jones was almost giggling.

'Why didn't you?'

'I will, next time.'

The bus driver had deposited them in the centre of Dumfries, not far over the Scottish border. It was a cold, bright day, and they spent some time leaning over the bridge that spanned the broad, shallow river.

'We are not really going back to Carlisle tonight, are we?' asked Mrs Rokeby-Jones.

'Do you want to?' said the woman, still looking at the brown water below.

'I'd rather go on,' said the other, 'if you want to. The country gets better all the time. And colder, though.'

The tea-cosy hat nodded.

'Yes. Shopping tomorrow.'

They were silent for a little, the sun on their backs.

'Watching water is like watching time run away. You want to stop it, and have time to enjoy it before it goes,' said Mrs Rokeby-Jones.

'Old thought?'

'No, a new one. I used to think that watching water was just a good way of making time pass. You know, when Sherry fell in, that day, that was what I was doing. Poor Sherry. I never asked you, how did you find him? I tried so hard. I suppose he was swept downstream, and I was looking in the wrong place.'

'No, under the weir,' said the woman.

'*Under* it? Is there a shelf or something?'

The woman nodded.

'And he got himself on to it?' Mrs Rokeby-Jones drew her breath sharply through her teeth. 'Poor little dog. I was very fond of him. He was fifteen, quite old. I got him as a puppy, as soon as my husband died.'

'Your first dog?'

'Yes, actually. Well, the first one of my own. There were dogs at home, when I was young. My father loved dogs, and so did I. So I got a puppy as soon as I could. From a dogs' home.'

'Never before?' The woman turned round, leaning against the parapet of the bridge, facing the winter sun, with her arms outstretched on either side and her eyes shut.

'No,' said Mrs Rokeby Jones. 'You see, my husband . . . Well, there were valuable carpets in the house and lovely furniture. My husband felt, quite rightly of course, that a puppy might damage them.'

'An older dog?' The gentle prompting went on.

'Well, possibly, but . . . Somehow . . .'

'Whose house?'

'Bloomfield? Well, mine, in fact.' Mrs Rokeby-Jones sounded almost apologetic. 'Though of course, being married, one shared everything. But it had been left to me by my parents. I was an only child.'

'Whose rules?' The questions were asked not with a note of curiosity but as if they followed a plan, to be asked in turn, without expression.

This last one seemed to break some spell.

'How do you mean? Who made the rules?' said Mrs Rokeby-Jones, frowning and looking at her interlocuter. 'I don't know quite what you are getting at. You must realise that I was a very ignorant and inexperienced girl. My father had recently died, and my husband was a mature, very splendid man, who knew a great deal more about the world than I did. I was enormously lucky that he took me on. And of course we had an extremely interesting life. He was very widely travelled, and knew so many fascinating people. Friends from the army, mainly, and their wives. He kept very closely in touch with his old regiment. He used to invite them to stay at Bloomfield after the war. He liked to entertain them.'

'You enjoyed that?' Very gently, but it still seemed to offend.

'Well, of course I enjoyed it,' said Mrs Rokeby-Jones, her colour heightening. 'I was very privileged to meet these people. Most girls of my age were . . .'

'Yes?'

'Well, you know, just getting jobs and things like that. I was extremely lucky in that I was looked after hand and foot. I never had to earn my living. I had a comfortable

home, and plenty of money, and a . . . I don't know why
you are going on like this.' Her voice suddenly became
sharp with annoyance. 'It is none of your business. I
resent all this questioning. Why do you want to know,
anyway?'

The woman shrugged, and walked away. Mrs Rokeby-
Jones felt angry, and disturbed, and did not follow her.
Instead she walked down to the river bank and sat on a
municipal bench, and for the first time allowed herself
to wonder what she was doing. With an ability that
stemmed from years of self-discipline, she had so far
kept her thoughts focused only on the immediate, and
never allowed them to stray beyond the next few hours.
It was a survival technique that had kept her going for
most of her life. In any case, she had been so exhilarated
by the strangeness of the experience of escape from her
normal life that she had felt no pressing need to question
her own motives. Or lack of motive, she thought, which
was why she had no urge to wake up from this strange,
dreamlike situation. What had no purpose could not go
wrong. She was certainly not harming anyone. She did
not suppose she was even worrying anyone, though they
might be wondering where she was. That possibility gave
her a definite sense of satisfaction. They can just wonder,
she said to herself, and felt a charming feeling of – yes,
naughtiness, as she did. It was a sensation that rushed
her back to her childhood. In a moment from long ago
she sat in the top branches of a mulberry tree in late
summer. The front of her smocked cotton dress was
stained with juice and the warm dark mulberries were
rich on her tongue. She heard her mother calling, and
knew there would be trouble later. She also knew that
it would be a small price to pay for the present joy,
which she would extend to the last possible minute. Mrs
Rokeby-Jones smiled, and stretching her arms along the

bench held her face up to the sun. In this windless spot it was positively warm.

'Most unseasonable weather for January,' she said aloud, and giggled.

'That's so,' said the woman's voice. She was standing just behind the bench, and Mrs Rokeby-Jones was strangely pleased.

'Chips,' said the woman.

Mrs Rokeby-Jones did not reply. She was trying to remember why she had felt so annoyed.

'Smell them?' said the woman.

They both inhaled deeply.

'Is that what it is? Lovely.'

The smell of frying fish and chips wafting towards them from the line of shops on the other side of the riverside road was mouthwatering, and irresistible.

'Shall we?'

'Mmm.'

Some time later Mrs Rokeby-Jones was licking her fingers and sighing.

'It is funny that something as prosaic as fish and chips should be so utterly delicious. I don't think I have tasted them since I was a girl.'

They stayed the night in Dumfries, sharing a room in a prim bed-and-breakfast house on the outskirts of the town. Mrs Rokeby-Jones looked at her clothes in the morning.

'I'm getting awfully grubby,' she said. 'I really need a change of everything.'

'Yes, it's time,' said the woman.

They went first to a cashpoint, and then to Marks and Spencer. The woman chose the racks and counters, Mrs Rokeby-Jones obediently selecting clothes from them.

'This is much more fun than going to a dressmaker. You know, my husband always decided what I should wear. I would have loved to have come to a place like this, and chosen my own. He had a wonderful eye, of course, and I really have very little taste in that way.'

'Green one?'

'No, I think the blue.'

Mrs Rokeby-Jones put on a long padded anorak, and looked at herself in the mirror.

'I look – I don't know – younger, don't you think?'

'How do you feel?'

Mrs Rokeby-Jones laughed. 'Yes, and I feel younger. It is really quite strange. I am thrilled at the thought of wearing the trousers. My husband did not like women in trousers. He liked women to look . . . No, not a pattern. I think you should have the brown one. Or the red – that's rather nice.'

They climbed on a bus, laden with green plastic bags, and got off it again at a stop in open country some way up the valley of the Nith. Down by the river bank, which was lined with scrubby woodland, they found a clump of tall gorse bushes that provided some shelter from the wind. There they changed all their clothes, shivering in the bright January sunlight. The woman took their discarded ones and, looking around her as she went, disappeared for several minutes further upstream.

'All gone,' she said, as she returned.

'How?'

'Rabbit holes.'

'Poor rabbits – what a shock.'

'And look!'

Ruth pointed out into the river, and floating, half submerged in the current, Mrs Rokeby-Jones recognised the tweed of her old coat.

'And there goes my personality,' she said with satisfaction, looking down at her new, blue, showerproof self.

Ruth looked very different too. She was now slimmer, her clothing still rather anonymous, but no longer shabby.

'You look quite different,' said Mrs Rokeby-Jones. 'Oh, and you've taken off your glasses. Can you manage without them?'

'Yes,' said the woman, and offered no explanation.

They walked along the road, in their new thick rubber-soled boots, for about an hour. Another bus came by, and stopped to pick them up when they waved.

'I am quite sorry, really. These last few days you have been making me remember how much I once loved walking. My father used to take me up on the Downs, and we would go for miles. It was so beautiful, especially in the spring, when the whitebeams were coming into leaf. And in the autumn . . . the thorn bushes were swathed in bindweed, "old man's beard", you know? So pretty, and such a creepy name. My father called it flowering fog,' said Mrs Rokeby-Jones.

They sat in silence as the bus charged northwards through the Galloway hills.

Next day, some four hundred miles further south, Beatrice had decided to be firm. Beatrice being firm meant Beatrice sitting between Henry and the door to the staircase and refusing to be interrupted.

'Henry, will you do something for me?'

'My love, your every wish is my command.' He kissed one fingertip in her direction.

'Just sit down, then, and listen, without rushing off upstairs, and without – without *avoiding* everything. I have really a great many concerns at the moment, just when I am so busy, which is *so* unfair. But I really need to share them with someone.'

Henry looked at Beatrice with interest. This was a new

line. She did not normally consult him about anything important. It could, of course, just be a ploy.

'First, it's about Mother. I don't feel any of us are taking her disappearance seriously enough. Louise rang me last night and evidently she still hasn't turned up. It is now thirteen days since any of us spoke to her. You may well say she is an adult, and free to come and go as she wishes. But she never has.'

'Never has wished? Or never has come and gone?' said Henry.

'Pay attention, Henry. She has never done *anything* unexpected. She has just sat there, since Father died, in aspic, as it were. We all *know* what she does and where she is. And now, suddenly, we don't.'

'Might that not be a good thing?'

'How *can* you say it's a good thing? You know *nothing* about it. It may be a desperately *bad* thing.'

Beatrice was becoming emphatic. Henry resolved to concentrate, or at least to look as if he was concentrating.

'Any sign of her fair companion?'

'No, not her either. And we have no idea, even, if Mother is away on her own or with that woman. And where would she go? She has no friends, as far as we know.'

'Perhaps she leads a mysterious double life . . .'

'Henry,' signs of exasperation came from Beatrice, 'I am seriously worried. Do try to take this a little seriously yourself, if it's not too much effort. She could be dead in a ditch, or kidnapped, and we are doing nothing about it. I mean, we are her family, after all. We are responsible for her.'

Henry was thinking that Flora would have said at once, 'Why are people always dead in ditches?' and that he liked her for precisely that sort of question, despite her rudeness.

'Henry? Pay attention. As her family, we are responsible for her.'

Beatrice could always tell at once when his attention wandered, even for a second.

'Not in law, I suspect,' said Henry. 'Sorry. Why don't you ring the police, then?'

'Well, I want to. I suggested it ages ago, but Patrick is absolutely determined that we shouldn't. I *cannot* make out why. Do you think he's frightened of a scandal or something? That would be more like Lionel. It might affect his fearfully important electoral prospects.'

'It can't be the expense,' said Henry, 'which is the usual fuss with Patrick and Lionel. Telling the police is a free service.'

'No. I shall have to ring Flora, after all, although she didn't seem keen either. Somehow I feel she is rather pleased about Mother's extraordinary behaviour. Flora is so unpredictable. Oh dear. But I must get some sense out of someone.'

The mention of expense had distracted her, reminded her of her second theme. She clasped her fingers together in an attitude of prayer and started.

'Henry, I have another worry – no, don't go away. I hate to bring this up, because I know I mustn't chivvy you, but you really must talk to me.'

Henry kept smiling, but a heavy feeling of foreboding enveloped him.

'O mistress mine, do not speak roughly to your little boy,' he said.

'It's about money,' said Beatrice, leaning forward and looking earnest. 'I know you can't rush your book, but have you got any idea when it is going to be ready? If you carry on at the same speed as you have so far? Just a rough estimate, say? No, don't say anything yet. Let me just talk on for a bit.'

'Speak on, my love, and cursed be he who first cries, Hold! enough,' said Henry automatically. He sat back in his chair and thought longingly of the bottle of tawny joy that lay in his desk upstairs.

'Henry, listen, now. I do my best, you know I do, to stretch the money as far as I can, but you must notice how *shabby* the house is now. It is *years* since we did any decorating, and in places, the staircase for instance, the paint is simply flaking off the walls. How *could* we have Mother or anyone else to stay? I mean, I would be *ashamed* to let anyone use the spare bathroom with those awful cracked tiles. I know you say Mother wouldn't care, perhaps she wouldn't, but *I* would care. I mean, one has a certain standard to keep up. I know important books take time to write, and I am not chasing you, you know I am not, but . . . oh dear, there are so many things that need replacing. The washing machine, that's another thing, by the way . . .'

Henry tried desperately to keep his attention on what Beatrice was saying. It was not easy.

'I work, three days a week, Henry,' she went on, 'at a job I hate and that I find *debasing*, in order to keep things going. I mean, one of these days someone I *know* will come to one of those dinners at the club, and they will see me in the kitchen, and they will tell everyone. I do *like* cooking, but I don't know if I could stand the *humiliation* of all our friends knowing about it. And the family – I have always said it is all charity work that keeps me so busy – and the other is so *demeaning*. I have my pride, and . . . oh dear. They do pay me quite well, particularly when I do the private dinners, but twice round the supermarket with a trolley and most of it is gone. I am not *complaining*, Henry. I know how important your book is. I am very proud of it, though I know so little about it. And the last thing I want to do is to make you rush it. But it would be such a help for me to know, just roughly, how long . . . how much longer . . .'

Henry tried to look at her gravely.

'Oh, take that reproachful look off,' said Beatrice tearfully. 'You know what I mean. Oh dear. But Henry, this is the main thing, now. And you are going to have to forgive me. I opened a letter of yours. By mistake. Only half the name and address was showing through the little window, and I thought it was for me. I would never have done it on purpose.'

She had Henry's full attention now. He was leaning forward in his chair with his mouth slightly open. A quiff at the back of his thinning hair was standing on end, where the cushion had pushed it up.

'You didn't! You didn't open my letter!'

'Oh, don't be cross. It's so unfair. It wasn't on purpose, but I couldn't *help* seeing.'

Henry said nothing. His face was without expression now.

'It was from your bank,' said Beatrice. 'Thirteen thousand pounds. I knew we were in debt, Henry, and that you had made an arrangement with them, but honestly . . . I didn't even know they would *let* you have an overdraft of thirteen thousand pounds.'

'They won't,' said Henry. Then he rallied. 'It doesn't cost nothing, you know, to be a writer. I have been obliged to invest in a new word processor, and even mere foolscap is now comparable in price to the best vellum in the days . . .'

'When?' said Beatrice, interrupting him.

'When what?'

'When did you buy a new word processor?'

'Oh.' Henry suddenly had to clear his throat. 'Sorry. Not long ago.'

'Where did you get it? You never go shopping.'

Henry was for a moment without an answer.

'How did it get here? I didn't see it.' She was looking piercingly at him now.

'My dear, it was delivered. While you were out.'

Beatrice stared at Henry during a long pause. He was carefully demisting his reading glasses, breathing on them and polishing them with his handkerchief.

'I want to see it.'

'To see it?' he said. 'To *see* my word processor?'

'Yes.'

'My beloved Bea, queen of my heart and mistress of my house, versed as you are in the culinary and maternal arts, you would not know one word processor from another.'

'I want to see it.'

'Bea, you wouldn't know the new one from the old one – it's the same make.'

'No,' said Beatrice, 'but I can read a date on an invoice.'

Her tone was grim.

'Beatrice, my own.' Henry stretched a hand, palm upward, towards her. 'You surely cannot imagine, for a second, for a single split second, that I, your husband, would ever conceal anything from you? Mislead you, lie to you? My love, my inspiration? My own?'

'Henry, I want to see your book.'

'Ah, no, not that, my love.' He was smiling indulgently at her, shaking his head. 'You ask too much. Until my book is finished, no mortal eye shall fall upon a line of my pregnant phrases. My innermost thoughts, my deepest feelings cannot be exposed to the light of day until the pangs of birth are totally and finally stilled. Then, heart of my heart, light of my life, with my own hands I shall bear the fruit of my labours to your bower, and lay before you the unravelled threads of my innermost soul. Till that day, till the . . .'

'I thought,' said Beatrice, icy cold, 'that it was a biography.'

'Beatrice, my fair one, no work of . . .'

'Henry,' said Beatrice, in a voice from Arctic wastes, 'I want to see your book *now*.'

Henry made no attempt to follow his wife as she walked up the two flights of stairs to the attic room that had till this moment been his inviolate territory. But as he sat leaning sideways in his armchair, with one hand over his eyes, his mind followed her as she shuffled through the papers in his desk, pausing perhaps to peer into other unopened letters from his bank. She would be skimming through the pages of the typescript that he had abandoned so long ago. Soon she would find the key and open the cupboard, and might even notice the loose floorboards as she walked over them.

Henry got to his feet and went to the dining room. Opening a cupboard in the sideboard, he lifted out a cut-glass decanter, and struggled to loosen the once familiar stopper.

Lionel was alone in the London house. He and Louise had moved back up from Surrey two days earlier, when the parliamentary session had started again after the Christmas break. Louise had just gone out, after trying to persuade him to join her at lunch in a restaurant with their elder son. She was trying to rebuild relations with Rupert after their disastrous Christmas, and though she knew that Lionel's presence would make this harder, she felt nevertheless that he ought to be there.

'No, Louise. You seem to think just because the House has only just started sitting that I have no work to do. You fail to realise that . . .'

'All right, all right, I am sorry. I must go. I am late already. There is salad, and some cold ham in the fridge. And lots of cheese.'

Lionel, however, had neither worked nor eaten lunch. First he had telephoned St Stephen's Secretarial Agency, the stand-by for most MPs when their normal secretarial arrangements broke down or needed back-up. Then he had received a telephone call. Now he was sitting with his head in his hands, hearing again in his mind the final sentences of the conversation.

'I am not going to repeat the details on the telephone. You know the two options, which haven't changed. You will give me your promise, in writing, of one or the other, with your signature witnessed. Otherwise I go to the press. You have one week from today to decide which. And that's it. Don't ring me again until you have decided. And don't try to come and see me. I won't be here.'

Lionel's attempt to speak was met by the line going dead. The stream of invective he directed at the instrument had done little to make him feel better. He was overwhelmed by a sense of injustice exceeded only by his fear of the calamity that was rolling towards him like a dark bank of fog. He felt a desperate urge to ask Louise for help and advice, and found himself laughing hysterically at the thought. After the laughter came tears of self-pity mingled with anger directed mainly at life itself.

He started as the telephone came to life again. Half hoping, half fearing that he would hear the same voice, he grabbed towards it as if at a lifeline, then withdrew his hand. He let it ring several times before lifting the receiver.

'Yes,' he said coldly.

'What's up, Lionel?' said the unwelcome voice of his younger sister-in-law. 'You sound in a temper.'

'My dear Flora, why should I be in a temper? I am merely busy.'

'Well, you should know,' said Flora. 'Listen, Lionel, I want to talk to you. You're the only member of this family who can discuss Mother without getting emotional. I'm away for the weekend, but will you meet me for lunch this Monday, the sixteenth? *Without* telling Louise?'

Flora made Lionel feel nervous, and he was not inclined to refuse her request without good reason. She might check up on any spur-of-the-moment excuse. Also, he rather liked the idea that Flora thought of him as cool and unemotional.

'Well, I am extremely tied up at the moment, but I daresay I could spare an hour. Where?'

'Olivo's, in Elizabeth Street. Nice grub and you can usually find a parking meter there. One o'clock?'

'Er – Flora, I think, on the whole, I would prefer to be closer to the House of Commons. There is always a lot happening at the start of the session.' Lionel realised just in time that he would feel more in charge of the situation if they met on his own familiar territory. 'May I suggest you join me at the Kolossi, just off Millbank?'

On another day Flora might have said, 'I expect the PM likes to have you within earshot,' but she remembered that she wanted Lionel on her side, and compromised.

'Well, I had intended to give you lunch,' she lied. 'But if you insist, I am delighted to be your guest.'

Lionel cursed Flora roundly but silently, and said, 'Monday then.'

It was a recorded message.

'It's me, Terry. Just a quick one. No real breakthrough yet, but we are getting there. I need to know at once if there is any danger of being found. I need time, more time than I thought. Use the bleeper, but

91

only once. If you do, I'll get back to you as soon as possible.

'Incidentally, I've made an interesting discovery, which is that alcohol could be the solution. Bye now.'

Chapter Six

'You promised me,' said Patrick.

'I promised you,' repeated the youth who lay on his bed, pursing his lips primly, and wagging his head in mocking imitation of Patrick's manner and accent. 'Who said I keep my promises then? Anyway, *you've* promised *me* plenty you haven't done.'

Patrick paced up and down in front of the window at the sitting-room end of the double apartment. Looking out, he saw a dog amble off the pavement by the church opposite and sit down in the middle of the road to scratch itself. It would be so simple to keep a dog.

He turned and spoke through the archway towards the bed.

'I can't go on like this, Simon. It's your habit, not mine, and I just haven't the money to run it.'

'Sell something. You've got lots of junk here.'

The youth looked round Patrick's carefully furnished flat – black marble and white linen, meticulously placed splashes of red, dyed flax branches and woven Mexican cloth. Black swirls of contemporary Japanese lithographs adorned the walls.

'You're going to have to leave,' said Patrick firmly. 'I will always help you if you are trying, but you are not trying. I can't cope with this any more.'

'I don't believe this.' Simon's eyes opened wide. 'After

all I done for you, you think I'm going to just, like, walk
out, when you say so?'

'Listen, Simon.' Patrick walked firmly to the end of
the bed and gripped the black iron rail of the bed-
stead. 'I mean this. I have no more money to spare.
I have nothing to sell that would make any, even if
I felt like selling. And I am not going to have any
more of that filthy stuff delivered to my shop. It is
simply going to kill you. It's for your own good. You
say you can give it up any time. Well, prove it. I am
making a stand, but I am saving your life. I am quite
prepared to help you, take you to a clinic, anything
you need. But I am not getting you any more of that
stuff.'

'Listen, Patrick,' the same imitation, but more malevo-
lent now, 'I mean this too. You're so bloody stupid. You
think you can just stop, don't you? Nice clean Patrick in
his little white socks, got tired of that game, doesn't want
to play no more. Well, mate, the gate of this playground is
shut now. You're in for good. Locked in, and you'd better
learn to like it.'

'Don't try to play tough with me, Simon. You are no
good at it. You are not impressing me at all, and if you
want to stay here you stay on my terms. No smack, no
coke, no hash, no drugs of any kind. Otherwise out
you go.'

Simon smiled and pretended to try to catch the pointing, jabbing finger.

'And if I won't go?' he said.

'Oh, you'll go, all right.'

'Throw me out, will you?' The sneer in his voice was
disconcerting.

'I shan't have to,' said Patrick. 'The police will take you,
quite happily, when I ring them.'

'Oh, yes?' The youth settled back comfortably against

the piled pillows and locked his hands behind his head. 'As a witness, I suppose?'

'Witness? I shall tell them you are pestering me. Unwanted guest. I'm not going to shop you, you idiot. They won't prosecute you.'

'No, you're right there, Patrick, they won't prosecute me but they will prosecute you,' said Simon. 'They like to get the dealers, every now and again.'

'Dealers? What the hell do you mean?'

'Oh, Patrick, you're so fucking innocent. If I had used all that smack you've been bringing me every Thursday, you wouldn't have to get rid of me. Nature would have done it for you, love. Oh, no, you're a dealer, Patrick, one of the best. Look, I can prove it.'

He was out of bed and across the room to the pile of clothes on the floor, pulling a plastic-wrapped brown envelope out of a zipped pocket of his fleece. As Patrick watched his smooth brown body squatting there in a shaft of sunlight he remembered briefly how he had once felt about it. It seemed light years ago, but he could still feel a detached admiration. Simon stood up and walked to him, with an outstretched hand.

'Here,' he said, 'recognise anyone in those?'

Patrick saw himself in the photographs, front view, side view, half-profile, surrounded by antique furniture, undoubtedly in his shop, taken, he supposed, through the window. He was openly receiving two plastic bags, yellow-brown, Sainsbury's, nothing unusual. Another showed him handing something to the other man, some bank notes, hard to tell how much. A close-up of that, too. Another full-face, thanking, smiling. The other man's face was never seen.

'There's nothing there,' said Patrick, his throat dry.

'Oh, no, not much. Just a plastic bag in the box of Sainsbury's non-biological washing powder you get every week. Oh, no, nothing much. Only half a pound of heroin, ducky, and it's going up, from next week.'

Simon was back on the bed, sitting cross-legged on the pillows like a leprechaun.

'You're ridiculous. There is nothing to implicate me in this. I am totally innocent, and you know it.'

'Oh, yeah? What about this one?'

He flicked another print across the bed.

Patrick entering Lloyds Bank, in Kensington High Street.

'Anyone can go into a bank. That's my branch. It has my account.'

'That's right, Patrick, your private account, your business account, and your other account.'

'I have no other account.'

'You do, though. Here's your latest statement.'

The boy threw himself forward full length on the bed and took the photographs from Patrick's drooping hand. He held a folded page up towards Patrick, who snatched it from him. He read the words at the top.

'Who the hell is Martin E. Dawes?'

'Don't you recognise him? Look, here's his photo, in his passport.' Simon flicked a page over. 'Very like, too, I should say, as one what knows, though it must be a few years old. I see it's got listed the distinguishing mark on the left buttock, too. Very thorough. I like that.'

It was one of the blue UK passports that he held up, not a new EC one. The photograph Patrick recognised as one of himself taken for a ski pass not more than five or six years earlier. The signature seemed to be in his own writing. But the name was Martin E. Dawes.

'Same name as the statement, right?' the taunting voice went on. 'Must be you. And have you got the wedge!'

Simon took the statement from Patrick, and, getting to his feet in front of the older man, held it up so that he could read it. The figure Patrick saw was of a sum such as he had never before seen on a bank statement, even in his business account. He heard himself make a whimpering sound.

'Here's your pay-in book, too. Martin never goes into the bank, of course. Oh, no. He's more of a postal man, is Martin. Same address as you, though. Funny, that. Oh no you don't!'

Simon danced back as Patrick grabbed impotently at the documents in his hands. Suddenly he was serious, pulling on his pants and jeans.

Patrick leant heavily on the bed rail.

The youth pulled a T-shirt over his head and watched Patrick as he tucked it into his waistband. His face relaxed.

'Look, mate. We're in this together, you and me. I can't get out no more than you can. So why not relax? We can go on having a good time together. We have a good time, don't we, Patrick? You and me? Well then, Patrick. I been fair with you. I told you what you was getting for me, I just didn't tell you how much. And don't you worry about me. I can handle the stuff, anyway. Some people can. Like, you just carry on bringing home the groceries, to coin a phrase, and I deal with the rest of it. Sorted. No problem. Fair's fair. And no one else will know anything about today's little tantrum.'

Patrick, grey with shock, stared at the grinning face. Suddenly he felt a convulsive rising in his stomach and ran blindly to the bathroom. He dropped on his knees in front of the lavatory pan, and was violently sick.

Louise's lunch with Rupert had not gone well, not as a meal, anyway. To begin with he had been three-quarters of an hour late. Louise would not have minded this, but the glares that she had received from the waiters in the small but crowded restaurant, as she occupied a corner table without ordering, had made her feel thoroughly uncomfortable.

When her son arrived, dressed in jeans, a greyish-white T-shirt and a shapeless woollen jacket that looked as if it had been used to clean a car, Louise, in her MP's wife's 'meeting' suit, wished she had chosen a pub for their reunion.

'Darling,' she said, 'it's so good of you to come. How long is your lunch hour?'

Before Rupert could reply, a waiter interrupted.

'Your order, madame?'

'Ah, now, what will we have?' said Louise, picking up the menu, determined not to be flustered by him. 'What do you recommend?'

'The beef bourguignon's very nice, so's the veal Milanese. It's all good,' said the waiter, watching another table that was being vacated.

'Darling, what will you have? Something nice to start with? There's that bresaola that you like, or an avocado, perhaps, with roasted peppers and feta cheese?'

'Plate of spaghetti, please. I haven't got long. Got a rehearsal at three.'

Rupert worked backstage at one of the smaller and less successful pub theatres south of the river.

'Spaghetti,' said the waiter, his voice indicating eyes lifted heavenward. 'We have fettucine alla carbonara, farfalle al basilico, penne con pr . . .'

'Just spaghetti,' snarled Rupert, 'with tomato sauce.'

'And madame?'

'The same, please,' said Louise courageously. 'With a salad. A salade Niçoise, I think. And may we have the wine list?'

'Oh, Mother. House red. Or beer. No fuss.'

'Madame would like a bottle of the Valpolicella?' said the waiter.

'Yes, please. And some bread.'

As he walked away, Louise said, to lighten the atmosphere, 'I hoped he might say, "We don't serve bread with one fish ba-ha-hall".'

'*What?*' said Rupert, peering at her crossly.

'Oh, silly joke,' she said. 'An old song. Sorry. Darling, this is fun. Now tell me everything you've been doing. What about the play? Is it good? When does it open?'

'What play?' said Rupert.

'Well, I meant the one you are rehearsing.'

'I'm not rehearsing any play. I'm in admin. And it's not a play, anyway. It's a musical psycho-drama. It's a disaster.'

'Well, who's in this disaster?'

'No one you would have heard of.'

'Well,' said Louise, 'that disposes of that subject. Your turn now.'

'Mum, sorry.' Rupert reached out and squeezed her arm. 'And I'm sorry I was late. It's been a hell of a week, and I've got the push, anyway.'

'The push? The sack? You mean . . . Oh, darling, I *am* sorry. Is that definite?'

'I wouldn't go back, anyway. I'll just stay till I get my money at the end of the week.'

Louise fiddled with a bread roll and poured herself a glass of water. She was more than thankful that Lionel had refused to come. She was extremely fond of her son and was aware that sympathy was his only need at this moment, not questions.

'Stupid people. They didn't deserve you. Do you know where you'll go next?' She kept all anxiety out of her voice. 'For a job, I mean?'

'No. Back on the dole, I suppose. You'd better not tell Dad.'

'No. No, I won't. But you will let me know as soon as you have something, won't you? Oh, dear, I am so sorry.'

'You needn't be,' said Rupert. 'I hated the job anyway. It was a lousy company. They're a real bunch of sh . . . Sorry. I think I'll go abroad.'

'Abroad? Oh, darling. Why not come home for a bit first, just to sort yourself out? Then you won't have to pay any rent for a while. Just till you find a job. I'm sure it won't take you long . . .'

They were interrupted by the waiter, bringing their spaghetti and covering it with Parmesan from a huge grinder.

'That stuff makes it smell of baby's vomit,' said Rupert when he had gone.

Louise laughed. At least he was making jokes now. They ate for some minutes in silence. Then Rupert pushed his plate away.

'Mum, you know I can't come home. He gets on my . . . Sorry. He never leaves me alone. I can't take it. It's not you, you know that. But I just can't stand the way he . . . the way you . . . Oh, for crying out loud!'

'Darling, what is it?' said Louise, sympathetically, looking at his clenched fist on the tablecloth. 'I still don't really know what went wrong at Christmas, I just know it wasn't very happy.'

'It was the most godawful shitty Christmas I have ever spent anywhere.'

'Rupert! Keep your voice down!'

'Sorry. Forget it. I've got to go.' He reached for his jacket.

'Rupert, you can't just go like this.' Louise reached a supplicating hand across the table. 'What *is* the matter?'

'What is the matter? The matter?' He was hissing now, and leaning forward. 'The matter is that you are totally and utterly blind. You can't see what is going on right under your nose. What's been going on for years behind your back. Everybody knows, everybody but you, and you just don't seem even to want to see the way you are being humiliated, we are all being . . . I . . . I . . .'

To her horror Louise saw that he was nearly in tears, her large, brawny, tough son.

'Meet me in the street, Rupert,' she said calmly. 'I'll pay the bill.'

He apologised outside the restaurant, and after a short drive they walked arm-in-arm across Clapham Common together, closer than they had been for years.

'Of course I knew,' said Louise, 'ages ago. Years ago. But for some of us it is easier to put up with something like that than to lose everything. I have you two, you see, and that makes it all worthwhile. And he hasn't been a bad husband, not like some. He has this weakness, so many men have. But I would rather that than that he drank, or gambled, or whatever. Are you surprised? You shouldn't be. I have just ignored it, as far as I can. It sometimes amuses me that he thinks I don't know. Actually, I think *he* worries about his womanising – nice old-fashioned word, isn't it? – far more than I do. He's really terrified of being found out, of there being a scandal in the constituency. He sees everything, you see, in terms of his majority, of the votes he might lose.'

'How can he care so much about a seat in that place?' Rupert kicked a stone in front of him.

'Oh, it's compulsive, the House of Commons. It gets under their skin. I have seen it change people completely. They become emotionally numb, so that moral issues are seen in terms of the strength of a lobby rather than in terms of personal conscience. Their consciences may still be there, but they are in abeyance. They have to be, or you would never get agreement on anything. Someone has to govern, after all. It's quite a hard life, you know, even for the idlest.'

'And he's one of those,' said Rupert.

'Yes, I'm afraid so,' replied his mother, with a rueful smile. 'But he does do some good, for individual constituents, quite often.'

'He's so pompous, Mum.'

'Yes, now. He wasn't originally. Don't you remember, when you were small? There is quite a nice man somewhere inside it all. But his pomposity and bullying manner is a sort of self-defence. It helps him to feel important. He has never got as far in politics as he hoped. He has never been a minister, or even got on to a parliamentary committee of any significance. He is fighting against feeling a failure. And his . . . well . . . girlfriends . . . give him one kind of success.'

Feeding pigeons scattered in front of their feet and bustled back behind them to fight over the crusty end of a loaf.

'You're quite different, Mum, when you're talking like this,' said Rupert. 'I never knew you were so philosophical. Or so sensible, really. That's not meant to be rude – but you and Dad seem to be in a bit of a mess. Matt and I just wish you would get your act together.'

'Our act, yes. It is all a bit of an act, most of the time,' said Louise. 'But he needs me. And we all need to be needed. That is one certainty that keeps me going. I know that he would collapse totally if he didn't have me to rely on. He trusts me, and in a funny way I know I won't let him down. I'm still quite fond of him, you know.'

'So you wouldn't ever leave him?'

'Probably not,' said Louise. 'In fact, certainly not. In any case, they say leaving your partner is as hard as changing your newspaper. Or have I got that the wrong way round?'

They both laughed, and Louise could sense the almost palpable relief in Rupert. This in itself would have been justification enough for putting up with Lionel. And she knew she would go on putting up with him, though God knew he would never change, because the benefits of being married to him still outweighed the deficits.

'Rupert,' she said, 'thank you for coming, darling. We should do this more often.'

Their lunch, she thought, had achieved the *rapprochement* that she had wanted, though perhaps not quite in the way she had planned.

Before they parted, she pressed a cheque for a hundred pounds on her reluctant son.

'Just to tide you over. You can pay me back when you're rich. You will get a job, I know you will. Keep in touch.'

She thought ruefully and unregretfully how angry Lionel would be if he knew. Well, he wouldn't know.

The shores of Loch Fyne were aglow in the sunlight, and though the trees were leafless there was colour everywhere. The bare branches were all shades of pink and purple, with green spruce, tawny gold larches, silver trunks of birch trees on the shore mirrored in the blue water, under a deeper blue sky.

The loch was still, almost without a ripple, until the odd lazy sigh of wind breathed across the surface, momentarily ruffling the reflection of the steep hills around. A light dusting of snow lay on the tops of more distant mountains.

'I wish I had some paints,' said Mrs Rokeby-Jones. 'Oh dear, what an ordinary reaction that is to beauty. It is predatory, really, like souvenir-hunting: a need to take something away with you. Photography is the same, I suppose. But with painting you really do take it away, inside you, as well as on the paper. Painting is a very sensuous activity, I always think. It makes you feel the landscape with your eyes, fondle it, touch it all over, investigate it visually. You have to, to get it on to the paper. And afterwards, you know it so well that you feel as if you own it. And your relationship with it has totally changed.'

'Do you paint?' asked the woman, still looking at the view.

'Oh, I used to, long ago. Just watercolours. I learnt a bit, as a girl. I gave it up after I married.'

'He didn't like it?'

'That's right. He liked me to do useful things, more. He knew a lot about art, of course, and I really wasn't very good at it. He showed me that.'

'Enjoyed it, did you?'

'I loved it,' said Mrs Rokeby-Jones with unusual passion.

'Well, then?'

As usual the woman seemed to be pressing her with questions, and often she felt as if she were being pushed into a corner of some kind; a dark corner, and it disturbed her.

'Oh, you wouldn't understand,' she replied dismissively. 'I only did it for fun, and . . . somehow it didn't seem fun any more. It didn't seem to work. Anyhow, with our very busy social life I didn't have time for that sort of thing.'

They were sitting side by side at a wooden table in front of the Loch Fyne Oyster Bar. They had eaten fresh herring in fried oatmeal in the old converted barn and shared a bottle of dry white wine. Then, feeling pleasantly relaxed, they had carried cups of coffee outside into the still warm sunlight. Only in the shade did it feel like winter.

'What were we talking about, before we got on to painting?'

'Louise,' said the woman.

'Oh yes, Louise.' She thought about her middle daughter. 'She looked very like my husband when she was small.'

'My husband,' the woman repeated. 'What was his name?'

'My husband? Surely you know. Lieutenant-Colonel Robert Rokeby-Jones. I have told you that, I am sure.'

'What did you call him?'

'I called him Robert, of course. What did you think I would call him?'

She turned to look at the woman, now a different creature from the shapeless figure who had turned up at Bloomfield. Her trousers fitted slim hips and without the tea-cosy her hair seemed to have settled down into a neat shiny cap. She found her hard to place. She was like no one she had ever known before, giving away so little of herself.

'Bob? Robbie?' suggested Ruth.

'Oh, goodness. No.' Mrs Rokeby-Jones half laughed, and then frowned.

'Why not?'

'Really! I do not like these personal questions. You are always asking personal questions. Please do not . . . pry. Why do you do it?'

'Conversation,' said the woman, shrugging.

'Well, let's talk about something else. You, for instance, Ruth. You haven't told me anything about yourself. I know nothing about you, really.'

'Ask, then,' said the woman, dipping a piece of sugar into the bottom of her coffee cup.

'Well, for instance, do you have children?'

The woman shook her head.

'No, I'm sorry. How silly of me. Of course, you're not married.' The hands on the knees of the blue jeans beside her had no rings. 'Not, of course, that that matters, I mean you might . . . um . . . Have you other close relatives?'

The woman laughed.

'An uncle. That do?'

'Oh, really? How nice. I never had an uncle. Aunts, but abroad. I hardly knew them. Do you know your uncle well?'

Somehow she could not imagine this self-contained woman having or needing any relations at all. Yet she must have some.

'What's "well"?'

'Well, I meant . . . do you get on with him?'

'Yes.'

The conversation did not seem very fruitful, and Mrs Rokeby-Jones gave up.

'You know,' she said, 'you seem to get younger. When you first turned up at Bloomfield, I thought you were much older. You looked older. And now . . . Perhaps it's the clothes. Why did you come to Bloomfield?'

There was no reply, and she felt guilty.

'I am very, very glad you did, of course.'

The woman looked at her quizzically, and then said:

'Time to move.'

'Where to now?'

'A walk, now. To Inveraray.'

'Is it nice? It's on the loch, isn't it?'

'You'll see. I like it.'

'Do we spend the night there?'

'We could.'

Mrs Rokeby-Jones hummed as they walked along the road that followed the side of the loch, and pointed with pleasure to a heron as it flapped lazily overhead.

The woman, two paces behind her, wondered.

Chapter Seven

Beatrice's reaction to what she found in Henry's attic workroom had been quite different from what he had anticipated. There were no tears or recriminations, no outpouring of self-pity or demands for explanations of how he could do this to her, when she was so busy. She had spent some time upstairs, and then gone out of the house. She had not reappeared for several hours. It was after dark when she returned, and by that time he was not capable of being either worried or frightened any more.

Beatrice had eased and dragged him up the stairs to their bedroom, and wordlessly removed his clothes and rolled him into bed. She had slept, or rather lain awake beside him, and then allowed him to sleep it off until he had woken naturally the following day at about midday.

She came then, and sat on the side of his bed, and stared at him.

'I couldn't *believe* it,' she said. 'One hundred and seventy-three bottles. How did you do it without me *knowing*? I simply can't *believe* it.'

Henry groaned, and shut his eyes again.

'I must be *mad* to have believed you. Just because you told me you had stopped, I *believed* you. Well, when they . . . retired you from the ministry I was *sure* you had stopped. I mean, who in their senses would go *on* after that? Even that doctor told me you had stopped. He should be *sued*. They know *nothing*, those people. They take your money, and they know *nothing*. How long has this been going on? A hundred and seventy-three bottles doesn't run up an overdraft like that. Tell me, Henry. How *long*? Two years? Three? Four? How *long*?'

Henry groaned again.

'Henry?' There was no mercy to be heard in Beatrice's voice.

'Two, three. I don't know. It's not like you think.'

'Indeed it *is* like I think, Henry.'

'I will stop, Bea, really I will.'

Beatrice considered these words, and by sheer force of personality made Henry meet her gaze, though his bleary eyes ached to close again.

'No you won't. You can't. I realise that. I have been in the library, reading it all up. Somehow I am going to get you into a clinic, a private clinic. Drying out, it's called. Detoxification. And you're going to go whether you want to or not. Until you're cured.'

'I can't do that. There's no money.'

He put an arm across his eyes.

'You don't have to tell *me* that,' said Beatrice bitterly. 'I have been struggling for years to keep up appearances, drudging away, for both our sakes, *and* the children's, while *you* have been spending our money on poisoning yourself. And you tell *me* there is no money. Thank you so much. Well, there is going to *have* to be money. I am going to have to speak to Mother.'

Henry groaned again and Beatrice left the room.

Lionel and Flora arrived simultaneously at the Kolossi restaurant, Flora by taxi and Lionel on foot.

'Is this your local?' said Flora. 'I haven't been here before.'

'I think you'll enjoy it,' said Lionel. 'Greek food, but not entirely.'

'Love it,' said Flora.

'A lot of us come here, MPs, lobby correspondents, top civil servants. One usually sees some interesting people, whom I dare say you will recognise. It is very conveniently near the House and they have a division bell. They know the form, of course, and they understand if one has to dash off to vote in the middle of the meal.'

Lionel was happy that he had insisted on this restaurant. He felt that Flora was impressed, which might make her less difficult than usual. He led the way downstairs into the restaurant, and waved to the head waiter, who bore down upon them, beaming.

'Ah, Andreas, my friend, there you are, 'said Lionel, the cosmopolitan man.

'Mr Leetham, sir, it is a pleasure to see you. I trust you had an enjoyable festive season? I have kept your usual table for you, of course. And madame, may I relieve her of her coat? A pleasure, madame. We are honoured to meet any guest of Mr Leetham's, of course. If you will kindly follow me . . . We have missed you, sir, during the recess. I am sure you will be very busy during the new session, but we hope you may find time to honour us with a visit every now and then. Always a pleasure . . . There you are, sir. Which seat would madame prefer? Of course, thank you so much . . .'

With an expert flourish he flicked pink damask napkins across their laps.

'And would you like to see the wine list, sir? Thank you so much. May I give madame a menu? A pleasure . . . Some water? Still? Carbonated?'

'Fizzy, with a slice of lemon, Andreas.'

Lionel's eyes were sliding around the other tables,

hoping to find someone well known to whom he could give a casual wave.

'For you, anything, Mr Leetham.'

The head waiter snapped his fingers at an underling and swooped off to greet another customer.

'What a creep,' said Flora. 'How can you stand it? Lionel! I do believe you like all that lick-spittle stuff! Yuk!'

'It doesn't matter,' said Lionel. 'He's a good fellow.'

He felt disconcerted. Damn Flora.

A junior Cabinet minister passed their table and nodded at Lionel, which made him feel better. Unfortunately Flora was looking at the menu. When she looked up he said:

'I expect you recognise the Transport Minister over there.'

'Oh yes? What's he doing here? Shouldn't he be on a train somewhere?'

Lionel gave an indulgent laugh.

'My dear Flora, even Cabinet ministers have to eat. From the look of it, I would say he was being given lunch by the *Observer*. A lot of journalists meet us MPs for informal briefings here. Time is precious in Parliament, and every meal is a working meal.'

'Nice work if you can get it. Jolly good menu.'

Lionel noticed with annoyance that she was looking at the à la carte.

'Rather a good sole in the set menu, I seem to remember,' he said hopefully.

'Hello, darlings!'

Lionel glared up. Patrick was standing over them, wearing an unsuitable bow tie.

'Oh, it's you,' said Lionel, looking at him with no pleasure. 'What are you doing here?'

'Joining you, old love.'

'I am afraid I only booked a table for two,' Lionel said coldly.

Patrick looked at Flora, who said, 'Oh, I asked him, but I didn't tell you, because I didn't think he would come.'

'All right, Lionel?' Patrick said, as he sat on the chair that a waiter was placing behind him. 'I'll have a dry martini, please, and some olives.'

'I did not invite you, but if you want to have your lunch at our table, you may of course do so,' said Lionel, not attempting to disguise his annoyance.

'Well, isn't that nice?' said Flora, beaming.

Once their meal was ordered, Flora leant her elbows on the table and interlaced her fingers.

'Right. Lionel, as you have just said, this is a working lunch, and I propose to chair it. Let's have no fudging the issue. I don't want to leave here without a plan to find Mother, get her home and then get her to agree to sell Bloomfield. I don't care if she goes into a flat, a cottage or a retirement home, though I can't see that, personally. And I will fight for her right to decide. But it is quite ridiculous having her sitting in that great place when she doesn't need half of it, it costs a fortune to run, she can't get help, or not help that stays, and that is one thing we all agree on. How about it?'

'It is not often, my dear Flora,' said her brother-in-law, 'that I agree so wholeheartedly with you, but this time I do. I have been saying the same for years.'

'OK, Lionel. I knew you would. Patrick?'

Before Patrick could answer, Lionel said, with an effort at casualness:

'As a matter of interest, what do you think Bloomfield might sell for?'

'Don't worry, Lionel, even in the present housing market it must be worth all of five or six hundred thou,' said Flora.

'Mmm.' The answer was so interesting to Lionel that he was unaware of the contempt in her voice.

Flora turned to her brother.

'What about you?'

'Yes, of course,' said Patrick. 'She must be made to move.'

'Oh?' Flora, surprised, looked speculatively at her brother. 'Usually you say the market is too depressed and we'll do better by waiting. Or you get all pseudo-whimsy about her trusting you, and her feelings and that sort of thing. What's changed?'

'Nothing's changed, I just think you are right. I think it is time we persuaded her.'

'Suddenly.'

Patrick flared up. 'No, not suddenly, Flora. I just . . . do. Why are you complaining? It's what you want.'

'I'm not complaining. I'm just interested. Lionel, what you don't know is that Patrick and I went to see Mother's solicitor, to find out what was in our grandfather's will about the house.'

'Ah!' said Lionel. He was not entirely sure of the implication of this, nor how to react to it. He broke off a piece of French bread and put it in his mouth.

'But we couldn't,' said Flora. 'He wouldn't let us see it. Pompous idiot, he wanted Mother's permission first. So we just don't know. There must be something in it about what happens when Mother doesn't need the house any more.'

'Could be left to me. Her only son, after all,' said Patrick, to annoy.

'You and your descendants, you mean?' said Lionel, sneering.

'Now, now, boys,' said Flora. 'I think that's unlikely, Patrick, given that you were not even born when our grandfather died. In any case, we are all agreed that we have to see the will before anything can be done about the house. And to do that we have first to find Mother.'

Slivers of smoked trout were placed in front of them, dwarfed by the accompanying half-lemons wrapped in muslin for easy squeezing.

'No, no bread, thanks. Do you realise,' Flora went on, when the waiter had gone, 'that it's been nearly three weeks, and none of us have the slightest idea where she is? I wasn't worried before, because, well, she had only been gone a few days. And why shouldn't she? I assumed she was back, anyway, because Bea would have been bleating away by now if she wasn't. One can always rely on her to be fussing. But it appears that Bea is in a stew about something else, I haven't found out what, yet. But she has put Mother's absence on her back burner, so it must be big. In any case, I think it is worrying, now, and that means we are going to have to do something.'

Lionel had remembered while Flora had been talking that this was his lunch party, whether he had wanted it or not, and that he had a perfect right to play a major role in it. He decided to assert himself.

'Well, personally, I think the whole matter is now extremely serious,' he said. 'An elderly lady, still in control of her money, leaves home, without informing any of her relations, possibly in the company of a half-crazed tramp, and nothing is heard of her for three weeks. In another sphere of life one would be informing the Social Services. In ours, I fear it is now a case for informing the police.'

'No!' croaked Patrick, and cleared his throat. 'No. Definitely not. I cannot possibly agree to bringing the police into this. It – it would be highly embarrassing for the whole family. And – and not necessary at this stage. No.'

'Look, Patrick,' said Flora, 'this morning I rang every

known relative I can think of, and most of her neighbours. *Nobody* knows where she is. We have a real problem. If you have time to drive round the country looking for Mother, I haven't. So we need help. But actually, I don't think the police *would* be much good, unless we could suggest to them that that woman has kidnapped her, which isn't exactly likely.'

'That's right,' said Patrick. 'They would not be in the least interested, and we would only make fools of ouselves. I veto the idea, anyway.'

'Your veto is not exactly at Security Council level, my dear Patrick,' said Lionel.

He smirked at his own wit and was spared an inevitable riposte from Patrick by the waiter bringing them their next course. He delayed as much as possible by sampling the claret very slowly, with much rolling round the tongue, sieving through the teeth, and asking to see the label on the bottle again. By the time he had finished, and the glasses were filled, Flora had once more taken charge.

'I've got a better idea. One way to find her is to get a photograph in the papers. We'll invent some juicy story, like she's lost her memory, or taken a gun in her handbag, and tell the press.'

This time it was Lionel who reacted with alarm.

'That is an extremely bad idea, Flora. I cannot possibly sanction that. You have to realise that in my position any press interest would be highly embarrassing. It would produce a great deal of undesirable attention, and since I am not an unknown figure, that is, I have a certain public persona, and . . . and no, certainly not.'

'Then – what – Lionel – do – you – suggest?' said Flora, each word venomously enunciated through bared teeth.

'There are other ways,' said Lionel,' of finding missing people. There is a Missing Persons Bureau, for example.

That's it. I will tell my secretary to find out . . . Well, it can't be hard to find out, anyway.'

'We could hire a private detective, I suppose,' said Patrick.

'Yes, indeed,' said Lionel. 'Quite right. Of course that's the answer. Leave it to me. If necessary, we can hire a private detective. That's it. That would be the most satisfactory way to handle it. These agencies are very discreet. I will deal with that.'

Flora, with one finger to her lips, was looking thoughtfully at her brother and then at her brother-in-law, aware that she was missing something with both of them. Normally she had a pretty good idea of what her relatives were up to, if only instinctively. As far as Patrick was concerned she had never been fooled by his regular visits to their mother's house into thinking that he was a caring son. She had long suspected another motive. Why, then, his sudden willingness for the house to be sold? And what was behind his fear of the police? Fascinating. And Lionel, talking of engaging a private detective – actually being willing to spend some money and, odder still, to take trouble over it. It was all quite out of character.

The table next to theirs became occupied, and they were obliged to talk of other things. This produced stilted conversation, and they unanimously rejected pudding and coffee.

To Lionel's relief Patrick, unprompted, laid some money on the table, and Lionel wrote a cheque. As he handed it to the waiter, he caught sight of a couple walking into another part of the restaurant from the hall. His jaw dropped and the colour drained from his face. His eyes fell to the table, and he sat for a moment oblivious of his companions.

'Who was that?' asked Flora, her antennae twitching.

'Oh . . . a . . . a . . . journalist I know,' said Lionel, in a voice of deep shock.

'Who was the girl? It looked rather like what's her name . . . your secretary. Was it?'

'No, no. I don't know. Could be anyone. I think I must go. I have a lot to do.'

As they left, Flora could see that Lionel was attempting to get another glimpse of the couple. He spoke quietly to the obsequious head waiter, and she heard him reply, 'That's right, Mr Leetham, sir, Miles Sorrell, from the *Evening Echo*. One of our regular customers.'

Standing in the street with Flora, watching Lionel's back as he walked towards the Embankment, Patrick said:

'You don't think something really has happened to Mother, do you, Flora?'

'Yes,' said Flora,' actually, I do. But not necessarily the sort of thing you mean. Still, we need to be sure.'

Her eyes and thoughts were on Lionel, however, whom they could now see turning left towards the Houses of Parliament.

'The Honourable Member our brother-in-law, though . . . I don't know what it is,' she said thoughtfully, 'though I think I can have a stab at guessing. That Lionel has got something serious bugging him. And I suspect that's why he needs some dosh quick. Intriguing . . .'

'God, Flora,' said Patrick grimly, 'he's not the only one with a problem. You know as well as I do that even if Mother turns up tomorrow, even if we can persuade her to get out of Bloomfield, it will be ages before we actually get the place sold. And if I don't get some money soon, my problem is going to be more than just serious. See you.'

And he too left her standing in the street.

*   *   *

A little later that afternoon Beatrice dialled a London number, which was answered with efficient speed.

'Mr Asprey, please,' she said. 'What? Oh, Mr Asprey senior, I think . . . Mrs Henry Fordham. Beatrice Fordham, you'd better say. Thank you.'

She chewed a fingernail impatiently.

'Mrs Fordham? This is Wilfred Asprey. How can I help you?'

'Oh, Mr Asprey. You knew me once as Beatrice Rokeby-Jones.'

'Indeed, Mrs Fordham. Or Beatrice, if I may be so bold. I remember you well.'

'Ah, good,' said Beatrice. 'Of course you would. And I remember you coming to Bloomfield after my father died, but I don't think we have met since then.'

'Alas, no. And to what do I owe the unexpected pleasure of this call?'

'Well, to tell the truth, Mr Asprey, I wanted some advice. You know that my mother is getting on now, and we all worry rather about what is going to happen to her. She does not find it easy to manage on her own now, you see.'

'Indeed?' said the solicitor. 'She has given me no indication of that. I trust she is well?'

'Oh yes, thank you,' said Beatrice. 'She's fine. It's just that, with her memory being very poor now, she asked me to find out what was her position over Bloomfield. Can she sell it if she wants to? Or does it pass automatically to one of her children? And she can't remember which one, if so. Or does it go to us all? If she has a life interest, can this be concluded before her death? It would be a great help to know, she says. And the other thing was, when she really can't cope, how do we go about seeking power of attorney? Does one have to have a doctor's certificate?'

Beatrice had a pen and pad at the ready, and a second

set of questions noted down depending on what answers the first ones should elicit. About selling items of furniture, among other things.

'My dear Mrs Fordham, ah, Beatrice,' said Asprey, 'it seems to me that you are asking a great many questions at once, on your mother's behalf. Speaking as her solicitor, I think it would be better if she put this request in writing to me, and I will of course reply to her. It is not information, you will understand, that I keep in my head.'

'She doesn't write letters very much,' said Beatrice glibly. 'Her eyesight is not at all good at the moment. I mean, she has got to visit an oculist. That is why she asked me to ring you.'

Beatrice was playing triplets with her fingers on the arm of her chair, and trying not to sound impatient.

'I understand, of course, Mrs Fordham, what you are saying. Well, may I suggest that either she telephones me herself, or that you draft a letter for her, to which she can append her signature? You see, I am placed in rather an awkward position here, since I cannot release information without my client's authority.'

Beatrice frowned. The conversation was not going in the manner that she had planned. But she kept the smile in her voice.

'Oh. She really wouldn't mind, you know. After all, I am her eldest daughter. Possibly even her heir.'

'I hear what you say, Mrs Fordham. But I fear I can only repeat what I have said.'

'Damn. I don't suppose she has been in touch with you recently, has she?'

'No, Mrs Fordham. Not recently.' Asprey's tones were not those of one disposed to be helpful.

'I see. Well, thank you. I will of course do as you say. I mean I will write a letter for her. Next time I see her.'

'Goodbye, then, Mrs Fordham. Next time you see her. And thank you for ringing.'

'Goodbye, Mr Asprey. Thank you.'

It was all so unfair. Life seemed to be loaded against Beatrice, even when she decided to take action.

The door of the office of Cockerill Private Investigations Ltd. was not entirely unfamiliar to Lionel. He had visited this particular street near Clapham Junction on two previous occasions when it had not been possible to satisfy his interested curiosity without professional help.

Wallace Cockerill was not displeased to see the familiar bulk once again in his waiting room. He never hesitated to make it clear to other clients that he was patronised by at least one member of the House of Commons, no names mentioned, of course, discretion was his middle name, but it did, he felt, no harm to his business to indicate that he was trusted in high places.

On this occasion, however, he was surprised at the nature of the assignment.

'*Two* ladies, you say, this time, Mr Leetham, and not ladies in their – ah – first youth?'

'Do I have to repeat myself, Cockerill? One is my mother-in-law, and no, of course she is not young, and the other woman – God knows how old she is. Middle-aged, I suppose.'

'And you don't actually wish them to be watched, on this occasion, more – how shall I put it – located?'

'Found, man,' said Lionel. 'I want you to find them. And very quickly. It can't be hard. Two women, they may be coming and going from the address I will give you, or they may be moving about. They won't be hiding, or anything like that. It's no problem, but I am concerned about them and I am far too busy to do it myself. I don't suppose it will take you long. Just find them.'

'Of course, Mr Leetham,' said Cockerill hastily. 'It will be a straightforward assignment, and I am sure you will be entirely satisfied with the result. May I have a description of the clothing your mother-in-law normally wears?'

'Clothes? Well, dresses, wool dresses, I should think. That sort of thing. Ordinary sort of women's clothes. A coat, I suppose, at this time of year, sort of blue, I think. And the other one much the same. But shabby, that one. Very shabby, I believe.'

'Thank you, Mr Leetham. Rokeby-Jones, for the files, of course. Discretion is our speciality. And perhaps you would be so good as to fill in this form with all the relevant details.'

After Lionel had gone Cockerill's receptionist/telephonist/girlfriend burst into his office.

'Go on, Wally, tell us, what's it this time?'

'Different, I can tell you that,' said Cockerill. 'There's somethin' new every day in this business. I thought it was a nice bit of kinky, at the start. But no, it's just bizarre, that's what, really bizarre.'

'Terry? Anything happening?' The enquiry was anxious.

'I think so. It's starting, anyway. I'm not giving you anything now, though. Any activity at your end?'

'None at all that concerns you.'

'None? I don't believe it.'

'I didn't either. It's even worse than I thought. Don't go yet. I want to ask you a few questions. Just ring off if it gets difficult.'

'I warn you, I may not answer them all. What you don't know you don't have to lie about. Fire away, then.'

Beatrice thought about it all overnight before telephoning her brother, reminding herself that involving Patrick in anything resulted in it becoming public knowledge. But in the end she decided that she needed his help more than she feared his indiscretion.

To her relief it was his own voice that answered. You never knew, with Patrick.

'Patrick, it's Bea. What is happening? Have you been on to the police about Mother? I don't think we should.'

'Well, that's a change,' said her brother. 'You were so keen on it before.'

'Well, I'm not now. I don't think we should let everyone know that she has disappeared. I mean, it is just inviting burglars, isn't it, to say the house is empty.'

'Well, I agree, as you know. Don't worry. No one's been to the police. But go on, what's the real reason?'

'Another reason,' said Beatrice firmly,' is that I have been speaking to her solicitor on the telephone. You remember him? Asprey? Well, he doesn't know she's disappeared, and I didn't tell him. If we went to the police now, they would probably track him down, and he would say I hadn't told him and it would look odd.'

'So that's it! You want me to back up your little deceit, Bea. Just like the old days, big sister. "Patrick, I have broken a pane of glass in the greenhouse. Will you say you saw a strange dog in the garden? I'll give you half my Mars Bar."'

The imitative whine in Patrick's voice was slightly obscured by the fact that he was lighting a cigarette from the butt of the one he had just finished.

'Patrick?' squeaked Beatrice, as his voice faded.

'Don't worry, I'm still here,' he said, 'and I'm not telling the police. But you tell me something. Why were you ringing Asprey?'

'Oh, just to see if he's heard from her. You never know. Patrick, that's not important. How on *earth* are we going to find her? What can we *do*?'

'Bea, Flora told me you'd gone all relaxed about it.
Funny. Well, don't worry, it's all in hand. Lionel has
got one of those private detective agencies on to it. All
they seem to have established so far is that Mother and
that gypsy woman were standing at the bus stop on the
road into the village a few days after Christmas, probably
the twenty-eighth. Someone saw them and they were
talking, but we don't know whether they got on a bus.
It's not much, but they have only been following it up
since yesterday.'

'Mother going on a *bus*! It seems so *unlikely*.'

Beatrice's astonishment was high-pitched.

'It's a start, anyway,' said Patrick. 'I suppose they will
check with the bus companies next.'

'Do you think we *ought* to tell the solicitor, Patrick?'

'No. Definitely not, darling. He's not going to help.
Flora thinks he's likely to side with Moth . . .' He stopped.
Too late.

'Does Flora know him? What's this? Have you and
Flora been talking to Mr Asprey? What about?'

Patrick brushed her suspicion aside with an easy back-
hander.

'Oh, same as you. To see if he had heard from her.'

'That's funny,' said Beatrice. 'He never mentioned it.'

'Bea, darling, I must dash. Oh, horrors. It's half seven
already. Hundreds of delicious people coming to dinner
and I'm nothing like ready. Just tell me something. Why
is Flora so keen to get Mother out of Bloomfield?'

'Well, money, I suppose, like the rest of us. And
– and concern for her wellbeing, of course,' Beatrice
added.

Patrick ignored the second point.

'But Flora is the one member of the family who doesn't
need the money. With her lodgers and her counselling
rubbish, she's rolling in it. But she has been going on

about moving Mother for as long as I can remember. What's in it for her?'

'I don't know,' said Beatrice, 'and I don't care. But at least we've got her helping for once, so let's not complain.'

Patrick replaced the receiver and stubbed out his cigarette without thinking.

'Shit,' he said, and lit another. He decided to go to the pub to take his mind off things. He could not stand the thought of an evening on his own, worrying. He felt that he was being carried at high speed towards Monday.

Chapter Eight

'You can't do this to me.'

Lionel was sweating. His plump face was shining and his collar felt a size too small. The handset was sticky in his hand.

'Can't I? You are not very fussy about what you do to me.'

The voice at the other end of the line was almost without expression.

'I saw you with that bastard Sorrell from the *Echo*,' said Lionel in a voice which by contrast was laden with desperation. 'What were you up to? You said you would give me a week to decide. What were you doing with him?'

'Oh, jealous, are we?'

'Mandy, for God's sake.' He was almost bleating.

'Why should I tell you, Lionel, what I was doing with him? He's a friend of mine. I can go out to lunch, can't I?'

The calmness of her voice was almost the most frightening thing about it. Until recently she had merely been petulant.

'But why with him, Mandy? You know how he feels about me.'

'Oh yes. He reminded me about his little tiff with you. You got him sacked from the *Evening Star*, he says, over some expenses fiddle. Talk about the pot and the kettle!'

Lionel swallowed. 'What have you said to him?'

'Nothing. Sweet nothings,' said the girl. 'But I have suggested that I might make it worth his while to give me lunch again on Monday.'

'Mandy,' Lionel whined, 'you said you would give me a week to decide. I need more time – I have to work some things out. Don't you see?'

'It will be well over a week, on Monday. I know you, give you more time and you will want more still.'

The MP mopped his forehead with his handkerchief, and then blew his nose.

'Can I come and see you? Please? You must feel something for me, Mandy. You never used to be so cruel.'

'If I didn't feel anything for you, Lionel, you wouldn't have the two options. I am going against my better judgement just speaking to you. I will not see you. All right, Lionel. One more week. Till the following Monday. But that's it. That's final. If you don't get that letter to me, with everything agreed and signed and witnessed, by midday on Monday week, you know what happens. Goodbye, Lionel.'

Lionel let the hand holding the receiver fall on his knee. He ran his finger round the inside of his collar and wished for an earthquake, a general election, anything that would distract attention from what was shortly going to happen to him.

He dialled again, the number for Cockerill Private Investigations. Only his mother-in-law could help him now.

During a long, wet bus journey towards Inverness Mrs Rokeby-Jones wondered, not for the first time, whether she had not got into the habit of opening her heart just a little too much to Ruth. She was such a good listener, and so easy to talk to. Those two evenings in Oban, in the restaurant on the pier, and perhaps especially today over lunch before joining the coach in Fort William, when they had again shared an excellent bottle of wine: she was aware that she had said possibly more about Louise and Patrick, in particular, than was entirely necessary. No family, after all, was perfect, and she was so lucky to have a family at all. She hated to think that she might have been guilty of disloyalty. In any case, any personal problems she might have were nobody's business but her own.

The seats near them were all empty, so it seemed a good moment to reassert her privacy.

'I feel, Ruth, that I may have been giving you a rather misleading impression of my family. Sometimes we have been talking late in the evening, or after we have had a drink or two, and in those circumstances I think I am prone to exaggeration.'

The woman looked at her, and made up her mind.

'You mean it's not true?'

'What's not true?'

'Everything you have been telling me. That your family is a bunch of ungrateful, grasping, spoilt parasites who have succeeded in sucking you dry and are now picking the flesh off your bones? And who won't be satisfied until you are a nice, clean skeleton?'

Mrs Rokeby-Jones gasped. This was the longest sentence she had ever heard the woman utter, and certainly the most startling.

'Ruth! I have never said anything like that!'

'It's what you have told me, though,' said Ruth.

'But this is absolutely untrue!'

'You have told me, or allowed me to see, that Louise is married to a fairly useless MP who is unfaithful to her and who bullies you. That she is incapable either of dealing

127

with him or of protecting you from him. And, indeed, she seems to have no wish to.'

'But surely I should be capable of protecting myself,' said Mrs Rokeby-Jones with an attempt at haughtiness. 'It is hardly Louise's business. And in any case, Louise is devoted to me.'

The woman gaped at her.

'Louise? She lives not much more than twenty miles from you, and yet you only see her every few months, and then only when she wants something.'

Mrs Rokeby-Jones grasped the back of the seat in front and leant her head against it while she thought. She must not give way to this battering.

'No,' she said carefully, 'it is not like that. Louise is a very busy wife and mother. She has a lot to do.'

'Such as?' the woman persisted.

'Well, she has to support Lionel in his constituency work, and attend a great many different events, there and in London. And that as well as look after two houses. She has very little help in the house, you know. And she does secretarial work for him, a bit, too, I believe.'

'Two houses, and they resent you living in just one?'

'No! You are making this up. You are jumping to conclusions.'

The shores of a dark-watered loch streamed by through the rain-streaked window. They both looked at it, but neither saw it.

'Louise never did more for you than just enough to keep her conscience quiet,' said the woman. 'You know that, don't you?'

'That is a terrible thing to say. And quite untrue.'

'Oh, yes? And Beatrice, your golden-haired, blue-eyed baby. How is she repaying your love and care for her? Long, haranguing telephone calls about how busy she is and how she can't possibly get over to see you because of

all her committee meetings. And as for asking you to stay
– when did you last go down to Dorset?'

'Ruth, what has got into you? I have never known you
like this.'

'Go on. Tell me. What does Beatrice do for you except
nag you?'

Ruth was watching her closely now.

'*You* have no business to harangue *me* like this,' said
Mrs Rokeby-Jones heatedly, 'and talking about people
you hardly know. I see I am right and that I have
been far too free in my confidences to you. You have
misunderstood the whole situation. It may be my fault,
indeed, but you have been quite misled.'

She sat back in her seat and smoothed down the front
of her anorak. She calmed herself before speaking again.
The woman waited.

'Beatrice,' said Mrs Rokeby-Jones, 'has serious problems in her own life. Henry, you know. He had to leave
the civil service because of drinking. Please keep this to
yourself, Ruth. It was a tragedy, really. Of course, it was
hushed up and Henry pulled himself together, but has
not been able, I fear, to find himself another post. It is
humiliating for a man, and at his age. Beatrice makes the
best of things, which is entirely admirable, and hardly
complains. Doesn't complain. Henry is now trying to
keep them by writing, but unfortunately I don't really
think he is very successful at that.'

'So you send her money to keep them going.'

'How did you know that?' The older woman swung
round on her companion.

'I guessed you would.' Ruth nodded with satisfaction.

'She could not manage without it.'

This was said defensively.

'So she may say. But is she grateful?'

'She doesn't have to be grateful,' said Mrs Rokeby-Jones with some spirit. 'I am her mother, after all.'

'Of course, I forgot,' said Ruth. 'You are only her mother. She never had to be grateful to you for anything.'

'You always twist my words. I am proud to be her mother. I am proud of my family. I am very lucky to have so many and that they are all so supportive of me. Many women at my age are quite alone . . .'

'Supportive? Patrick?'

Mrs Rokeby-Jones swallowed.

'I know I mentioned to you that he has occasionally asked me to invest in things that have turned out to be unsuccessful. But that is the nature of the stock market, and hardly his fault. I mean, I am sure he, and the others, are only thinking of me, in their way. Patrick is very fond of me. He is very affectionate, you know. He was such a dear little boy.'

There was a touch of desperation in her voice.

'He is no longer a dear little boy,' said Ruth, ignoring it and twisting in her seat to speak straight at her companion. 'He is now a manipulative and self-centred fully grown man. You can never say no to Patrick, can you?'

'Patrick has his own problems, as you know. You were very wrong to make me tell you about his private life. It is his own business that he is not the marrying kind, as they used to say. Of course that is bound to make his life more complicated.'

'Is that why he removes things from your house at almost every visit?' said Ruth.

'You don't understand,' said Mrs Rokeby-Jones defiantly. 'I told you – that is to avoid death duties. If I give him presents, and live for seven years, there is no tax to pay. In any case, they help to furnish his shop.'

'Oh, yes? He doesn't sell them, then?'

'I – I have no idea. I don't suppose so.' She spoke defiantly now. 'I don't care, you see. They mean nothing to me. They were mostly bought by my husband.'

'With your money?'

No reply from Mrs Rokeby-Jones, but her lips tightened.

'Flora,' said the woman, changing tack. 'Now of course Flora would never do that, I suppose?'

There was a long pause before the answer came.

'Flora has never taken anything from me.'

'Really?' said Ruth derisively. 'And how do you know what Flora is doing while you are asleep?'

'I do not need to know,' said Mrs Rokeby-Jones. 'Flora has never spent a night in Bloomfield since she left home in 1968.'

This stopped the woman in her tracks. She flopped back in her seat, still looking at her companion.

'Nineteen sixty-eight? Heavens, she can't have been more than . . .' For once Ruth sounded genuinely surprised.

'Sixteen. It was one week before her seventeenth birthday.'

As Mrs Rokeby-Jones said this, the bus swung left and stopped at a filling station. It was windless, but drizzling. A huge sheet of water could be seen in the distance through the white trunks of a birch wood. The driver informed his passengers that they could 'have a wee break here. Time just to do the necessary.'

Back in their seats, and trundling north-eastwards, the woman and Mrs Rokeby-Jones sat in silence for an hour. Then Mrs Rokeby-Jones said, tonelessly:

'Why are you so intent on tearing up all my memories?'

The question hung in the air for a moment, before Ruth said:

'Am I doing it, or are you? I have said nothing that you have not told me.'

No answer.

'And are they memories,' she continued,' or are they just a series of curtains you have hung in front of your memories?'

There was another long pause.

'There are some things,' said Mrs Rokeby-Jones, 'that just don't bear looking at.'

'It certainly takes courage,' said Ruth.

'I am not very brave.' Mrs Rokeby-Jones lay back against the high back of the seat, and shut her eyes. After some minutes tears started to seep out beneath her lids, and ran down her cheeks. 'I'm sorry,' she said.

'Don't be,' said the woman. 'I think you *are* quite brave.'

And she too lay back and shut her eyes.

Patrick stood staring through the rain-drenched window out into the street. He was waiting, though it was after the time that he should have closed his shop, for a visitor. He was not normally late. In fact he usually came on the dot of five thirty every Monday so that Patrick could simply take the bag, lock up and go home. Why was tonight different? Perhaps he had been held up in the traffic. Rain always seemed to bring London traffic to a standstill. But he always came wearing a motorbike helmet, so traffic would hardly slow him.

He turned away and picked up a duster, flicking it idly round the gleaming surfaces of the antique furniture that crammed the small showroom. He had had a good day, an ormolu clock having fetched more than he had dared hope, and in cash. He had split the wad of notes four ways, and concealed them all separately.

The small bell above the door tinkled. He was there. In

a raincoat, dripping on the carpet. The plastic Sainsbury's bag was gleaming wet.

'Do get on to the mat,' said Patrick irritably. Then he looked up in surprise, as the figure stood where it was. This was not the man he was expecting.

'Well. Won't you ask me in?'

'Who are you? I don't know you.'

'Oh, please don't worry about that,' said the man. 'I know you, after all. We are not strangers.'

Patrick had the feeling that he had heard the soft, slightly affected, nasal voice before. He also had a feeling that he didn't like it, though until recently it had merely been linked to a twinge of jealousy, as always when Simon had received telephone calls. He edged towards the desk and the alarm button.

The man moved forward fast.

'No you don't,' he said sharply. Patrick drew back his hand.

'You're all right, Patrick. What are you worried about? It's just that Len couldn't make it tonight, that's all. I brought your shopping for him. I was doing my own, and I'm always willing to help a friend.'

'Who are you?'

'Just a friend of Len's, I told you, didn't I? Hey, Patrick, let's go into your back room there. I have a touch of pinkeye, and I don't like all these bright lights. Never did.'

The eyes in the narrow sallow face were hidden by round dark lenses. Reluctantly, Patrick led the way into the tiny cubbyhole that was his office. As the man passed through the shop he picked up a heavy glass door-stopper that was displayed on a side table.

'I like that,' he said. 'That's really nice. Antique, is it?'

Patrick's mouth was dry and his legs felt weak. He sat down at his desk, spreading his hands out on the leather

133

top to steady them. He was entirely unprepared for the blow when it came. He screamed and threw himself back in the chair, holding his smashed fingers against his chest. Sobbing, he looked down at them. Blood was oozing out from under his fingernails and beginning to drip down his wrist.

'Oh my God, what have you done?' he moaned. 'Get away! Get away!'

He retched and doubled up. The pain was excruciating and surged right up his arm.

'All right, Patrick. That's all. No more. I'm not going to give you any more. Not this time, anyway. That's just a little warning, see? It won't happen again, not if you behave, not if you're a good boy. Who had a fiddle with the top of the packet last week then? That won't do, that won't do at all, will it? You just deliver the groceries as they are. No fiddling, and you won't have any more trouble.'

'I didn't open it,' Patrick moaned. 'Anyway, I only wanted to look.'

'And you were spotted, weren't you, by our little friend, trying to have a look, right? No more looks, no more trouble, Patrick. Got the message? Right. Now let's have the money. Groceries don't come for nothing.'

Still hugging his throbbing hand, Patrick went to a drawer of a Queen Anne tallboy in the showroom, and returned with a bundle of notes.

'How much?' asked the man.

'You know. Two hundred and fifty.'

'Not enough, Patrick. You were told, weren't you? It's gone up. Inflation, you know. It's affecting everyone. Dreadful problem. Seven fifty.'

'Seven fifty? You must be mad! I can't manage seven hundred and fifty pounds a week!'

'Oh dear, Patrick. That is very unfortunate, very bad.

I think you had better have a little think about that, before next week. I do hope Len will be able to make it himself next week. Otherwise I might have to come again, mightn't I, Patrick? Now, get the money.'

The voice was no louder, but the tone was suddenly quite different. Patrick went straight to a porphyry vase, and with his undamaged hand drew out another wad of notes, which he thrust at the man.

'That's right, Patrick, much better,' the man said as he flicked through it. 'I knew you'd see sense. And when Len comes again next week, you won't give him any trouble, will you? No, of course you won't. You're not stupid, are you, Patrick?'

He turned with his hand on the street door.

'Are you, Patrick?'

Patrick was still standing at the door of the office, nursing his arm, which ached agonisingly to the elbow. He shook his head reluctantly. The brown and orange Sainsbury's bag, bulging with vegetables and household goods, lay on a table between them.

'Good night, Patrick. Oh, and do get something done about that hand. It looks so painful.'

And he stepped out into the night.

As Patrick left the casualty ward three hours later, the nurse said:

'You come back to Outpatients on Wednesday, then, to have it dressed. Any time from nine thirty. You shouldn't have too long to wait. Try to keep your hand up, and I'd stay away from car doors for a while, if I were you.'

Lionel's voice was high with irritation.

'You must have found out more than that by now, surely? How many men have you got on this job?'

He was talking on the telephone to Cockerill Private Investigations Ltd.

'Just the one, Mr Leetham. We would normally not put more than one operative on a case, but of course you can have as many as you want to pay for.'

Louise walked into the sitting room, putting down her shopping bags, and pulling off her gloves.

'Well, tell me then,' Lionel went on,' just what have you done so far? I know you talked to everyone in the village, encouraging gossip, no doubt. But since then? You said just a few days, it would take you.'

'Well, in a case like this a lot of the preliminary work is done in the office, you see, by telephone. We have been in touch with all the bus companies, the railway stations in the area, the taxi companies, and then we send someone to check any likely leads. It would help if you could confirm whether there are one or two ladies involved, we understand that there was some doubt about that, and give us a little more guidance on what they might be wearing.'

'One lady,' said Lionel grimly, 'and we think she may be with one – God knows – tramp, gypsy, traveller, whatever you call them. How can we know exactly what they were wearing? I gave you a rough idea, didn't I?'

'Let me speak, Lionel,' said Louise. She took the telephone from him. 'Hullo? This is Mrs Leetham . . . Well, that's very kind. We are, of course, rather worried. I can give you a good idea of what my mother would be dressed in. Almost certainly she would have on a light wool sweater, probably blue or mauve, or perhaps light brown. She could well have a matching cardigan over that, and possibly a string of pearls. She would have a tweed skirt, brownish or greeny-blue, perhaps, and brown leather shoes with a slight heel. Oh, and a coat. I should have looked to see what had gone.

Possibly a rather old camel coat, full length, with a belt. But more likely, actually, a three-quarter-length brown tweed . . .'

'Thank you, madam,' said the voice on the telephone. 'That is not at all what we have written here. Perhaps the first description was given when your husband was a little upset. Now we have some idea of the style of the lady. Would she have money with her? Credit cards?'

'I haven't the faintest idea. I suppose she took her bag. Yes.'

'And her personal appearance?'

'Well, she's quite tall,' said Louise, 'about five foot nine, I think, and slim. You know she's seventy? Yes . . . Well, greyish hair, in a sort of bun, but not grey at the back. Sort of blondey-chestnut. Rather wavy. She's quite handsome, really, and doesn't look nearly as old as she is.'

'Thank you. And the other lady?'

'Well, of course, we don't *know* that they are together. But if they are, she is quite different. Shorter, and . . . I don't know what shape she is. I have only seen her bundled up in a grubby old mac with a bit of string round the middle. And boots. Rubber boots, I think. Sort of indeterminate age. I can't remember her face, but spectacles and a thick sort of knitted woollen hat, with a pom-pom, pulled down.'

'That is very helpful, thank you, madam. Most observant. And a recent photograph of your mother would help, if you would send it to our office. I should say that we are not unhopeful. One positive identification, and we should have that soon, and then we will be moving fast and hope to produce a speedy and satisfactory result. Rest assured, madam. We will be in touch.'

Louise stared thoughtfully at Lionel.

'They want a recent photograph,' she said. 'I don't suppose Mother has been photographed for years.'

'Surely someone must have a snap of some kind? Stuck in an album?'

'I'll try Bea. She's the most likely. It will have to be recent, I suppose, but now the children are all away, no one takes photographs much.'

When Louise finally got an answer, the voice was Henry's.

'Henry? Why does no one ever answer your telephone? It's Louise.'

'Yes, I know. We've been out. Bea's just coming.'

'Henry, you sound awful!'

'I'm all right. We have only been shopping. Wheeling our little prams round the tin-lined galleries of the grossly misnamed supermarket. Nothing less super have I ever known. Here she is.'

'Who is it?' said Beatrice's piercing voice. 'Oh, it's you, Loopy. Have they found Mother yet?'

'No. I'll come to that. What's this about you dragging Henry out shopping? He never does anything like that. I can't even imagine it.'

'I don't know why not,' said Beatrice. 'One often sees men in supermarkets. I don't see why I shouldn't have a bit of help, anyway. And Henry and I have decided to spend more time together. To do things together, in fact. I get quite lonely sometimes, and Henry does too, don't you, Henry? Loopy, what about Mother? Has she turned up yet?'

'No, that's what I am ringing about. Have you got a photograph of her? A recent one? Mine are all about twenty years old. The detective agency wants one.'

'Heavens. I can't think. There must be something. What about after the funeral? Father's funeral?'

'That was about eleven years ago, Bea, and anyway you don't have photographs at funerals. Not like weddings.'

'No, I suppose not. Sorry. I was distracted.' She put her hand over the mouthpiece. 'Henry! Stay in the room, please, where I can see you. Yes, Loopy. A photograph. I have an idea Patrick took a photograph of her standing by the little walnut table, last summer. By the way, where is the walnut table? Do you think it has been moved? I am sure it was not in its usual place last week.'

'Oh dear, that's not important,' said Louise.

'Well, it is to me. Mother promised ages ago that she would leave it to me, in fact I happen to know that it has my name on a sticker underneath. I was going to ask whether she might give it me sooner.'

'Bea, let's worry about Mother now and tables later, shall we?' Louise sounded quite sharp, her normally lazy voice edgy with irritation. 'I'll speak to Patrick. We have got to get a photograph somehow.'

'I think I have found something,' said Terry, 'that could be important. But I can't quite make out what it is.'

'You are enjoying this, aren't you?'

'You know, against all expectation, I think I am. But it's harder than I expected.'

Chapter Nine

Patrick opened the door of his flat and stepped back into the narrow hall to let Louise pass him. She walked into the living room.

'I can't be long,' she said, looking round, 'I'm on a meter. I'd forgotten how hard this place is to find. Every street round here seems to have no-entry signs at almost every turning. Nobody in their senses would drive through here.'

'That's why I live here,' said Patrick.

'I have been wandering for ages, and I only came upon Cambridge Street by chance. Goodness, your flat really stinks. It's like a Hindu temple. What have you been burning? I haven't been here for ages. It looks different. Have you been redecorating? You could hide a zebra in here. I would get bored of all that black and white.'

'Is that what you came to say, Loopy?'

'I've only come,' said Louise, 'because I can't trust you to be quick getting that photograph to the agency. I'm glad you found it. Is it reasonably clear? They want to do photocopies of it.'

Patrick handed her a brown envelope.

'What's the sling for? What on earth have you done to your arm?' she said.

'It's not my arm, it's my hand, and I got it caught in a car door,' he answered wearily.

'Ouch. How careless. Is it bad?'

'Two fingers broken,' said Patrick, 'and yes, it is very painful, and no, it wasn't my car, and yes, it's lucky it's my left hand, and yes, I will probably lose the fingernails, which will look disgusting. Thank you for asking.'

'Why are you so touchy?' said his sister. 'I was only being sympathetic.'

'Darling, I'd never have known. Do you want some coffee or something?'

'No, I really can't wait,' said Louise. 'Let's have a look at this.'

The photograph was in colour, an eight-by-ten-inch enlargement. In the centre was a pretty cabriole-leg walnut table, and over to one side, with her fingertips on the table top, was the slim figure of their mother, half smiling at the camera.

'Well, I wouldn't exactly call this a portrait of Mother. But we can get them to cut out the table and blow up Mother, I suppose. Where is that table, by the way? Beady-eyed Beatrice says it has been moved. She says she couldn't see it when we were all down there.'

'It's being repaired,' said Patrick, taking a cigarette pack from the mantelpiece, his back to his sister. 'They take ages, these people.'

'Who broke it? One of those women?'

'It wasn't broken. The inlay was coming away at the back. Mother asked me to get it done. What's the news, Loopy? Have the sleuths done any good? It is quite ludicrous that she hasn't been found yet.'

As she talked Louise was walking round the room peering at things. Patrick's flat was unlike anything in her two chintz-bedecked homes. She felt slightly disapproving and more than a little jealous.

'Well,' said Louise, 'there is a report of two women who just might be them catching a bus in Oxford. It sounds pretty far-fetched to me. I mean, why on earth should they be in Oxford? I can't feel it is right to look for them this way. But if you and Lionel absolutely refuse to bring in the police or the press . . . Mother could be murdered, buried in the garden, and the murderer getting away all this time.'

'You don't really believe that, do you?' Her brother watched her irritably. He wished she would sit down. 'If you do, let's go down there and start digging.'

Placing a cigarette between his lips, he mumbled, 'Frankly, I am desperate to find her, alive or dead, if that doesn't sound too crude.'

'You smoke too much. It is crude,' said Louise, trying out a high black-enamelled ladder-back chair and concluding that its purpose was decorative only. 'It is crude, as you say, but we have to face it. We are all concerned about Mother, of course, and we all, for our different reasons, dearly need the money that only Mother and Bloomfield, one way or another, could give us. All of us, that is, except Flora. And that's a mystery. Flora, unmarried, on a high salary, valuable flat, no ties – why does she want Mother out of Bloomfield so much? Have you thought about that? She's been working on it longer than any of us. What's she up to? It's never simple with Flora.'

'Too right. And you're not the first person to mention it. I have wondered too. I thought it was just a general vindictiveness. She's always had a funny relationship with Mother. But we need her on side, assuming Mother turns up, so let's not worry about her motives.'

'She must turn up – anything else is really too awful to contemplate,' said Louise, contemplating it.

'If she doesn't, it takes simply years to get someone declared dead – you know that? Think of Lord Lucan.'

'That's odious, Patrick! How can you even think like that? Of course she is alive, and of course she will turn up. Oh Lord, my meter. It only had twelve minutes left. I'm off. If I can ever find my way out of Pimlico.'

In Inverness, Mrs Rokeby-Jones had said, 'We've come a long way.'

'Yes,' the woman replied, 'and we could go a lot further.'

'Where to?'

'It depends how far you want to go.'

'Let's go as far as we can. What happens beyond this? I'd like to see a map.'

'More of the same,' said the woman. 'More Scotland. Sutherland. Caithness. After that we could take a big jump to Orkney.'

'I feel like a big jump. I am in a jumping mood. I would like to keep on going, if you agree. Or, at least, go as far as we can without passports. Let's go to the furthest tip of Britain.'

Ruth laughed. 'That's Shetland, I think.'

'Wonderful! Let's go to Shetland. How romantic. We'll need to get some more money. And we'll have to find out how to get there. Ruth?'

'Yes?'

'I'd be very happy if you called me Meg.'

'I thought you were called Cecilia,' said Ruth, remembering.

'I am. It's my first name. My mother always called me Cecilia. And my husband. I was christened Cecilia Margaret. My father called me Meg, hardly anyone else. And after he died, it dwindled. But I think of myself as Meg.'

'All right. I'll call you Meg, if you like. And if you really want to go to Shetland, we had better find a travel agent first, and ask where you go from. For once I am stumped.'

* * *

The journey recommended by the travel agent, by boat from Aberdeen, was tiring and tedious. They both slept only intermittently in their bunks, but Meg was much more alert than Ruth when they met in the ferry's café in the morning.

'I got such a shock,' she said, 'when I looked at myself in the mirror just now. For a second I was looking at a stranger, seeing myself as others see me, I suppose.'

'Is the colour about right?' asked Ruth.

'Well, yes. Pretty well, but I'm afraid it is many years since it was like this all over, with no grey. Rather mutton dressed as lamb, don't you think?'

The session with an Aberdeen hairdresser the previous day had transformed them both. Meg's naturally wavy grey hair was no longer raised in a chignon, but cut short and bouncy and dyed golden chestnut, streaked with silver. Ruth's mousy fair hair was now very dark brown.

'No. Really not,' said Ruth, surveying her companion with approval. 'Your skin is good, much younger than your age. One would guess you had touched your hair up, but it really suits you. I like the silver highlights, by the way.'

'Thank you. I will allow myself to believe you. I don't think you are given to flattery.'

Meg looked across at herself in the long mirror that hung behind the food bar.

'It's such fun to change one's appearance. It makes you feel like a new person, and if you've got a bit tired of your old person, well . . . And these wax jackets. I find mine very consoling. It felt totally windproof when I was out on deck just now. I liked my anorak, too. Such fun. Such extravagance. Let's sit down.'

They chose seats where they could see through the window to the heaving grey sea.

'Blue sky to the north,' said Ruth, peering out. 'Thank goodness for that. I guess Shetland will be bitterly cold. So the coats are a necessity, not extravagance.'

'I'm so glad you suggested them. You are oozing with good ideas – and you make me do nice, stimulating things I have never done before.'

'Like thinking?'

'Now, come, Ruth. You talk as if I really had never thought before. I know I have been inclined to try to wipe my family's failings from my mind, but that is a very human fault.'

'It can also be dehumanising.'

'Let me get you some bacon and eggs,' said Meg. 'They are swimming in fat, and very nourishing. All right?'

'Thank you,' said Ruth.

She watched Meg's back as she walked to the counter, bracing herself against the movement of the boat. Ruth shook her head wonderingly.

Later, pushing away her plate, Meg folded her hands under her chin.

'I know you are right, of course. My family are singularly unlovable, all of them, to varying degrees. I don't know that they really deserve that particularly unattractive analogy you used – parasites, was it? – though I suppose there is a blood-sucking element in most of them. It is emotional, as much as anything. I feel sometimes that they will not allow me any emotions of my own. I think I do manage to love them, in a way, but probably there is not one that I would like much, if I were not related to them. And there is only one for whom I have any respect. It just makes me feel guilty to say it, or even think it.'

'I think there is more than that,' said Ruth. 'I think you have come to blame yourself for what they are. And because you can't face it all being such a failure, you pretend, even to yourself, that it is a normal, happy family.'

Meg thought about this for some time.

'I know,' she said. 'I do pretend. It is easier to cover it up and not look at it. I pretend that there is nothing out of the ordinary in our family. Failure is awfully hard to face, when you have nothing else.'

Ruth felt like putting an arm round her shoulders, but resisted. Meg would go on if left alone, she guessed. She was right.

'It has to be my fault, doesn't it, as their mother? I brought them up.'

'Single-handed?' said Ruth.

She had struck a wrong note, and Meg veered away.

'That makes no . . . Ruth, when it comes down to it, a mother owes something to her children.'

'Why? What do you owe them?'

'Loyalty, I suppose,' said Meg thoughtfully. 'My father thought that loyalty was the greatest of all virtues, and I think he may have been right.'

'Your children have shown no loyalty to you, that I have noticed.'

'Not really. No, not really, when I come to think of it . . . Well, only one, perhaps. Since you seem to find out everything, Ruth, I suppose you have realised that the older ones want to put me in an old folks' home. "Residential accommodation for retired gentry." God. Actually, it is my own fault to some extent. As a sort of defence against them I have always pretended to be even vaguer and dottier than I am. It gives me – how shall I call it? – some leeway when I'm dealing with them. I can appear to remember or not remember things they have said according to whether it suits me. Do you understand? I have probably been more convincing than I realised. Now I have them thinking, "Mother cannot cope with life any more. She would be better off in a home." You know what I mean? I suppose I have asked for it. But it is the one thing I do find very hard to take. I can't bear the thought of living in an institution. Lots of people have to, I know, and I suppose one day I may have to too. The thing that hurts, though, is that they should be so eager to do it to me. None of them has really asked me how I feel about it, if I would mind.'

Meg was no longer looking at Ruth across the table. Her finger was dabbling in a small coffee spill on the yellow Formica in front of her, dragging out its edges into a many-pointed star. The words too were dragging out painfully.

'It's the house, isn't it?' said Ruth, gently. 'They want their birthright. The need for money, even in the comparatively well off, is dehumanising too.'

'Yes, I am afraid you are right.' Meg sat up and laughed. 'Most of them just want the money, and my hanging around there stops them getting it. It surprises me in Henry, actually – Bea's husband. I can't see him proposing it. He really is a decent person, rather a dear. You see, if they only had the honesty to tell me why, to let me know what their problems are, I would sell the house like a shot and give them the money. But they lie to me about everything. No one in our family has done anything but lie to everyone else for years . . . and I am as bad as the rest, as you have so effectively pointed out. So, they pretend they want me out of the house for my own good.'

Ruth was listening with a broad grin on her face. Meg was in full flow. She looked intent and determined, not an expression that she was often seen wearing, and it became her.

'Despite what you and they may think, Ruth, I am not yet senile. Surely I am the one person who knows something about my own good. I am not particularly fond of Bloomfield, as Flora constantly points out. In fact I am not at all fond of it, but it is mine and I will not be coerced out of my home. I know you think I am very weak, but one has one's pride.'

'One certainly does!' said Ruth.

'You are laughing at me.'

'I really enjoy hearing you get angry!' Ruth was indeed laughing.

'It is not a familiar feeling,' said Meg with a rueful smile. 'I think I have never dared be angry. I was taught by my parents that anger was wrong. Anyway, there has always been someone capable of greater anger than me.'

'Who?'

'That's not the point. But I think I shall practise more anger in future. I shall rather enjoy it.'

'And pride?' said Ruth.

'Should I be more proud too?' Meg asked.

'I think pride, of a kind,' Ruth was suddenly serious, 'is your greatest problem, both lack of it and excess of it.'

'I don't understand you.'

'No, but you will. I think we will be there soon,' said Ruth.

Meg looked out of the window.

'I see islands, misty islands, and the waste of seas.'

'Scott,' said Ruth. 'Do you read Scott? That was only the Hebrides he was on about. Inshore stuff, by comparison. The seas are much more wasty here. Shetland really is sea-girt and remote. There's nothing much between here and the North Pole.'

'Flora? This is Lionel Leetham here, ringing at two twenty-five p.m. on Thursday. If you get this message before this evening, call me, please. I want the name of those solicitors of your mother's. I will try to get it from Patrick. Louise doesn't seem to know it, to my amazement. I am at my office in the House. You have my number. End of message from Lionel Leetham.'

* * *

'Patrick.' Flora rang her brother as soon as she came home from work. 'What's all this? I found a message on my machine. Lionel's trying to see Asprey. Have you heard about this? What's he up to?'

'Relax, Flora darling. I've told him where to go. Don't be so suspicious. There have been major developments with the private eye people. They have found Mother's spoor.'

'What! Where is she?' said Flora.

'Well, all they know is where she was, about two weeks ago,' said Patrick. 'But it's a start.'

'Go on. She's all right, then?'

'It depends what you mean by all right. She is, believe it or not, still with that woman. The descriptions fit. It *was* them getting the bus from Oxford. They spent a night near Stratford, and, at some point, a night in Carlisle. In Carlisle – can you believe it? They have actually traced the bed-and-breakfasts where they stayed. But they are stuck now. Cockerill makes the point that Mother must have got some money, as presumably the bag-lady doesn't have much, and they want to have access to her bank record. And of course the bank won't play unless the police are involved, or unless they have instructions from her solicitor. So that's what it's all about.'

Flora thought briefly.

'Well, I hope Lionel has more luck with Asprey than we did. It was rather like trying to get a pearl out of an oyster with a toothpick.'

'Yes, well,' said Patrick, 'there was no luck involved. Our forceful brother-in-law simply rang Asprey and told him that Mother has disappeared and we are trying to trace her. So after a bit of humming and hahing Asprey has agreed to write to her bank and give them authority to show Cockerill her latest statement. So far Mother has paid their way in cash, no cheques. But the statement will at least show where they are getting the cash, unless she had a stash of it, which seems unlikely.'

'That'll take days,' said Flora. 'I'm glad she's all right.'

'No, not necessarily days. Cockerill seems to be moving quite fast now.'

'You bleeped me.'

'Yes, problems I am afraid, Terry. The honeymoon may be over. I had an unpleasant call here today. You are going to have to take evasive action.'

'Don't worry, I have. You'd be amazed.'

'Have you got much of what we want?'

'Yes, a lot. Not enough, but a lot. But I think I can get it all.'

'I'll hold the fort, don't worry, though it's getting harder. I'll make sure you have time to get it all. There's just one other problem. You can't have any more money.'

'I have anticipated that. I thought it was too good to be true.'

'There's always the "hollow tree" trick.'

'With luck, we can do without.'

'Will this weather hold?' asked Meg.

'It is hard to know,' said the owner of the small restaurant, as he accepted payment for their meal. 'At this time of year anything could happen. You should make the most of the weather while you have got it, I would advise.'

They walked down Commercial Street, through the stone-paved centre of Lerwick, and along the harbour front. They watched groups of men working on their fishing boats, using the winter sunlight to prepare for the spring.

'The Shetlanders have quite a different accent, don't they,' Ruth said, 'from the rest of Scotland? I suppose it isn't really Scotland. You know, in the library someone told me that there were beautiful beaches on the mainland, and I thought he was referring, rather pointlessly, to the mainland of Scotland. But he wasn't. The island we are on now is the biggest of all the Shetland islands, and it's called Mainland!'

'There are even better island names than that,' said Meg. 'I have been looking at that map. What about Yell? Tomorrow, I am going to Yell! Or Muckle Roe – sounds like a delicious fish dish. Papa Stour! There are some wonderful names round the coastline, too, like Fitful Head, or The Slithers. I can't wait to explore. And did you have any idea that there would be a town as lovely as this up here? It is really charming, with these beautiful old buildings, and the way some of them seem to grow out of the water. What fun, don't you think, to have your boat moored to your house wall?'

'I have to admit, there is much more here than I expected. I thought it was just trout fishing and oil rigs. Not a rig in sight!'

They moved up from the waterfront, and strolled up narrow streets between the handsome fronts of eighteenth-century houses. Almost all were built in stone, and there were few modern additions to spoil the look of the centre of the town.

'You know the book that I got in the library, about Lady Franklin?' said Meg. 'She leant from the window of one of these houses, throwing money to women in the street. They only needed ten pennies each for cheap emigration tickets to Australia, so she wanted to help them. There's hands-on philanthropy for you!'

'I think I'd rather have stayed here,' said Ruth.

'Not in 1849 you wouldn't. It must have been pretty rough. Sheep, fishing and not much more.'

'I'd like to see what happens beyond Lerwick.'

'Shall we go north tomorrow,' said Meg,' and do some

island-hopping? Do you know there are about a hundred islands in Shetland?'

'Let's not do them all, please,' said Ruth. 'It might make sense to hire a car, unless with your new passion for walking you want to do it on foot. I suppose there must be ferries linking the islands to each other.'

It was more or less dark by three o'clock in the afternoon, and they spent much of the evening reading the books they had borrowed from the library. Later, after eating, looking for warmth but reluctant to go so soon to their lodgings, they came by chance on a small pub off the main square. It was dark and smoky inside, noisy and friendly. They shared a table with two elderly men, who asked them where they were from, polite enquiry rather than plain curiosity. They chatted over glasses of dark-golden whisky, and after a while one of the men produced, from beneath his seat, a violin. In the hours that followed, they heard fiddle music such as they had never heard before, wild, restless folk tunes, gentle melodies and ranting jigs. Everyone seemed to play, and to have their own variations on the tunes. The fiddles passed from hand to hand, with much laughter and applause. It was late into the night when Ruth leant forward at last and called into Meg's ear.

'Can you do without sleep? I don't think I can.'

'What an evening!' said Meg, after they had made their farewells and left. 'I think I may come and live in Shetland.'

'I think I may not come and live in Shetland after all,' she said on the following day, as they drove northwards. It was barely light at ten in the morning.

'Different in summer, when it never gets dark,' said Ruth.

'I wouldn't mind that.'

Meg was driving, and they travelled fast, along wide, well-maintained tarmac roads. They paused occasionally, to look at an especially fine view out over the North Sea, but soon the road swung inland. The country was hilly rather than mountainous, boggy, with coarse grass and heather. Small sheep with concave profiles grazed upon the verges. On every slope they saw signs of peat-cutting, the land sliced like black cake, with drying peat bricks stacked into neatly built walls.

'No reliance on oil-fired heating, I notice,' said Ruth.

'Peat's free. And think of the lovely smell. No fools, the Shetlanders.'

'What was this Lady Franklin doing here?'

'She was the wife of Sir John Franklin,' said Meg, 'the man who discovered the Northwest passage to America, round the top of Canada, from Greenland. He never came back, so she came here to see if any of the men who worked on the Greenland whalers had news of him. I read the book years ago, but being here I thought I'd read again about her time in Shetland. She was an amazing woman. Very tough.'

'Where did she go?' said Ruth.

'The way we are going. She took the ferry from this island, Mainland, to Yell, and another one to Unst. That's the most northerly of the big islands.'

'Is that where we are heading?'

'I'd like to, if you agree. I can't believe this bright, cold weather will last, but if we are quick we might get to somewhere I would dearly love to go.'

'I'm in your hands,' said Ruth, smiling to herself.

Beatrice had hardly slept for several nights. Neither had Henry. They sat in the kitchen of their Dorset house, he shaking and unshaven, she haggard and drawn. The tension between them was near breaking point.

'Please, Bea. Please, I implore you. I can't go on like this.'

'You said you would try. You know how I have tried. Oh, it's so unfair. Do you think it is *fun*, watching you all the time, never being able to do anything, or leave you for five minutes, in case you have a bottle somewhere?' Her voice was rising. 'Do you think I *enjoy* this?'

'Do you think I do?'

'You said you would *try*, Henry.' She leant forward, knocking over her cup of black coffee and ignoring the stain that spread across the tablecloth, shrieking at him, 'You said you would try! I tried to believe you, and I tried to help you to try. I thought you *meant* it. And you couldn't even be trusted to go to the lavatory!'

She pointed an accusing finger at the near-empty whisky bottle she had retrieved from the cistern.

'If I hadn't seen the thing dripping, you would have drunk it all, and where *next*? Where else have you got the filthy stuff? *Answer* me . . . Oh, o-o-oh, what am I to do?'

She was sobbing, tearfully, messily, wiping her eyes with her palms.

'You could just leave me alone,' said Henry. 'Just go away and leave me. It's no good. I'm no good, and the sooner you face that the better for both of us.'

'Hah! That's what you want, is it?' Beatrice glared wetly at him. 'So you can blame me for deserting you? *That's* it, is it?'

'No, Bea,' said Henry wearily. Despite his dishevelled state and shaking hands he was far more in control of himself than she was. 'I would never blame you. But I just want to give up now. I haven't the strength, or the will, to go on. I have never been able to live up to what you expect of me, and I don't see that I ever will. I have know that for such a long time. I went on pretending for far too long.'

He looked across the table at her, his bleary eyes compassionate as he went on.

'You wanted to be married to a success, of course you did. To someone with a name to be proud of, someone *you* could be proud of. I have tried, too . . . at least I used to try . . . but you set me such impossibly high standards. Now I can't even live up to your minimum requirement, which is just to keep sober . . . There is no point in going on like this, Bea, each making the other suffer. It won't work. The greatest kindness you could do me now is to leave me.'

'What do you mean, leave you?'

'Divorce me, and get away from me. And it is the greatest kindness you could do yourself and the children, too. There's not much, but the house should fetch a bit. I wouldn't ask for anything, I promise.'

Beatrice was no longer crying. Her wet face was still with shock.

'You're just saying that . . . this is some trick. I know your tricks . . .'

'No,' said Henry, 'no more tricks, I promise. I have thought about it. I can still think, you know. I am sure that would be best for us all. There is nothing else, really. We can't go on like this, you know that.'

Beatrice did not answer for a while, then, hiding her face with her hands, she spoke again, in a small, toneless voice.

'Is that what you really want?'

Henry looked at her, and nodded.

'Yes, that's what I really want.'

'You would go on drinking, and just . . . and die, without me.'

'Does that matter?'

Another long pause.

'I don't want you to die. I don't want you to leave me.'

'No, no. I wouldn't be leaving you. You would be leaving me. There is no shame in that.'

'Henry, you don't understand what I am saying.' Beatrice's normally strident voice had sunk to the point of near inaudibility. 'Henry, I need you.'

She lifted her face, a hideous, pathetic face, with pink swollen eyelids and a wet, twisted, quivering mouth. A child's face, grubby and tear-stained.

'Oh, come, Bea,' he said wearily.

'Henry . . . I can't do without you.'

Henry walked blindly to the window, touching chair-backs as he went, as much for reassurance as for support.

After a long time he said, without turning round:

'You will have no trouble in doing without me.'

'Henry . . . Oh, Henry, please . . .'

'What are you saying, Bea?'

'I am saying . . . I am saying . . . that I love you.'

'I thought you were. Or something like that. I think . . .' his voice faltered, 'perhaps you are just feeling emotional. I don't really know . . . If it's true, I . . . I don't advise it. Bea, there's not much of me left. I think it may be too late.'

Chapter Ten

Lionel had been at his worst all morning. The small house in South End Row in Kensington, bought many years ago, had been entirely his choice. They had been unable to afford one within division-bell distance of the House of Commons, which he now in some oblique way seemed to consider Louise's fault. In addition, today nothing in or about the house seemed to please him, from the noise in the vacant industrial premises opposite to the excessive number of washing-up brushes in the kitchen sink.

Louise's reminder that the house was now worth vastly more than the sum he had paid for it seemed to cast him into an even deeper gloom.

'Why the blazes can't we have door knobs that don't come away in your hand?' he said, kicking one of the kitchen cupboards.

So when the telephone rang Louise answered it with some relief.

'Yes, speaking. Oh, Mr Cockerill . . . Yes, please do. I am listening . . .'

Lionel grabbed the receiver from her hand.

'Give me that. Cockerill? Lionel Leetham. Have you found them?'

'Well, not exactly found them, Mr Leetham, but I think you will agree that we are making very substantial progress, when you hear . . .'

'Oh, go on, man.'

'I was about to tell you.'

Cockerill hated to be hurried out of his syntax. He took a particular pride in the clarity of his reports, both written and oral.

'Go on, then,' said Lionel again, crossly.

'We have now,' said Cockerill in the same measured tones, 'had an opportunity to study the subject's bank statement, and this shows six transactions since December the twenty-eighth. These include four withdrawals of cash from cashpoints in the following locations: Newbury, Warwick, Carlisle and Oban.'

'My God, those are all over the country!' Lionel's voice rose to a squeal.

'Yes, indeed,' said Cockerill. 'The last location is in Scotland.'

'I know that,' 'Lionel said forcefully. 'The point is, it could be *anyone* using my mother-in-law's card. It could be the tramp woman on the run. She'll milk it dry! We will have to freeze her account – ring the bank.'

'I would advise against any impetuous action of that kind, Mr Leetham. I think when you hear the rest of my report you will agree that a significant and helpful trail is being left by the use of the bank card. May I continue?'

'Yes, yes. Go on. Be quiet, Louise.'

Louise, frustrated, went up the stairs as fast as she was able and threw herself across their bed. She quietly lifted another telephone and held it to her ear, careful not to breathe into the mouthpiece. Cockerill was speaking.

'. . . volved sums of less than one hundred pounds. A subsequent transaction in Inverness on January the twenty-fifth, however, involved a cash cheque for the sum of five hundred pounds.'

'Oh, God,' said Lionel, 'it's a disaster. We have got to stop this. Can't you get a move on?'

'I understand your concern, Mr Leetham,' said Cockerill, 'being as you are so fond of your mother-in-law. You are concerned that Mrs Rokeby-Jones may have been a victim of theft, possibly even of violence, and that the card could be in the hands of another party. However, our operative on this case reports one possible and one positive identification of the subject, which lessens that likelihood. A further transaction was a payment by cheque, supported by the bank card, and took place more than a week earlier at a branch of Marks and Spencer in Dumfries, in south-west Scotland. Two females – I beg your pardon – two ladies answering reasonably to the descriptions provided by yourselves, bought a number of items of clothing, presenting a cheque signed C.M. Rokeby-Jones, and the bank is satisfied that the signature is that of the account holder.'

'That sounds fairly definite,' said Lionel. 'What about the other?'

'We consider that to be only a possible identification, Mr Leetham. The definite one is that the lady who cashed a cheque on this account in Inverness is described as tall, slim, with silver-brown hair swept up in a bun, wearing a blue anorak and jeans.'

'Blue anorak! Jeans!' Lionel's doubt of Cockerill showed in his voice. 'That doesn't sound like her.'

'Remember the clothing purchased in Dumfries, Mr Leetham. Unfortunately the items were not specified, but it does not sound unreasonable.'

Cockerill had had an exchange of opinion with his employee who had gone to Marks and Spencer in Dumfries and failed to establish just what clothes had been bought, in which the expressions 'dickhead' and 'bloody amateur' had been prominent. He kept talking hard in case the same thoughts occurred to Lionel.

'The personal description fits, the signature is once

again authenticated, and remember that the ladies do like to change their style occasionally.'

'It's possible, I suppose,' said Lionel grudgingly. In his mother-in-law's absence he found no difficulty in transferring his ire to the detective agency.

'The conclusions that our operative draws from the information collected so far, Mr Leetham, are that your mother-in-law is not acting under duress, and that the ladies, having in all likelihood turned south in Inverness, are now heading towards England again. He has been unable to ascertain their movements since that identification, as they are presumably now paying their way with cash. However he is pursuing his enquiries in Aberdeen.'

'If he is simply using the bank statement to track them, we could have done that ourselves,' grumbled Lionel.

'On the contrary, Mr Leetham,' said Cockerill. 'All along the route our operative has been checking with all local bus and taxi companies and at the railway stations. On several occasions he has achieved identifications that have subsequently, on investigation, proved unreliable. Scotland appears to be full of ladies travelling about in pairs. There is also, of course, the problem of regional accents, which causes certain problems when interviewing witnesses, and which slows the operation down. As I think I mentioned, he is one of our best operatives, and extremely thorough. But he is from Epping.'

'So you think she's on her way home?' said Lionel hopefully. He had no fondness for Cockerill. Previous investigations done for Lionel by the agency, always concerning affairs of the heart, had yielded no pleasure for the MP, but they had at least produced conclusive results.

'So it would appear, Mr Leetham, but we shall of course continue to monitor her progress very carefully, and report back to you.'

'Right, well.' Lionel looked towards the door and lowered his voice. 'Er, listen, Cockerill. There is a bonus in this for you if you get her back here and in touch with me within thirty-six hours. Do you understand that?'

'A bonus, Mr Leetham?'

'Yes. Let's see. Two hundred, no, three hundred pounds, in cash, if you get her back in that time. If you can get her to telephone me, a hundred. You got that? Home, or on the telephone, within thirty-six hours.'

'Thank you, Mr Leetham.' The sneer in Cockerill's tone was hardly disguised. 'We will be in touch, sir.'

After Lionel had put his receiver down, Louise, upstairs, did the same, thoughtfully.

The news spread fast round the family.

Louise told Beatrice, and Lionel told Patrick, who told Flora. Louise also told her son Rupert, who had dropped in to use the washing machine.

'I think it's really cool,' he said, 'Granny doing a runner like that. Good for her.'

'Darling,' said Louise, 'it's terribly worrying for us, you must see that.'

'Why's it worrying?' said Rupert. 'That's the problem with your generation. You always want to keep tabs on everyone. You can't cope with people doing their own thing. No wonder we all freak out.'

'Don't you think you should unroll the sleeves before you put them in, darling? No? Sorry. I'm fussing. Is that fair, Rupert? After all, we are talking about an elderly woman, already, apparently, showing signs of senility, who appears to have fallen into the hands of a dirty old female tramp who seems to be making her behave very strangely. I can't believe all this is Granny's idea. It's all so out of character, and so undignified, too. I mean, what could she see in the woman?'

'Hey, do you think Granny is a closet dyke? Brilliant!'

'Don't be disgusting, Rupert. You know, Granny could be in real danger. Look, let me just check there are no coins in your jeans pockets. They block the pump.'

Rupert made giving-up signs with his hands and Louise took over the laundry business.

'How, in danger?' he said, scoffingly. 'In danger of losing your patrimony, you mean – or would it be matrimony? That's all you and Dad ever seem to think about, the money.'

'Darling,' Louise protested automatically, 'that's so untrue. And anyway . . .'

'It's not untrue, Mother. I heard Dad saying that the woman could be getting her to sign papers and that she wouldn't know what she was doing, and then there would be no money left for anyone. But anyway, I don't think Granny is half as senile as you all say she is. I don't actually think she's senile at all. When I went to see her last summer she was perfectly normal, I thought. Quite good value, actually, when she relaxes. I just think she's lonely. And now, at last, she seems to be having a bit of fun, and all you lot want to do is stop her.'

Rupert hoisted himself on to the edge of the sink where he sat swinging his legs and watching his mother.

'Fun?' said Louise, pausing. 'That's not a thought that has occurred to me, somehow, that Granny might be having *fun*.'

'Well, I think it should occur to you,' said Rupert, lighting a cigarette. 'And I'll tell you another thing that should occur to you.'

He pointed his finger accusingly at his mother.

'You and Granny have got a generation-gap problem. Just like my generation is meant to think yours is too old for sex, your generation thinks the next lot up don't need to have any fun. Why shouldn't Granny have fun? Well,

I don't mean raves and whatever, but her kind of fun and a few laughs. I bet she'd laugh like hell if she saw you all flapping about like mad hens trying to find her.'

Louise gazed into the cup of detergent in her hand.

'Well, in this case, her fun is our worry. Oh dear, Rupert. I hear what you say. You have another view, and it's a perfectly fair one. It's true that I hardly know my mother, or even what her idea of fun is, if she has one.'

She slammed the door of the machine and pushed some buttons.

'I wish I could talk to your aunt Bea. But you know she is so weird at the moment too. Instead of the usual overreaction she seems to have completely lost interest in your grandmother.'

After Rupert had gone, Louise realised that he had managed to make her feel guilty. No, in fairness, he had simply activated the latent feeling of guilt about her mother that she had long been in the habit of suppressing, with Lionel's very active help. She had never been at all close to Meg; but she could discern little real feeling in the concern shown by any member of the family over her disappearance, and this was beginning to make Louise feel very uncomfortable. What was more, she found Lionel's urgent pursuit of the mother-in-law for whom he had no affection increasingly distasteful.

Flora asked Patrick at once, 'When did they leave Inverness?'

'I don't think we know. We just know she was in a bank there a few days ago.'

'How long do you think till she's home?'

'I am guessing within a day or two.'

'You could be right, Patrick.'

'Monday or Tuesday at the latest.'

'Probably,' said Flora.

They were both thoughtful.

They did not know it, but their minds were working along the same lines.

Once again Meg was up and about before Ruth. They had been unable, the previous afternoon, to find any obvious place to stay on Unst, and in the village of Haroldswick they had asked for help in the post office.

'Mary-Ellen Leask, up at Valsgarth, she takes a few visitors in the summer, so I've no doubt she'd get a room ready for you. Would you like me to give her a call?'

They accepted with gratitude, since dark had already fallen and the idea of sleeping in the cramped discomfort of their small hired car had not appealed.

At nine thirty next morning Meg was standing outside Mrs Leask's bungalow in the chill air, looking at the first glimmers of dawn lighting the slopes of the hills to the north.

'Mrs Leask has been up for hours, you know,' she said to Ruth as she came through the front door. 'She must think we are very lazy.'

'No I do not.' Mrs Leask's round, cheerful face appeared round the doorjamb. 'You're on holiday, and you have the right to sleep as long as you like. Come away in now. I have a good breakfast ready for you to eat before you set off.'

'I wasn't sleeping, actually,' said Meg, 'at least, not for the last hour or two. I have been reading a fascinating book that I got in the library in Lerwick, about Lady Franklin. Do you know about her?'

'Oh yes, I have heard all about her, though I haven't read the book. She stayed with a family just down the road in Baltasound, and got them to take her out to Muckle Flugga. I've never been there myself. There's not much. Just the rock and the lighthouse. She was a sad lady, right enough. The old people remembered her, tall and pale, with a very sad face. There was a song we used to sing, "Lady Franklin's Lament".

'And now my burden, it gives me pain,' she sang, 'For my long lost Franklin I'd cross the main . . .'

She hummed a few more bars in a low, pretty voice.

'You are all so musical here,' said Ruth.

'Well, it's the tradition. We have a lot of music in Shetland. That's because we had to have something to do in the long, long evenings before we had the telly.'

She laughed, and placed huge helpings of bacon, sausage and egg in front of them.

'That'll keep you going for your walk. And I've made you a wee bag for your dinner. You'll get hungry going all that way. And just you keep an eye on your watches. You southerners forget how short the day is here in January, and Hermaness can be a dangerous place, especially if the weather changes and the mist comes in.'

'It looks good, though, doesn't it?' asked Meg anxiously, looking out of the window.

'It does look good. Very settled. But don't waste any time. You eat up, now.'

She left the room.

'You really want to get there, don't you?' said Ruth.

'I really do,' said Meg.

It was almost full daylight when they reached Burra Firth, the long sea inlet that cleaves in two the northern end of Unst. They left their car parked at the end of the tarmac road, by the low stone wall that rings the shore-station building for the Muckle Flugga lighthouse. The sky above them was uniformly blue, but a bitter wind encouraged them to move at once. Following a signpost, they started along a stony track dotted with sheep's droppings, winding uphill among clumps of mahogany-coloured heather.

'In the spring this place is alive with birds,' said Ruth. 'I had a natural-history lesson from the librarian in Lerwick while you were chasing Lady Franklin. The whole of Hermaness is a bird sanctuary. Great skuas nest all over the high ground – they call them bonxies here. There are arctic skuas, too. I think they are the same but blacker.'

Despite the wind it was hot walking. They were warmly dressed and the sun, almost at its midday peak, though not far above the horizon, had some heat in it. It was a relief to reach the top of the hill, and to be walking across the rough plateau of short grass and heather, pitted with deep peat holes. After an hour the land began to fall away.

Meg looked at the map.

'I think we are here, just above these cliffs, where it says Saito.'

'I know where we are,' said Ruth, excitedly. 'The librarian told me about this. If we go out on that promontory we should be able to see the cliff face.'

Sitting on the ground well back from the sheer drop they could look down at the folds of the huge cliff that rippled away from them to the south. Most of the dark granite rock was white with bird droppings.

'In the breeding season,' said Ruth, 'there are hundreds of thousands of gannets on those cliffs, all jammed up against each other, nesting on every possible ledge and cranny. And the noise is evidently quite deafening. They have particulary raucous voices.'

'What are gannets like? They don't seem to have heard that birds never foul their own nests,' said Meg, staring in amazement.

'Gannets? Big birds. Terrific divers. Look, you can see some down there.' Ruth pointed.

Far below them, large white birds, with disproportionately long, black-tipped wings, were reduced to tiny size as they glided over the surface of the wrinkled sea.

'It is one of the biggest gannetries in the country, or is it the world?' she went on. 'I forget how many thousand birds, but the boffins have some idea. I can't think how they count them.'

'It is quite awesome, isn't it, the thought of all those identical birds in one place,' said Meg.

'Aha, I hoped you would say something like that,' said Ruth. 'Listen to what he told me, the librarian. In among all those gannets on the cliff each spring is another bird. It has been coming for years, and it appears to think it is a gannet. But it's not, it's an albatross – the only Black-browed albatross in the northern hemisphere, in fact. How about that?' Ruth was enchanted by her discovery.

'The only one? All on its own? There must be others, somewhere?'

'Yes, but in Antarctica, and places like the Falklands. Not exactly within dining distance for this poor thing. No one knows how it came to be here by itself.'

'Oh, how tragic,' said Meg, genuinely moved. 'I can think of nothing sadder than to be alone like that, with no fellow beings. No wonder it has come to think it is a gannet. Sort of self-defence, do you think? Or just self-delusion?'

'Fascinating, isn't it? I would love to see it, wouldn't you?' said Ruth, gazing down into the depth of the cliff, and imagining a whirling turmoil of wings below, as there would be in a few months' time.

'I think if I were an ornithologist,' said Meg, 'I would somehow get hold of it and take it, by hook or by crook, to where there were other albatrosses. Or else bring another Black-browed albatross here.'

'Yes, it would be quite a temptation. Risky, though. It might not work, you know, interfering with nature.'

'But it's not natural for it to be alone,' said Meg stoutly. 'I would risk it.'

'But what if it is content as it is, believing it is a gannet?'

'I would be prepared to show it that it is an albatross. I think it would be happier. Particularly when it realised that it wasn't alone in the world.'

'Lots of people would argue with you about that.' Ruth was smiling. 'But, as it happens, I wouldn't. I most definitely wouldn't. Let's go on. I'm cold.'

'That's it. We are there,' said Meg, some time later.

They had walked on northwards, keeping to the high ground, perhaps a mile and a half along a central ridge of hill. It was easy walking, on short, springy heather. The cliffs dropped away and the slope ran more easily down to the rocky shore. From this point of Hermaness, still high above the ocean, they could see below them the straggle of small rock islands with which Great Britain finally stutters to an end. The largest, Muckle Flugga, crowned with the white warning finger of its lighthouse, lay not more than a mile to the north.

They sat in the lea of a low mound, leaning their backs against a little sandy cliff that sheep had clearly used for shelter.

Ruth flicked dried droppings down the slope.

'So this is where she came, your sad, pale Lady Franklin?'

'Well, if she sat up here, there is no record of it. All she wanted to do was get out there, to Muckle Flugga. And that wasn't easy, even in July. Look at those waves. It was days before it was calm enough to land. They made several abortive expeditions before they got there. The locals must have thought her fairly mad. She was absolutely determined.'

'Did she have a family, this woman?' asked Ruth.

'No, just a niece, who travelled with her.'

'If she had had a family,' said Ruth, 'I suppose they would have stopped her.'

'Like me, you mean? A family who stopped her doing anything she ever wanted to do?' Meg's sudden anger surprised Ruth.

'I didn't mean that actually. I meant a family who worried about her for her own sake. What's this, though? Do you see yourself as a sort of deutero-Lady Franklin? Is that why we are here? Perhaps you *are* rather alike.'

Meg laughed bitterly.

'No, indeed. There is a fundamental difference between me and Lady Franklin.'

'What's that?' Ruth turned to look at Meg, sitting slightly above her.

She waited for an answer that didn't come, so she said instead:

'What did she do when she finally got to Muckle Flugga?'

Meg did not reply at once. Her eyes as she turned to look at Ruth suggested that her thoughts had been in another direction.

'Didn't I tell you? She made them take her to the rock called the Outstack – do you see it there, where the waves are breaking? – beyond all the others.'

Meg pointed to the distant rock, the most northerly point of the British Isles. For all its significance, the Outstack looked tiny and vulnerable in the huge spread of heaving grey sea. Like the other islands, it was all rock, and at that distance they could see no sign of green on its surface. It looked bleak and inhospitable. With each wave that broke upon it the spray flew high and wild.

'She made them land her on that rock – imagine them, in an open rowing boat,' said Meg. 'She is said to have stood there, facing in the general direction of Greenland, and thrown a wreath into the sea. I think that was the moment when she finally accepted that her husband was dead.'

'You said she went on hunting for his body, all the same,' said Ruth.

'She wouldn't give up,' said Meg. 'She went on raising money wherever she could, bullying the Admiralty, sending expedition after expedition to northern Canada for years afterwards. She needed to prove his death, of course, to get his pension. But there was more to it than that. I think she found it impossible to stop. It was an obsession.'

'Why did she do it?' said Ruth.

There was a long, long pause. Meg Rokeby-Jones half turned away from Ruth and gazed a while at the distant rock where the waves crashed silently, and the spray rose high. Then she answered.

'You know why.'

'Why? Why did she do it?' Ruth was quietly insistent.

Meg's voice when she eventually answered was so low that the words were barely audible.

'Because she loved him.'

After another pause, a gap in their talk that they both knew was a cathartic moment, the woman said, gently:

'That's the fundamental difference, isn't it, between you and her? She loved her husband. Do you want to finish it now?'

'Yes. Ask me. Make me say it.'

'Did you love him?'

'No. I hated him.' The words came out flatly, but with intensity.

'Did you ever love him?'

'I was blinded by him. I never loved him.'

'What did he do to you?' Ruth's questioning was almost monotonal too.

'He reduced me, slowly, bit by bit, to nothing.'

'With words?'

'Yes, at the beginning. With words.'

'And then?'

'With other things.'

'Go on.'

'He beat me.'

'Once?'

'Often.'

'Where?'

'Not where it would show. On my body.'

'With his hands?'

'Sometimes. Sometimes with a stick. One of those thin riding sticks, whippy, you know.'

'Did you cry?'

'Of course. I had to. If I didn't, he would go on till I did.' Meg's voice was still low and almost without expression.

'Why did he do it?'

'He needed to. It . . . you know . . . what they say now . . . it "turned him on".'

'So that he could . . .?'

'So that he could, you know . . . You know the words. I can't say it.'

'Say it all the same. 'Ruth spoke urgently. 'It doesn't matter what words. Say it the easy way . . . go on . . . say it . . . so that he could make . . .'

'No! I won't say it like that!' Sharply, loudly, Meg's voice rang out. 'He didn't know what love was. He couldn't make love, he made hate – hate – hate! He wanted me to hate him. He *needed me to hate him*. He could only function on hate, and fear, and disgust. And I hated him! I hated him! I hated him!'

Meg had risen to her feet, and her voice too rose as she repeated the words, till she was screaming them out. The sound carried on the wind to mingle with the shrieks of the gulls on the rocks far below. She waved her arms at the empty sky and shouted again and again, 'I hated him! I hated – hated – hated – hated hi-i-i-iiimm!'

Ruth lay back in a clump of heather, smiling, and shut her eyes.

'Well done,' she said quietly.

'Do you know,' said Meg, after a while, 'I feel like taking all my clothes off, and running about naked?'

'Well, do,' said Ruth.

'Too bloody cold. I would, if it wasn't so cold. I would, really.'

'I believe you,' said Ruth. 'You can always come and do it another time. My friend in the library told me that in the spring, when they are nesting, the great skuas dive down and attack walkers here quite viciously. I expect they would love to have a go at a naked woman.'

Meg giggled. 'It would make a charming surrealist painting: Nude, with Skuas. Elderly Nude, with Skuas.'

She lay half on her side by the little pit in which Ruth sat, gesturing in the air with one hand. The laughter dwindled, and subsided into sobs, then tears. Ruth let them go on for a little.

'Why didn't you try to stop this, what he did to you?'

'I didn't know. I thought I had to put up with it.'

'Oh, Meg. What about your parents? Tell me.'

The gentle sympathetic encouragement from Ruth was quite different now from the deadpan questions of the woman of days ago, or indeed from the merciless probing on the Inverness bus.

'Don't you see, my father was dead . . . He would have helped me, he always helped me, but he was dead . . .'

The tears were still wet on Meg's cheeks. She did not seem to notice, and made no attempt to wipe them away. Her voice was fairly steady, however, with long gaps between phrases.

'I went to my mother, but she wouldn't let me talk . . . She said a wife had no business to talk about private matters of marriage to anyone but her husband . . . She went out of the room . . . There was no one else. I couldn't tell his friends. They wouldn't have believed me, anyway . . . And I had no friends of my own. He had made sure of that.'

'How long did this go on for?'

'Oh, years it went on,' said Meg. 'There were gaps, of course. When I was pregnant he left me alone, mostly. I don't know whether it put him off, or whether he didn't want to injure the child, somehow . . . He wanted children, you see. "Pledges of our love", he used to call them, to his friends. Our love!'

She laughed bleakly.

'I didn't mind,' she went on. 'It was such a relief, each time I knew I was having a baby. Then once, some time after Patrick was born, I pretended to be pregnant, and I got away with it for a long time, and then he found . . . you know . . . pads. And he guessed. I pretended I had had a miscarriage, but he beat me all the same. And about a year after that I really did have a miscarriage, at six months. They couldn't save them in those days. He was furious, and blamed me. And then he had to keep away from me for a bit.'

She paused.

'Go on.' Ruth was huddled low behind the little bank, her hands tucked deep into the opposite sleeves. Meg, sitting upright now, seemed oblivious to the biting wind.

'The next miscarriage came in the year after Flora was born. A genuine one again. He was frantic with rage. He thought I had had hot baths or something to get rid of the baby. But I was quite ill, and I had to go to hospital. So I was able to think, quietly, by myself. I realised that it was just going to go on and on. I was young, you see.

I could go on having babies for years. He wanted that. I think he saw himself as a sort of Victorian paterfamilias, ten, twelve children, and a wife worn out by childbirth and . . . other things . . . It was all part of his virility thing . . . his compensation for his eye – I told you he had lost an eye? – and leaving the army and all that . . . And I realised I couldn't do it – I couldn't face it. I would rather die. I remember lying in that hospital bed during endless nights, looking at the ceiling and wanting to die. I tried saving up the sleeping pills they gave me, but they found them. They didn't guess, they just thought I didn't want them, and took them away.'

The tears had long stopped, but Meg's words went on, in an unceasing flow.

'And then something one of the nurses said, talking about herself . . . I forget what was the context . . . "We don't get another chance at life", that was it. It made me think, and I just knew that I had to do something. So, still in hospital, where he couldn't see me, I wrote a letter. I put it all in, how he treated me, the things he did to me, everything. And I copied it. And I sent one copy to the wife of the commanding officer of his regiment. I knew them, you see. They used to come and stay, and they were better than the others. She was a kind woman, and I knew she knew I wasn't happy. She encouraged me to talk, but I had never said anything. I was so frightened of him, you see. Somehow he always seemed to know everything that was going on in the house.'

'What about this letter?' said Ruth.

'Yes, the letter. I sent it in a sealed envelope addressed to the General, inside a covering letter to his wife. I sent them both to her, you see. I trusted her. I told her that the envelope must never be opened unless they got a telephone call or a note from me about it, or unless something happened to me. Then when I was home from hospital I gave the other copy to my husband . . . to Robert. I told him first what I had done. And then I watched him read it.'

'You were very brave.' Ruth looked up at Meg, whose eyes were still fastened on the rocks to the north.

'Yes. I had never done anything so brave in my life. But I was desperate. I was beyond being frightened. He was completely flabbergasted. I don't think he had ever dreamed that I could do such a thing. He was so angry, I thought he would have a stroke. Then I thought he would choke me – he got me by the neck and I couldn't even scream.'

Meg was shaking, but it was nothing to do with the cold.

'But he stopped. He let me go. But he didn't touch me, didn't hit me, I mean. He knew that I was telling the truth about the letter, that I meant it all. He was so shaken, that after a bit I could talk to him. I still hardly know how I did it. I told him that he was never to come into my bedroom again. I said that if he didn't come near me, no one would ever know, and we could carry on as normal.'

'Did he agree?' asked Ruth.

'I didn't know. He was too angry to say he agreed. But he didn't come again. I started locking the door, in case he changed his mind, when he was drunk, perhaps. But he never did. He cared about his reputation in the regiment more than anything in the world, I think.'

'So no more sex?'

'I don't know what he did. He used to go away, for days, sometimes. I never knew where he was. He didn't tell me anything. He stopped talking to me, really, as if he wanted completely to blot me out.'

'Did you mind?' Ruth was so cold she could hardly think, and shivering inside her double layer of clothing.

'Mind? It was the best thing that I had known for years.'

'What did you do?'

'Not much. I moved into the bedroom I had had as a child, away at the end of the wing, where I still sleep now. I read a great deal – I still do – and looked after things at home. It was peace, in a way, the first peace I had known for a long time.'

'Were the children still at home then?'

'Only Flora.'

'M-my teeth are chattering,' said Ruth.

'Yes, you look cold. It is cold, actually. We'd better move,' said Meg. 'And look at the time. We'll have to get back before it gets dark.'

'Thank God,' said Ruth.

'Why?'

'I had an awful feeling that you might want to go to Muckle Flugga. And I had an awful feeling that I might not be able to stop you.'

They took a shorter route back, across the top of Hermaness, following a track. The wind was still strong, and clouds were beginning to gather on the horizon. It was hard to talk with the wind in their faces. As they reached the downward slope towards Burra Firth, the sun had sunk low in the sky. The shadows were stretching far across the water as they approached the car. Meg had not spoken for some time, but Ruth's interest had revived as movement had sent the blood flowing back into her limbs.

'Go on,' she said, settling into the passenger seat.

'What?'

'You said "only Flora". Only Flora was left at home.'

'Must I talk about Flora?' asked Meg.

'Don't you think you should, Meg?' said Ruth.

'Do you think I have to?'

'Don't you think you need to?' Ruth persisted.

'I suppose so. Later. Sometime.'

'Whatever you say.'

178

Chapter Eleven

A white van was travelling slightly too fast, with dipped headlights, through the network of West Sussex lanes. On its side was written KPT SELF-DRIVE HIRE, KILBURN. At its wheel was Patrick, Patrick looking unlike his usual self. Patrick in jeans, a white T-shirt, an ancient donkey jacket and a back-to-front blue baseball cap. Patrick nervous and tense and fired with an unusual determination.

If he was ever to take action, it had to be now, quickly, before it was too late. If it went wrong, he would hardly find himself in a worse situation than he was in already. If it went right, then disaster could be staved off for some time to come. He just needed a breathing space, to give him a chance to think of something. Anything.

He had left London at one o'clock in the morning. There had been virtually no traffic on the road, and he was now within a mile of Bloomfield. He had turned left off the A24 some while back and was approaching Bloomfield from behind. He had no intention of letting the van be noticed by some prying busybody in the village.

He knew the lanes well. They had been his bicycling ground as a child, and yet twice in his haste he overshot a turning, and cursed at the wasted minutes.

He entered Bloomfield by the back gate, closing it behind him. He turned the van in the yard, and reversed it as close as he could to the kitchen door.

He got out and stood for a few moments, looking and listening. The house was in darkness, and there was no sound. Satisfied, he took a crowbar from the seat, then a pair of black leather gloves, and put one on. The other he abandoned after a minute's struggle. He could not get it over the bandages that still covered three of his fingers. Opening the double doors at the back of the van with one hand and some difficulty, he took out several cardboard wine boxes, which he piled up on the doorstep.

He saw that there was still a pane missing from the small window by the door, but did not attempt to reach through it to the lock. Instead he tried to insert the point of the crowbar between the door and its frame just above the handle. He could not get any purchase, so he went back to the van and got out a hammer. Muffling the end of the crowbar with a folded handkerchief, he tapped it with the hammer, first gently, and then harder. He had to give it a resounding blow before the point was forced into the wood. Alarmed by the noise, he stood for a few moments, aware that his heart was beating fast, listening for any sound, any indication that he might have been heard. He knew that the house was empty and that there were no other houses nearby, but there was always the remote possibility of someone passing in the lane.

Hearing nothing, Patrick applied all his strength to the crowbar handle, and to his satisfaction, with a cracking and tearing sound, the lock gave, and the door swung open.

Carrying the boxes in, he pushed it shut behind him with his foot. The lock being no longer operative, the door swung open again, so he propped it shut with the crowbar.

He took out of his pocket a slim pencil torch, and shone

its narrow beam down on the floor. He moved across the kitchen towards the door into the passage that led to the front hall. He passed through it to the dining room, and put the boxes down. First he took the inlaid mahogany knife box that stood on the sideboard. This took up most of one cardboard box, and he filled the remaining space with the table silver from the drawers. He wrapped the spoons and forks in pages of newspaper to stop them rattling. Anything initialled or crested he rejected, and the bone-handled knives he also ignored. Silver salt cellars and pepper pots he squeezed into the top, and closed the box before he carried it back to the kitchen.

He worked at speed in the almost complete darkness. He had planned this in detail, and everything was going exactly according to plan. Feeling his way as carefully as his bandaged fingers would allow, he removed the Sèvres tea set from the glass-fronted cabinet in the hall, wrapping the delicate porcelain with loving care. He knew where everything was, and what he didn't want, the two pieces of spurious Meissen, for example, and a Staffordshire figure that was almost certainly not Enoch Wood. The rest was superb.

Wasting no time, and careful not to let the beam of the torch rise from the floor, he now turned his attention to the furniture in the drawing room. First he drew all the curtains and, even though he knew his light would not be seen, he kept the beam low. A Sheraton work table was moved to the kitchen. He slid his hand, longingly, over the top of the little Bechstein boudoir grand, and settled instead for the fruit-wood music canterbury, emptying its contents on to the floor. He folded the drop-leaves of a pale Sutherland table and carried it through, and returned for the semicircular folding card table with the delicate scrolled inlay that stood behind the sofa to one side of the fireplace. It was as he was lifting this, with the torch gripped between his teeth, that he kicked something heavy and metallic which fell over on to the carpet. A gurgling sound was followed by the pungent smell of petrol.

'What the h . . .' The torch fell from his mouth and rolled away sideways on the carpet, its beam clearly lighting up a metal can lying on its side, the remains of its contents trickling out into the large dark puddle that lay around it. Patrick stood in silence, unable to move from sheer fear. His heart was pounding and his mind could make no sense of what had happened. There was no sound of any kind. He shone the torch beam round the floor of the room. Not a sign of anyone, just this mysterious can.

His instincts told him that it was time to leave, but his greed made him pick up the table to take it with him. It was then that he realised that between the table and the sofa back was crouching a dark figure.

At his whimper of alarm it rose to its feet and pushing him violently aside made for the door into the hall. Patrick was unable to move for some seconds, and then, emboldened by the flight of the other, he rushed into the hall and shone his torch beam down the kitchen passage after the fleeing figure. All he could tell was that it was dressed in black from head to foot, and was not very large. He followed, as much angry as frightened. He arrived in the kitchen to see it wrench at the door, which stuck partly open. In attempting to squeeze through the crack, the intruder tripped on the crowbar, and fell headlong on the doorstep, hitting its head with a loud crack against the door frame.

Seeing no movement, Patrick took one foot and pulled the body back into the kitchen. It was less heavy than he had expected. Shining his torch fearfully at it he saw a woollen hat, a blackened face, black sweater, dark jeans, black gloves. The eyes were shut, but as he bent to feel if it was breathing, they flickered open.

A dark hand rose slowly to the side of the head, and there was a long groan.

'Who the hell are you?' said Patrick fiercely. He could deal with a smallish, groaning burglar. 'I have a gun on you. Turn over on your face.'

Instead the figure sat up, both hands to its head. It pulled off the woollen hat, and short dark hair fell into place.

'I have a gun,' said Patrick again, petulantly. He was not quite sure what to do with a called bluff.

'Shut up, you fool,' said a voice he knew. 'God, my head. You bloody cracked my skull.'

'Flora!' said Patrick weakly. He felt for, found and sat on a wooden chair.

'What did you hit me with?' Angry white eyes glared at him from the blackened face. The torch now lay on the table, its narrow beam reflecting light back from the white Aga front.

'Christ! You're the frigging burglar!'

Patrick, taken by surprise, answered, but not quickly enough.

'No . . . no. The burglar got away. He must have hit you as he ran out.'

'You bloody liar,' said Flora with sudden realisation. 'I saw you. And I heard the van. I saw it just now, standing outside, before I fell. That's you, not a burglar, stealing the furniture. Look at all that!'

All round them was the evidence, standing on the kitchen tiles.

'You filthy thief,' said Flora, getting to her feet. 'Christ, my head.'

'And what do you think *you* are doing, sweety-pie,

creeping around like a member of the SAS? Let's have *your* explanation,' said Patrick.

Now Flora hesitated. She pulled a chair out from the kitchen table and sat down. Her mind began to work.

'I'll tell you exactly what I was doing, Patrick,' she said. 'I had an idea that Mother might be back, and I wanted to find out precisely what has been going on between her and that woman without either of them seeing me.'

'Then what were you doing hiding in the drawing room? How did you get in, anyway?' said Patrick.

Despite the pain in her head Flora knew she was thinking faster than her brother.

'The window pane by the back door, of course. We broke it last week, remember? You can stick an arm in and reach the lock. I had only just got in. I heard the van, and raced through to the drawing room to hide. I thought it might be the police, checking the house. I didn't want to have to explain to them what I was doing dressed like this. If I had known it was only you . . . Anyway, you've been found out now, Patrick, at your grubby little game. I had a pretty good idea that this sort of thing was going on, but not on this scale. So, what's it worth to you for me to keep quiet?'

'Flora, listen.'

As usual his sister was in charge of the situation. He was going to have to throw himself on her mercy. God knew, he could do with someone to talk to. With difficulty, he told her about Simon, the grocery deliveries, the reason for his broken fingers, the gist of what had happened to him in the last few months. He told, for once, the truth.

'I've got to have money, Flora, don't you see? They could shop me to the police at any time, unless I keep up the payments. I'm in the red as it is, at the bank. There's nothing I can do. I know Mother would help me if she were here.'

To his surprise Flora seemed to understand and even to sympathise.

'I do see,' she said. 'You are in a pretty tricky position, though you're a damn fool to get into it. All right, I'll forget it, and I suppose I'll give you a hand. You load this stuff up. I'll get the brass clock from the drawing room for you. That should be worth a bit. My torch is along there.'

Flora disappeared up the passage. Patrick was so relieved that without stopping to wonder at this unexpected reaction he started at once to move furniture out through the door. As he picked up the Sheraton table he kicked something metallic that skidded across the tiled floor. He shone his torch after it, and saw it was a metal screw top. He realised what it meant and the smell of petrol came back to him. In a wild flash of understanding he leapt for the passage door. He reached the drawing room in seconds and by the light of a table lamp saw Flora standing by the sofa, and heard the match striking. He threw himself at her, and together they fell over the sofa and landed on the floor in front of the hearth.

'For God's sake, what are you doing?' he shrieked, holding her down, half lying on her. His broken fingers had jarred against the floor.

'Get off me!' croaked Flora.

'You can't do that. They'd never pay – they can tell when a fire has been lit like that. We'd never get the insurance, you fool. You'd have burnt the house for nothing.'

Flora's white eyeballs rolled in the dark face as she laughed hysterically, a wild, mad laugh that made Patrick slightly loosen his grip on her.

'Money!' she gasped. 'It's all you ever think of! There's not one of you deserves a penny of her money.'

She raised her knee sharply, a fairly well-aimed blow at Patrick's groin, enough to make him fall backwards with a grunt. She rolled away, and on to her feet. In pain, he lunged forward, still on his knees, and pulled himself up by the sofa, but this time he failed to reach her before the match was struck. She dropped it on to the huge stain on the carpet.

The speed of the blaze astonished them both. The flames shot up with a roar to the ceiling as, clutched together, they fell back to the door. Flora's hair was crackling and her hands had been seared by the fire.

Patrick threw her on to the floor of the hall and leapt for the fire extinguisher that stood in the corner.

As he dragged it to the drawing-room door he felt Flora's hand grab his ankle and heard her voice screaming, 'No, no!' He kicked out viciously and pulled the pin from the extinguisher with his good hand. Painfully, he squeezed the handles together, and a stream of water shot from the nozzle towards Flora, who was thrown back by its force.

Free of her grasp, Patrick turned the water jet on to the base of the fire. Within half a minute the roaring flames that had seemed about to engulf the room were reduced to smoke and steam at floor level. A burning picture frame was easily drenched and extinguished, and Patrick then soaked the smouldering back of the sofa.

As he finished he became aware of an extraordinary sound. Flora, her face washed almost clear of the black colouring, was lying on the hall floor, making a strange howling noise and tearing wildly at her clothes and her hair, as if she were distraught with grief or pain. Slowly her writhing and animal wails subsided, and she lay, a black, sodden pile of trembling clothing, sobbing uncontrollably.

Patrick went to the dining room, turned on the light, and, taking the top off the first bottle he could find, took a long swig of sherry. Although he was still shaking with shock, he found his torch and turned the lights out. Then he went back to the kitchen and finished loading the van. He returned to the hall, and found Flora still lying there on her side.

'Flora?' he said.

She did not reply.

'We've got to get out of here,' he said. 'I'm going back to London.'

She opened her eyes and stared at him.

'Are you coming?' he said.

She nodded. Her hands were red with scorching but she did not seem to feel any pain as she pushed herself on to her knees and then to her feet. She appeared dazed, but walked down the passage after him and followed him out to the van. She stood by it with her head lowered, waiting for Patrick to open the door for her.

'Haven't you got a car?'

'Oh. Yes.' She looked round. 'I think it's in the lane.'

'I didn't see it.'

But it was there, in a lay-by, half under a bush.

'Are you all right to drive?' said Patrick doubtfully. 'You had better put that coat on. You are wet.'

Flora nodded, and got in. She sat staring over the steering wheel.

'You'd better follow me,' he said.

Cockerill held his pencil like a dagger and stabbed it repeatedly into the top of his desk. Scars of previous rages were all over the surface. The girl at the desk in the waiting room, the only other room of his small office, raised her eyes towards the sky and got a new pencil out of a box in a nearby drawer. Then she turned back to her horoscope.

'They have been leaving a trail as wide as a herd of bloody elephants and still you lost them,' said Cockerill heatedly into the telephone. 'You are a flaming disaster,

Mick. I should never have taken you on. I thought you said you'd done this kind of work before?'

The high-pitched voice whined out of the receiver at him.

'I told you, didn't I, I was best at the marital stuff. This fuckin' country is full of old women on buses, and they all look the same. It's like a barrel full of mackerel. *You* try findin' two of them without some decent equipment. Look, Wally, I 'ad to wait 'alf an hour to get into this bleedin' call box.'

'Look, lad,' said Cockerill, 'on our margins we don't run to mobile phones. And don't call me Wally. Mr Cockerill to you. You get your arse down to Dundee sharpish and check that lead. Call me after four. It's all very bloody well for you, messing around up there. I've got this bleeding MP breathing down my neck.'

It was on the boat back to Aberdeen that Ruth brought Flora's name up again. 'Tell me about her.'

'I hate thinking about Flora.'

'I know,' said Ruth, 'but I think you know that you have to face it all, now.'

'Oh, I know. Scour it all out. You don't have to explain.' Meg sighed heavily, rubbing her eyes with her fingertips.

'I think I feel most guilty about Flora. She was much younger than the others. When they were small, the house was full of noise and bustle, and I suppose they were all quite happy, in a way. Robert paid them a lot of attention, gave them presents, spoilt them, bribed them. He was at home all the time, you see, except when he went to meetings. There was no pattern of going to work, coming home from work, like ordinary husbands. And all the time he was quite merciless in his determination to make them like him and despise me. And he would undermine any effort I made to teach them anything. He always made me feel such a fool, and they imitated him, and it made him laugh. I didn't try to fight back, in the end, because it only made him angry. I was a coward, I know, and I knew it even then. Can you understand if I say that I had no foothold, no support at all on which to base a counter-attack, not even my mother?'

Ruth nodded.

'One needs someone, or something, to back one up,' she said.

'I could see,' Meg went on, 'that I was losing them, and losing any chance of influencing them, but he was just too strong for me. Then, when the others went off to school, just Flora was left, being quite a bit younger. She would have to have been blind and deaf not to feel the misery in the house. When she left home I was so relieved. She was doing what I was too . . . too weak to do myself.'

'How old did you say she was?' asked Ruth.

'She was nearly seventeen. She was supposed to be going to university, but she left home, so that didn't happen.'

'She just left? Was there a row?'

'I shall have to tell you it all, I suppose. It makes me feel so ashamed.' Meg drew a deep breath.

'Flora and I were very close. I don't really know why, but he let me have Flora, if you see what I mean. He thought she was plain, and he didn't really like her. She was very affectionate, very demonstrative when she was young, a dear, skinny little person. But as she got older she gradually changed. She no longer liked to be hugged. She was sharp, and observant. And critical. Robert insisted that she stayed at day school, unlike the others. Perhaps he couldn't face being left alone with me. I didn't let him know how grateful I was, or how much I needed her. She did well at school, really well. But they were always concerned about her. They called her a loner.

'She knew, of course, that Robert and I hardly talked to each other, except in front of other people. And that we didn't sleep together, in the same room, I mean, like other people's parents. She didn't bring other children home from school. I tried to encourage her to, of course, but I couldn't blame her for not wanting to, with the sad, sterile atmosphere there was in the house. So she was lonely. And she minded about us, Robert and me. She even wanted to "bring us together", as they say. When she was nine or ten she would ask leading questions, at mealtimes. "Father, was it romantic when you proposed to Mum?" or "Mum, why don't you and Father ever go to the theatre?" and then stare at us both. He would pretend he hadn't heard, or would talk about something else. He couldn't cope, and I always covered up for him, telling her we didn't like the theatre, or whatever it was. I pretended to her that we were normal, and happy, whatever it might seem like. She would say, "Do you and Father love each other, Mum?" and I would say, "Of course we do, darling. What a ridiculous question." '

'Could you have told her the truth?'

Meg gazed into her cup of coffee, cold on the café table in front of her. It slopped gently from side to side with the movement of the boat.

'I am sure now that I should have told her the truth, or some version of it. But I don't think I was capable of it. Ruth, don't you see, my whole upbringing was geared to pretence. My mother believed in "a woman's role": smiling in the face of adversity; supporting their husbands in all things; it was a woman's duty to keep the home together, above all. Some of it may have made sense, once. But oh, so defeatist. And my father, who was a dear, good man, if not very effectual . . . he was much the same. He taught me in clichés, to "keep my chin up", to "put my best foot forward". I must never let anyone see if I was hurt. "Keep up the façade." Do you see what I mean? I believed, I sincerely believed that it was right to hide my problems. I thought it was my duty to keep up a brave pretence. It seemed one way of protecting the children – I think I even felt I owed it to Robert, so brainwashed was I. And I also felt deeply ashamed of what had happened to me . . . ashamed of my failure to make our marriage a success.'

'Your failure! You had done nothing wrong.' Ruth had been shaking her head sadly during this narrative. 'I talked about your pride before, and this is what I mean – you were too proud to admit your marriage had failed, and yet if you had had more self-esteem this foolish shame would not have come into it, and you would have seen that you had as much right to happiness as anyone else. To talk about failure! You had done nothing wrong, Meg.'

'Except, as you have shown me, by hiding it all. Until it was too late. Until I couldn't talk about it to anyone, not even myself. I think in the end I almost made myself believe the things I have been pretending for so long. And after Robert died it just seemed easier to keep up the act, to be a typical widow, after a typical marriage. I was so used to it that I wouldn't have known what else to do, anyway. I was in the habit, you see.'

She looked at Ruth, pleading for understanding.

'I blame your mother, 'Ruth said. 'If she had listened to you at the start . . . if she had not pushed you into that incredible marriage . . .'

'I don't blame her.' Meg shook her head. 'She didn't know any better. I should have seen for myself that it wasn't right to marry someone I didn't love. But I was too gullible. And I was used to doing as I was told. My mother was a remarkably determined woman.'

'So what happened with Flora?'

'Well,' Meg sighed heavily again,' as she got older, and

prettier, perhaps twelve or thirteen, he started to notice her. He bought her presents, offered to drive her here and there. She always refused, which made him even keener to make her like him, and to detach her from me, just as he had the others. She used to ask me, "Why don't you do things with him? You're his wife, aren't you?"

'She changed during those years. She became very sullen and unhappy herself. She had a very sharp tongue, and she couldn't resist saying cruel things.

'Then came a stage when she let me know that she knew our marriage was – you know, awful. She would keep pointing it out. I don't know how much she guessed. There was one time when she saw him beating a dog that kept coming into our garden, poor thing. And Flora saw the horrid pleasure he got from it. And he used to shout at people who worked for us. He had this need to subdue people. Flora saw me crying after he had bullied one poor girl quite dreadfully, and I think she . . . Oh, I don't know. But after that she used to say things to me, bitter, critical things. She tried to incite me to face up to her father. She said I was a coward . . . that she despised me. And then she would go and spend all her money on presents for me. She was in such a muddle, poor little Flora.

'You see, I couldn't talk to her, not without bringing the whole edifice I had built up crashing down around us all. That was too frightening. I had to go on pretending. I think perhaps she couldn't forgive me for not being frank with her. Perhaps she still can't.'

'What made her leave?' asked Ruth.

'Oh . . . dreadful,' said Meg. 'I told you he paid her a lot of attention as she got older. I should have guessed what was going on. He went to her room one night. He was drunk, of course. I don't think anything very much happened, but it was bad enough. She turned up in my bedroom, and screamed at me. She said it was all my fault, and why hadn't I left him years ago, and why were we both such hypocrites, and she hated men, and hated the whole world, and all that sort of thing. And she left, then, in the middle of the night.'

'Just walked out?'

'She took the car, and dumped it a few miles away.'

Meg's eyes were bleak with the memory.

'I think she probably thumbed a lift. And that was it. I was in despair, of course, but she rang a few days later, saying she was all right, and not to look for her. That was kind of her. She was not really unkind, just very, very unhappy. And she wasn't even seventeen.'

'Poor Flora.' Ruth found herself for the first time in sympathy with another member of Meg's family.

'Yes, poor, poor Flora,' said Meg. 'God knows what she did at the start. I hardly saw her again until her father died. I didn't want her to come home, of course. The other children were all away from home by then. They let me know how she was. I don't think she told them much. They just thought she was going through a teenage phase. She turned up at her father's funeral, to my surprise, just to the service. She didn't come back to the house. I think I told you, she has never stayed the night in Bloomfield since she left. I think she hates it very deeply.'

'Do you think that is why she wants you out of it?'

'Ruth, you know, I wonder. It could be. With the others, I think it is just the money they want. You know, after Robert died, Flora stayed in touch with me. She started to come, just brief visits. And she still comes, at once, if she thinks I need help. Sometimes I wish she wouldn't. We don't talk easily. She occasionally even invites me to meet her in London. We go to a film, or a play. But we have never talked about what happened. I don't think we could. I know very little about her private life. We just talk on the surface. But, although she is very sharp, very edgy,

I like her. I really do like her. I like being with her. She is an interesting person, and very noticing, perceptive. She is also less like Robert than all the others, in looks and in manner. I would like to know her.'

'Meg,' said Ruth, 'can I ask you something personal?'

Meg laughed, despite herself.

'I thought everything you have asked me, or everything you have somehow made me tell you, has been extremely personal!'

Ruth smiled. 'This is different. Have you ever been in love?'

'Ah,' said Meg, 'I see what you mean. Yes, that is different. In love? Yes, I think I was once really in love.'

'Before you were married?'

'Oh, yes,' said Meg. 'And after, too, I'm afraid.'

'This man,' said Ruth, 'whoever he was, was he in love with you?'

'He said he was. Yes, I know he was. He got married though, rather more happily than I did.'

Meg looked at her watch.

'It won't be long till we're there,' she said.

'Did he ever ask you to marry him?' Ruth persisted.

'Yes. And I wanted to marry him, too.'

'So why didn't you?' Ruth was incredulous.

Meg laughed bitterly. 'My mother, of course. No money, no prospects, she said, too young, and he was about to be called up. The war, you see.'

'So?'

'So she made me write to him, and say I had changed my mind. She wrote to him too, though I didn't know that till years later. She told him not to write to me ever again.'

'This is brutal,' said Ruth. 'Go on.'

'He wrote, of course,' said Meg. 'She intercepted all his letters. I wasn't told about them. I thought he had forgotten me. After the war he wrote again, and asked why I had never answered. I was married . . . I wrote back, just the kind of letter my mother might have dictated . . . saying I was happily married, and that he must never talk to me about love again . . . It nearly broke my heart. But what else could I do?'

Ruth gazed out through the misty window of the ferry boat, wondering if she felt more saddened than irritated.

'Have you ever seen him since?' she asked.

'Oh, yes,' said Meg, smiling. 'Quite often. I still do.'

'And you have never said anything?'

'I told you. He married. His wife died, some years ago now. I think they were happy,' she added, wistfully. And then, more briskly, 'Indeed, I hope they were.'

'You have never asked much for yourself, have you?' said Ruth, smiling.

'No,' said Meg. 'But there's always time to learn.'

The boat suddenly shook and juddered as the engines were put into reverse. They were docking at Aberdeen.

Chapter Twelve

When Jinny Fordham telephoned her parents and told them she was coming home for the weekend, she was astonished when Beatrice said no.

'What do you mean, Mum, you're busy? What sort of busy? Do you mean you've got a meeting or something? That doesn't mean I can't come home, does it? It never has before.'

'No, you don't understand,' said Beatrice. 'We are fully occupied, all weekend, and we just don't want anyone else here at the moment. I will explain another time.'

'Mum, this just doesn't sound like you. Or like Dad, for that matter. Are you all right?'

Jinny was surprised and slightly hurt by a reaction she had never heard before from her mother. Beatrice was usually overjoyed to welcome her children on their fairly rare visits home, and would drop any engagement in order not to miss a minute of their time.

'Yes,' said Beatrice, 'we are perfectly all right. Please don't come home this weekend. I will ring you next week. All right?'

And she put down the receiver and cut off her bemused daughter.

'That was a little unkind, wasn't it?' said Henry, putting a hand on her shoulder.

'Darling, I can't face the children at the moment,' said

Beatrice, reaching up to touch it. 'Sorting out your and my future is by far the most important thing just now. The children can wait.'

Henry could not remember any previous occasion when Beatrice's and his own concerns had taken priority over their children's.

'Our future. Yes,' he said.

'Shall we talk a bit? Do you feel like it?'

'Yes, I think so.' Henry sighed deeply.

'You know I have been reading all these books.'

'I know. I am very touched.' He meant it.

'I think, love, you have got to ask yourself whether you really want to get off the drink. You know they say that no alcoholic can be cured until he, or she, really wants to be cured. It is no use me asking you to do it. You have got to want it yourself, nothing to do with me.'

Henry gazed at the glass in his hand. Beatrice had insisted that, whenever he needed a drink, he should drink it in her presence, and not alone in his room. And she would often have a glass with him, but not every time. She had been horrified to see how often the now recognisable signs of his need came round again. She did not try to stop him drinking. She just tried to talk with him when he was at his most lucid.

'It is very odd,' he said, moving to an armchair. 'I feel different now that you use that word – alcoholic. Me – an alcoholic. I have shied off it before, even in my thoughts. I suppose one does. But in a strange way it makes me feel much better to be able to say it, and to hear you say it. I feel, what . . . understood, I suppose. And much closer to you.'

'I know,' said Beatrice. 'I know. Me too. And I really don't want to lose that feeling again. So you know I won't try to persuade you, but if you want to try, or when you do, I will do everything I can to help you. If you want me to, that is.'

She got up and pushed a log into the fire with her foot, and stood for a long moment watching the rising sparks. For the first time for many years she felt no sense of urgency, no need to bustle or make lists. She had spent so many years being indispensable, coping, complaining, and impressing on herself and everyone else how busy she was that she had come to believe in her self-created persona. Now, possibly for the first time, she found herself, however precariously, in a situation when she might genuinely be needed. It was a strange sensation. She felt an unusual confidence; focused, that was the word, but unhurried.

Henry watched her. This new, calm Beatrice took a bit of getting used to. It was strangely easy to talk to her. She was suddenly more like the person he remembered a long time ago, the person he had once loved and felt close to. The feeling of closeness was there again now, and the other, well, perhaps he might even be capable of that. Who could tell? Everything seemed to be changing.

'I just know I can't do it myself,' he said. 'I have tried before, you know. Well, I don't suppose you would know. But I have. I can't make twenty-four hours on my own.'

'You think you do want to stop, then?' said Beatrice. 'It's a very long, hard haul. All the books say so. It takes an awful lot of courage. And staying cured, that's a job for life. For both of us.'

'Bea, I would like to stop. The thought frightens me, more than I can say. But if you will help me, I will try. I would like to stop more than anything.'

'Do you really mean that, do you think?' said Beatrice. 'You may just be saying it. I would understand that.'

'I mean it. At this moment, with the courage of a drink in my hand, I mean it. But I cannot promise I will mean it tomorrow.'

'Bugger tomorrow.'

'Bea!' Henry laughed aloud. 'You really are different, suddenly. I have never heard you say "bugger" before.'

'Not saying words doesn't mean you don't sometimes think them. I feel different, though, too. I feel like fighting for you. And I will, if you'll let me. I love you, and I know you are worth fighting for.'

She looked at him, searching his face with her eyes, as if she hardly knew it. He met her gaze, shaking his head gently in disbelief, and took another mouthful from his glass, his hand shaking slightly.

'Listen, dear,' Beatrice went on, 'they think Mother is on her way home. As soon as she is back, I am going to ask her to help pay for a clinic for you. We can't possibly afford it. I have been ringing around, and it is at least seven hundred pounds a week, at the cheapest sort of place, but I know she will help.'

'No. No, Bea, no!' His voice at first emphatic, then rising almost to a shout, Henry stood up. He looked down at Beatrice in her fireside chair. 'I am not taking any more money from your mother. We have been sponging off her for years, and I will not add any more to that endless debt.'

'It's not a debt, love,' said Beatrice, gently. 'She won't want it back.'

'To me it is a debt. I am not going to one of those posh health farms on someone else's money. People who can't afford them don't go to them. Bea, listen. I know I have lost my self-control, and if I ever had any dignity I have lost that too. But when you are in a hole like that you don't, as they say, go on shovelling stuff out of the bottom. I have some vestige of self-respect left. I will be cured. With your help I will be cured but I want you to promise me that whatever happens you will keep your mother out of it.'

Beatrice gazed up at him, astonished.

'If you say so. But what do we do, then?'

'Will you come with me to the doctor, tomorrow? The family health clinic in Winchester? I think we need some advice.'

'Yes, Henry, of course I will. Oh, my dear, my dear. Of course I will.'

As the tears came to her eyes Beatrice realised that she was filled with admiration for her husband. Again, it was a new sensation. It was not just her usual determination that others should admire him, should think that Beatrice had married a unique and splendid man and envy her. This was something different, an upswelling of genuine respect for a Henry that she had not known existed.

'Henry?' she said, when she could speak. 'Henry, I want to say something. I think they would give me more work at the club. Every day, I mean. Don't frown. I know I moan about it, but that's just me. I actually really enjoy the work. And I'll do it, and I don't care who finds out, and who knows it. And if anyone says anything unpleasant I will put chilli powder in their soup.'

Henry's eyes were warm as he smiled at her.

'I do believe you would,' he said. 'But I think the people who matter would be impressed. Just as I am.'

'Mr Leetham? Mr Leetham, should I answer the letter or not?'

There was no reply.

'Mr Leetham? Are you all right?'

The woman who had spoken looked at her husband, who was sitting beside her. On the opposite side of the table sat their Member of Parliament. His gaze was unfocused and he seemed to be staring straight through them.

'Mr Leetham?' She spoke again, louder.

'What? Yes? I'm sorry, what did you say?'

Lionel Leetham's attention returned, and he looked anxiously at the couple.

'The letter. The letter I gave you.'

'Of course. Of course. I'm sorry. What did you say again?' He looked down at the letter he held in his hand.

'Mr Leetham,' said the woman after another meaningful glance at her husband, 'I don't believe you have been listening to a word I have been saying.'

'Indeed I have,' said Lionel earnestly. 'Every word. You must forgive me. All these late nights, you know . . . My attention drifted but just for a second. The letter. Of course. Let me read it, now.'

'You have already read it, Mr Leetham, and if you are not going to take this matter seriously I shall not waste my valuable time being made a fool of any longer.'

'No, no. I remember, now,' said Lionel. 'The letter is pure evasiveness, and I suggest that you, er, write to your district councillor and say that I said so. That I view the matter very seriously indeed, and that I will take it up with the Minister if they don't do as you ask. Definitely.'

'The letter is from the Inland Revenue, Mr Leetham, nothing to do with the council whatsoever. Give it to me, please. Come on, dear.'

Getting to her feet the woman tapped her husband on the shoulder.

'We are not going to get any help here, I can tell that.'

'That's right. Thank you for nothing,' said the husband.

The couple flounced out of the room, banging the door behind them. Lionel gazed hopelessly at the children's drawings that hung round the classroom wall. His fortnightly Friday-night advice surgery in the local school was the constituency duty that he liked least. But tonight had been particularly disastrous. He had been quite unable to concentrate on anything except the sense of doom hanging over him. He leant his elbows on the table and ran his fingers over his scalp.

After a few minutes, he realised that nobody else had come into the room. He opened the door and looked out to where his young constituency agent was sitting on the edge of a bench in the passage. He had not been in the job long, and was still nervous of the MP.

'That's the lot tonight, is it?' said Lionel with an attempt at heartiness. 'All the customers satisfied?'

'Er – there were another two waiting, but I think they decided not to – er – wait.'

He did not feel it was his job to say that they had left on hearing a furious comment from the woman who had just come out.

'That man has been drinking! I know where I shall put *my* vote next time. It's diabolical. I am going to write to the Prime Minister.'

Instead he helped Lionel on with his overcoat and said, 'No thanks, I brought my bike,' to the offer of a lift. Then he walked home in the rain.

On the following morning Lionel invented a heavy head-cold to get out of a coffee morning and bring-and-buy sale arranged by a branch of his constituency association. He was fearful of missing a telephone call from Cockerill. Louise went on her own, and as usual made convincing excuses for her husband. The constituency agent looked distracted as she explained what a bad headache Lionel had.

When she got home, Louise went into the kitchen where Lionel was sitting moodily.

'Here,' she said. 'They sent you the flowers from one of the tables to cheer you up.'

She handed him a plastic margarine pot bristling with blue and yellow flowers.

Lionel stared at them.

'I rang Cockerill, and he's not there,' he said.

'Well, it's Saturday. Presumably the office is closed.'

'But there must be some news! They must have found them by now! It's unbelievable!'

'Why are you so upset?' asked Louise calmly. 'We believe they are on their way back, don't we? Surely we can wait another few days.'

Lionel stood up violently, throwing his chair backwards, and crashed out of the room.

A minute later he came back in.

'I want to go to London this afternoon,' he said. 'There may be a message there, on the answering machine.'

'But . . . we're supposed to be here for the weekend. The Marshalls are coming to supper.'

But Lionel was already collecting papers and stuffing his briefcase.

'Ring them up. Make some excuse. Say I am ill, say anything you like. I am going to pack.'

Placidly, Louise complied. For some time she had felt that some sort of crisis was coming, and she knew that she must just go along with the flow of events. She felt unusually calm and strong, and she almost looked forward to the inevitable moment when Lionel turned to her for help. She felt all the more capable in the knowledge of her husband's inadequacy when under pressure. She only vaguely guessed at what was affecting Lionel, but it was clear that her mother's continued absence somehow had a major impact on his private affairs.

Being frank with Rupert about her matrimonial problems, after their lunch together, had made her feel strangely liberated. This had inspired her to think quite analytically about her relations with her husband and with the rest of her family, and to come to some helpful conclusions. She had no illusions about Lionel – those had gone long ago – but she did not find it impossible to live with his faults; she knew the depth of his dependence on her, far better than he did, and it gave her a pleasing sense of importance. Rupert's plea, speaking for himself and his brother, that his parents should 'get their act together' had affected her, and strengthened her resolution to maintain her marriage, assuming, that was, that this latest scrape of Lionel's was containable and bearable.

As for her mother, there again Rupert's words had struck a chord, and she knew that it was time that she listened to the voice of her own hitherto dormant conscience. She had resolved that she would, in future, not only set a better example to her husband in terms of care for her mother, but try to make sure he followed it. She felt much better for this decision.

There was no message from Cockerill waiting at the London house, and no answer from his office on the Sunday morning. Lionel hardly ate, and moved incessantly from room to room. By mid-evening Louise had had enough.

'I think, Lionel, that you are going to have to talk to me, whether you want to or not. You are going to have to tell me what has been going on. I might as well tell you that I have known for a long time that you have been having an affair with Amanda Bliss, and also that you were going to spend some time with her just before Christmas.'

Lionel was speechless. He stood and stared at Louise with his mouth slightly open.

'Sit down,' she said. 'You look as if you need to. I realise that something has gone wrong between you, and that it is somehow linked to your need to have Mother back. Quite why, I haven't worked out. So you had better tell me.'

'You knew about me and Mandy? How long have you known for?' He was as deeply shaken by his wife's calm manner as by the revelation, and did not know how to take either.

'Oh, probably since the start. May of last year, wasn't it? Not long after little Miss Windelow went back to Holland.'

This further knowledge of his private life shook Lionel still more.

'Does anyone else know?' he asked apprehensively.

'Probably,' said Louise calmly. 'You're not exactly good at dissembling. But don't worry, I am not going to make a fuss.'

Lionel stood up, and stared at his wife.

'Louise, I hardly know what to say.'

'No, I don't suppose you do, Lionel. But you'll think of something. Meanwhile, why don't you tell me why you need Mother so much? It's quite a mystery to me why her return is suddenly so necessary to you.'

'Louise, you know how fond I am of you.' Lionel approached Louise where she sat comfortably in an armchair. He laid a hand on her shoulder and spoke earnestly. She did not look at him.

'I don't know why I do these things,' he said. 'But I am a man, you know. It is different for women.'

'Oh yes?' She looked up at him now, with a face of rapt attention. 'Do tell me more.'

'Louise, don't be so difficult.'

'Difficult? Me? You call this difficult? I am offering to help you, for goodness' sake. And stop hanging over me like that. Do sit down.'

'Oh, God, I wish you *could* help me. I am in such a mess.' Lionel changed tack. He sat down on a stool near her knees, and buried his face in his hands. Soon he was genuinely sobbing with self-pity and exhaustion. He had truly not slept for several nights, but not as a result of late sittings in the House.

'Go on. Spill it out,' said Louise unsympathetically.

'She is blackmailing me. She is telling lies, of course, but she says I said I would marry her. You know I wouldn't, Louise. She's made it up – she says she has a letter from me. I expect she's forged it.'

'I expect she hasn't,' said Louise. 'You are quite capable of saying anything like that to get her into bed with you.'

'Oh God, I can't argue with you. You simply have no idea how bad it is.'

The face he lifted towards her was pink and unattractive. His slightly too bright chestnut hair had risen from where it was normally slicked down across the shiny top of his head. Grey showed at the roots, and Louise's resolve nearly faltered. He looked ridiculous in his despair, and despite herself she found it touching.

'Go on,' she said impassively.

'It's blackmail,' said Lionel. 'I mean it, Louise, really blackmail. Not just the expression. She says if I don't agree to marry her she wants a hundred thousand pounds instead. One or the other. She's given me till Monday, till tomorrow, to decide which. She means it, Loopy, I know she does. She says she will tell the press if I don't give her a letter tomorrow – tomorrow! – promising one or the other.'

'What has all this got to do with Mother?' asked Louise. 'Go on, tell me.'

'I thought,' Lionel's voice faltered, 'I thought if I told your mother the truth she would help me. If I told her our marriage was in danger, you know. And my career. She could sell something, furniture or something. Or think of selling the house, and then I could borrow from the bank, if she would just give me a letter. I am sure she would, to help us, if I tell her the truth.'

'The truth,' said Louise bitterly. 'Since when did you tell anyone the truth? By God, Lionel, you really have hit rock

207

bottom, haven't you? Going to your mother-in-law to ask her to pay off your mistress. Well, I can tell you, Lionel, that I may be a bad daughter, but even I would not take my mother's money for that.'

Lionel was thrown back by this attack, surprised by the violence of the emotion shown by his usually passive wife. But his own troubles kept him from dwelling for long on this change in Louise.

'Loopy, don't you see? Your mother is my only hope. I haven't got that sort of money, not to spare, you know I haven't. Mandy is serious, Louise. She was having lunch with a fellow from the *Evening Echo* the other day. I saw her. She was lining him up to tell him about me. He would lap it up – it's just the sort of thing they love. It would be all over the tabloids and I would be ruined. I would never get re-elected for Surrey Downs! And it would hurt you so much, which is even more important, of course. And the boys. Don't you see? Loopy, don't look at me like that.'

Louise had in fact turned her head away from him.

'Oh, Loopy, help me. She'll do it. She'll shop me to the press if she doesn't get the money.'

'Or if you don't marry her. That's the deal, is it?' Louise said flatly.

Lionel nodded miserably.

Louise was more shaken than she would have cared to admit. She looked at him, wondering why she had married him, wondering at her own weakness, wondering why she still had enough lingering attachment to him to want to help him. Her mind also touched briefly, not long enough to feel uncomfortable, on the knowledge that she would rather be an MP's wife than an MP's ex-wife or, worse still, a dejected ex-MP's wife. She would help him, of course, but not too cheaply.

'Why don't you marry her, then?' she said coldly.

'You don't mean that, Loopy! I'm married to you!'

'Oh, you noticed,' said Louise.

'Oh, Louise, please forgive me. You know I love you. Please help me, oh please . . . What am I going to do?'

She looked at the crouched, snivelling figure for a long time.

'You don't deserve my help, Lionel,' she said at last, 'or Mother's help or anyone else's. You make it quite clear that you despise my mother, but expect her to bale you out when you're in trouble. Why should she? I am not going to put up with your treatment of her any longer. She has more decency in her little finger than you have in . . . Oh, what's the point? You'll never change. You deserve to stew in your own stinking juice, and if I weren't a total fool I would let you do just that. You don't give two pins for what all this does to me, or the boys for that matter. All along you have only thought about what it does to you, and your life, and your reputation. You are despicable. Am I right? Answer me, am I right, Lionel?'

Lionel was not so stupid that he didn't see that the gaining of Louise's support depended on his total subjection here and now. He did not know what she could possibly do to help him, but he was at his wits' end. For the first time for years he submitted to her will.

'Yes, Louise, you're right,' he said meekly. 'I'm sorry. So sorry. I have been a . . .'

'Right then,' said Louise briskly, cutting him short, 'I think tomorrow morning you and I are going to pay a call on Miss Amanda Bliss. Now go to bed.'

Lionel tried to speak, but found he had nothing to say.

'Shall we fly?' said Meg on Monday evening in Aberdeen. The granite city was still enjoying the sun that had followed them from Shetland. They had wandered through the streets and eventually settled for their evening meal on a restaurant called Sorrento. Two seagulls had been flying above it earlier as they walked down a narrow side street, and the combination of the name and the birds was, as Meg said, irresistible.

Now they sat over their second cups of coffee.

'Fly? Go by air? Why the sudden hurry to get back?'

'Because I have nothing more to tell you,' said Meg, laughing. 'And because I have been doing a lot of thinking.'

'I thought you were unusually silent,' said Ruth.

'Don't tease. I suddenly feel full of action. I want to get back to Bloomfield before my determination goes, or in case it does. Just at the moment I feel very clear in my mind.'

'About what?'

'About what to do next. I have been static for far too long, and I want to get moving before I get any older. I am seventy, you know.'

Ruth looked at Meg sitting in the glow of the candlelight and remembered the sad, grey woman she had first seen standing dripping beside a stream in Sussex. The change was extraordinary, and the clothes and revived hair colour were only a very small part of it.

'You are twenty years younger than you were when I first met you, that's all I know,' said Ruth.

'I feel it. You have done more for me than you may think. You have spurred me into making some decisions I should have made aeons ago. I am going to sell Bloomfield. And I am going to see my solicitor and make some adjustments to my will. No, don't look alarmed. I thought it all out in bed last night. The children will have to wait for my money until I die. I might give them a bit now, but not much, because it won't do them any good. Perhaps just some of the furniture for the time being.

'I want a clean break from Bloomfield and all that, and I know I have the courage to start again somewhere else.

Perhaps in London – it doesn't matter. I am going to paint, for a start, and who cares how badly I do it? And write. I'd love to write. And travel, above all, I shall travel. And that is why I shall need money.'

'You really have no feeling for Bloomfield?' said Ruth.

'My feelings for Bloomfield are entirely negative,' said Meg. 'Even as a child. I wasn't born there, you see. My parents bought it just before the war. They had plenty of money. They both came from trade, in the Midlands. All my mother wanted was a big house and what she called "position", by which she meant social position. She was a snob, of course, you'll have gathered that. My father was called Jones, and she tacked her own name on to make it sound grander.' She smiled. 'Poor Father.

'When I first came there, though I was only four, I felt very strongly that I had been uprooted from the place I knew as home, which was a flat in London. But Bloomfield became home, eventually. Then, when my parents were dead, and they both died quite young, I moved back there with Robert. I didn't want to, but he did. Then it just became the place that I was stuck in with him. Its only advantage was that in the later years it was big enough for us to live separately in it.'

'Then why on earth didn't you sell it after he died?'

'I can't think.' Meg shook her head, and fiddled with the wax dripping from the candle on to the red tablecloth. 'The place was full of him, and I should have seen I couldn't escape him as long as I stayed. Almost every bit of furniture he had bought, the curtains, the carpets. He chose them all. I really don't know why I didn't go. Flora tried very hard to persuade me to move. I think I was emotionally atrophied by then, and the relief from his physical presence seemed to be enough. Then, of course, after a while, when I thought of moving, Patrick, and Lionel, were convinced the market would get better.

Then came the slump in housing prices, so I couldn't have sold anyway. I shouldn't have listened to them, but I really was not used to making decisions on my own.

'And now, recently, they have all wanted me out because of the running costs, and they all need money, and they are worried about death duties if I stay there till I die. Well,' she said, rubbing her hands together, 'I am not going to die there. I am going to live, and have some fun, before I think about dying.'

'Well done,' said Ruth, clapping her hands in applause. 'It is fantastic to hear you talking like that.'

'If I have changed, it is entirely thanks to you, as well you know. That is why I want you to come with me to see my solicitor. I might need your support to give me courage when I tell him what I want to do. To do him justice, he has tried to persuade me to move, too.'

'Fine, I'll come,' said Ruth. 'I would really like to be there.'

After driving the white van back to London, Patrick had gone back with Flora to her flat. Her lodgers were away, and her state of mind had been such that he had felt unwilling to leave her alone. He had parked the van in Prince of Wales Drive where he could see it from her windows. In the morning Flora was low and abnormally silent, but otherwise more like her usual self. Patrick felt anxiously that ascertaining her attitude on the future of the contents of the white van took priority over his shop opening on time.

After breakfasting on black coffee they went out into Battersea Park together. It was cold, and bright, and they walked for a while round the ponds without talking.

'We are a mess, both of us,' said Flora. 'I don't know which I hate most, you or myself.'

'Correction. I'm in a mess: you are a mess,' said Patrick.

'You haven't told me why you were trying to set fire to Bloomfield? This was no spur-of-the-moment decision, I gather.'

'Oh, can't you see, you cretin? To get Mother out. To stop her coming back to it.'

'We all want her out,' said Patrick, 'but that was a bit drastic, wasn't it? You say you don't care about the money, but why burn the house, if not for the insurance?'

'Why burn it?' Flora stood still, threw her head back and shut her eyes. 'Because I *loathe* that house. I loathe everything to do with Bloomfield. I want it not to exist. If I could I would stop it having ever existed.'

Patrick stared at her with no understanding.

'Well, fine, I'm not mad about it either. But we can at least get something out of it.'

'I wouldn't touch one penny that came from that place, however you got it.'

Flora spoke with a passion that Patrick had never heard in her before. He stood still and she walked on, up a side path between dark evergreens. He stared for a moment at a contemporary sculpture that said nothing to him.

'You're dotty, Flora,' said Patrick when he caught her up. 'I don't understand you. But if you don't want the money, all the more for the rest of us, that's all I can say.'

'Good God, what did she do to get a family like us? Listen, Patrick,' said Flora, swinging round and bringing him to a halt again.

She jabbed her finger at his coat buttons in a manner that might have seemed affectionate had it not been accompanied by her words.

'You are not going to get your hands on that money, nor Bea nor Loopy, if I have anything to do with it,' said Flora furiously. 'I will spill the beans about your burglary, and a lot more than that, if you put any more pressure on Mother.'

'What the hell do you think you were up to last night, then – was that pressure, or what?' said Patrick sharply.

'OK, OK, I tried to burn her out of the place, and I know it was stupid. I just felt desperate, and it seemed the perfect opportunity. I wouldn't do that again. I want her out, but I know she should leave Bloomfield when *she* wants to, and not a minute before. We've got to stop pushing her around. But when – if – she does go, *she* gets the money, no one else.'

'Flora, come off it. You have been pushing her to leave quite as much as the rest of us, whatever your motives. Listen, isn't it about time you told me what bugs you about Bloomfield? You sound paranoid about it.'

'If you don't know about Bloomfield,' said Flora, shoving her hands into her coat pockets as she turned away, 'God knows what you were thinking about in all the years you lived there. I mean, you're not stupid, or blind.'

'Well, all right,' said Patrick. 'It wasn't the cosiest marriage, those two, but they managed, didn't they? I wasn't unhappy, just bored.'

'Bored, he says! If only boredom had been the problem,' said Flora. 'I do believe you really don't know. Those boarding schools . . . but you *must* remember the holidays. Patrick, I spent more time in that bloody house than any of you. Do you know what it was like living all the year round with two people who loathed each other?'

'Oh come,' said Patrick, smiling uncomfortably, 'it wasn't as bad as all that. I know he bullied her a bit . . .'

'Bullied her! Well, you weren't there, you were at school, or staying with friends, or at college, so you just don't know – and it got worse and worse after you all went away for good. I was there – I *do* know!'

She stopped and turned to look at him, her face pale with anger.

214

'Do you realise that he wouldn't even get in the car with her? That he never addressed a word to her at meals, for *years*? Can you imagine for a moment the atmosphere, him drinking, and her moving like a zombie from room to room so that she didn't have to look at him? Mother was a perfectly decent, reasonable woman caught in a situation so intolerable that it reduced her to a – a husk, an empty husk! Even I couldn't communicate with her. I hardly can even now. She disappeared inside herself, and became a sort of puppet, just opening her mouth to say the right things. You recognise what I am saying, don't you, Patrick? And he did it to her, that man who was our father. God knows how he did it, because I guess we only saw the tail end of it . . . We probably never will know. Do you remember that photograph, in a frame, that used to lie about the attic? It showed she was a girl, once, a normal, cheerful-looking girl.'

Flora paused, and looked at Patrick.

'God, I hated that man. Did you know that when he was drunk he couldn't keep his hands to himself with anyone? *Anyone?*'

'Good Lord.' Patrick was shocked, despite himself. 'You mean *you*?'

'You're bloody lucky it wasn't you, too. Well, I got out. And I swore I would never go back, ever. I left her, Patrick, you see. I deserted her, and now I can't just let her die in that place. She has got to get out too. But not for your benefit, for her own. And the money is bloody well going to be hers for as long as she needs it. That's why I wanted to see her father's will, so I could make sure she knew her rights, because no one else is going to care about them.'

'Flora,' said Patrick, still incredulous, 'I want to get this straight. Have you been telling me that Father hit you? Or are you saying something worse than that?'

'Exactly. A lot worse than that. And he didn't succeed because in the event it was me who hit him.'

'Wo-o-ow,' said Patrick, 'if I may say so. You have certainly said a few mouthfuls, Flora.'

They walked a little way in silence, then stopped and gazed at the dark, leaf-filled winter water.

'It explains a lot, I guess. About you, Flora, for a start, why you did a runner from home. We all thought it was just teenage dementia. And about Mother too, I suppose. She has always seemed so . . . emotionless,' he said.

'I know. You can't talk to her. When her dog died, that's the only time for years I have seen her show anything. I'll tell you more, some day, when we have time.'

'Listen, Flora,' said Patrick, reminded, looking at his watch and reverting to his own troubles, 'it's nearly eleven o'clock. I have to have money by this evening – a lot of money. That stuff I got from Bloomfield, it's the only quick way . . .'

'No,' said Flora loudly. 'Let me think. Shut up, and let me think.'

They walked on, side by side, sparrows moving ahead of them in little bursts of flight. Flora's head was down, her hands clenched in her pockets.

'Right,' she said after a while. 'Patrick, if I get you clear of that lot – your drug-dealers – I want a written declaration from you that you will take all – and I mean all – that furniture back, and everything else you took. And then you will leave Mother alone. I'll write it.'

'God, if you could get me out of the mess I'm in,' said Patrick, 'I would sign anything. I'd do anything to get them off my back. But you don't know what those bastards are like.'

'I have a fair idea,' said his sister, nodding at his bandaged fingers. 'What day do they come?'

'Today – that's the whole point!' There was panic in Patrick's voice. 'Monday at five, every week.'

'Today . . .?' said Flora. 'We're going to have to move fast. Now, you are going to answer some questions. I want every detail of what has been going on. Start at the beginning, when you first met this Simon fellow. Did you approach him, or did he approach you?'

They sat on a bench overlooking the pond, with geese moving hopefully round their feet, and Patrick, because he had no alternative, opened his soul.

Chapter Thirteen

'May I have an appointment to see Mr Asprey, please?
. . . Mr Wilfred Asprey . . . Well, could it be on Wednesday of this week? . . . I quite understand, but I think if
you give him my name, he will make an exception . . .
No, I can't ring back, I'm afraid . . . Well, even if he is
busy, could you interrupt him and ask him? . . . Yes,
I'll hang on.

'Hello? Yes, I'm still here. Oh, good. Ten thirty a.m.
on Wednesday. Perfect. Will you tell him, please, that
I won't be alone? Thank you. Goodbye.'

On Monday morning Lionel and Louise stood on the doorstep of a block of flats in South Lambeth Road. As Lionel
rang the bell opposite the name Bliss, Louise wondered
how often his finger had pressed the same bell, and if the
name now seemed as ironical to him as it did to her.

'Yes?' A voice came from the intercom.

'It's me, Lionel.'

The voice crackled, and a buzzer sounded. Lionel
pushed the door, and it swung inwards.

'The lift,' he said. His voice was shaky, and his face
was grey and drawn.

'Pull yourself together, Lionel,' said Louise, as they
were carried upwards. 'And try not to speak. Let me
do all the talking.'

At the door of the flat she paused to give him time to calm himself. Then she rang the bell.

Louise had never seen her husband's secretary out of her working clothes before, and for a moment as the door opened she thought they had rung the wrong bell. Instead of the usual miniskirt and black collarless jacket that she had for some reason expected, she saw shrink-tight jeans and a close-fitting orange ribbed sweater with no evidence of anything underneath it except Amanda Bliss's opulent natural attributes. Somehow this gave her courage.

'Good morning,' she said, placing a foot firmly over the threshold. 'May we come in?'

Clearly surprised, Amanda Bliss fell back a pace, and Louise was inside the flat before she could reassert herself. Lionel hovered on the landing, and Louise said sharply, 'Come in, Lionel.'

Amanda shut the door behind him and turned.

'Mrs Leetham. I was not expecting you. What *is* this, Lionel?'

Lionel opened his mouth and said, 'Er . . . um.'

'I don't see why you were not expecting me, Amanda,' said Louise. 'As I see it, we are all three implicated in this. Shall we sit down?'

She led the way out of the narrow hall into the sitting room.

'May I?' she said, and took a seat on the arm of a chair with her back to the window.

Lionel followed, and stood awkwardly in the middle of the room. Amanda stood in the doorway facing them. She had composed herself.

'I don't know why you are here, Mrs Leetham, but it does not alter the position between me and Lionel. Have you brought the letter, Lionel?'

Once again Lionel opened and shut his mouth, and

looked apprehensively at Louise.

'For crying out loud, can't you answer for yourself, Lionel?' said Amanda. 'I warned you often enough, didn't I? I mean every word of it. I am not going back on what I said, and I have given you long enough to make up your mind.'

'Lionel can speak later, Amanda,' said Louise, pleasantly. 'It is naturally a very emotional moment for him, as I am sure you will understand.'

Amanda looked at her coldly.

'Do sit down,' said Louise. 'And Lionel, you sit over there. Now, Amanda, perhaps you will explain to me, in your own words, just what is the deal you are offering Lionel.'

'I want to know what is going on here,' said Amanda, sitting reluctantly in a chair opposite Louise, who noted her rising colour with satisfaction. 'Lionel knows what I have said. I have made it quite clear.'

'Very well, I will tell you the position as I see it,' said Louise. 'You have been having an affair with my husband.'

'He has used me, you mean. He took advantage of me, he said he was in love with me and he promised to marry me. I have it in his own writing. I have my self-respect. I can't be treated like that.'

'Keep calm, please,' said Louise. 'And, may I ask, do you love him?'

Amanda looked sharply at Lionel, who was hanging his head, unable to look at the two women.

'Well, of course,' said Amanda. 'I wouldn't have said I would marry him, would I? If I didn't love him? And he loved me. He said so often enough. That's why he wanted to marry me. That's why I . . . why we . . .'

'Went to bed together?' said Louise helpfully. 'I quite

understand. I am sure you would never have dreamt of going to bed with him if you didn't love him.'

Amanda was breathing heavily.

'So I can't be treated like this,' she said. 'He can't get away with this. And I have it in writing that he wants me to marry him.'

'Good. Now I am getting the picture. So you have said to him that if he won't divorce me and marry you you want a hundred thousand pounds in compensation, is that correct?'

'Well, I deserve it, don't I?' Amanda's voice was rising. 'You can't treat a person's feelings like that, walk all over them, and make promises, and then get away with it, just saying you can't let your family down and you've changed your mind. That's what he said, the rat, he'd changed his mind. Well, you can't do that. I have taken advice about that.'

She looked venomously at Lionel, who seemed to be shrinking into his collar. Sweat glistened on his forehead.

'And as I understand it,' said Louise, 'if he does not come up with the money, or a written promise of the money, today, you intend to sell your story to the tabloid press?'

'The *Evening Echo*,' said Amanda more confidently. 'There is a reporter expecting to meet me tomorrow unless I tell him it's all off. And I can tell you, he will make a meal of it.'

'I have absolutely no doubt of that,' said Louise. 'I can see the headlines now, and the photographs. I can imagine the reporters doorstepping me, doorstepping you, catching my children as they leave work. A real circus, it would be. My husband's letter to you printed in facsimile. Another bit of political sleaze – just what the papers feed on. It doesn't matter who is damaged by it.' She was looking at Lionel as she spoke. He pulled out a handkerchief and wiped his forehead.

'Mandy . . .' he started. Louise glared at him, but the girl interrupted first.

'That's right, Mrs Leetham,' said Amanda. 'I wouldn't enjoy it any more than you. And I want to avoid it too. So that is why Lionel had to come here this morning. I have given him long enough. Too long, in fact. When I get the money, I will go away, I promise, and start rebuilding my life. You won't see me any more.'

'Oh, no, Amanda.' Louise laughed cheerfully, 'Oh, no. You quite misunderstand me. I don't see any reason for you to go away. In fact, I don't see why you can't carry on with your career just as normal.'

Amanda stood up, frowning. She wanted to see more clearly the face of her opponent, who was silhouetted against the window.

'What are you getting at?'

'Well, of course, what you are suggesting is a particularly unpleasant form of blackmail, and you will be well aware of the implications of that, if Lionel and I were to report you to the police. We are both witnesses, now, of what you have suggested. I think we have all the details.'

The girl's eyes narrowed as she tried to assess Louise's meaning.

'You wouldn't dare,' she spat out. 'It would all be in the papers long before you could do that. You wouldn't dare.'

She turned mockingly to the abject figure between them.

'*He* wouldn't dare, would you, Lionel? Not with a majority of seventeen hundred, would you, Lionel? Not with that knighthood you are longing for if you manage to hang on for your twenty years, would you,

Lionel? Not with only two years to go. Oh, no, Mrs Leetham.'

She swung round to face Louise again.

'You won't go to the police. That's the last thing you will do.'

'No,' said Louise. 'You are absolutely right, Amanda. You are not a stupid girl. We won't go to the police if we can avoid it. But, unfortunately, we can't go to the bank, either. We simply cannot find a spare hundred thousand pounds for you, though I now realise that that is what you really want.'

'Oh yes you can, Mrs Leetham. You forget. I have been Lionel's secretary for two years. You are not stony-broke, if that's what you are trying to make out. You may not have the money in the bank, but you have got it in shares. It may clean you out, but you've got it. All you do is make a call to Lionel's stockbroker. It's as simple as that.'

'That's true, Amanda. You are even brighter than I thought. Maybe Lionel will not be getting such a bad deal after all. In any case, it won't be necessary to ring anyone, because the money won't be needed.'

'What do you mean by that?' Amanda's voice was menacing.

'I mean,' said Louise, 'that Lionel has quite rightly decided to behave like a gentleman and to stand by his promise to make an honest woman of you. He and I will get a divorce – it won't be difficult to prove irretrievable breakdown of marriage, you know how it goes – and then he will be free, after the least possible interval, to marry you.'

The effect was everything she could have hoped for. Amanda Bliss was speechless. Her mouth fell open and the colour drained from her face. At last she stuttered:

'Lionel, you don't mean that?'

Without looking at her, Lionel nodded.

'That's right,' he said.

'We have discussed it, and thought about it very carefully,' said Louise chattily, 'and we have both come to the conclusion that Lionel would be much happier with you. It is quite obvious that our marriage has not been successful. It happens to a lot of people at our age, and I shall make it quite clear in the constituency that it is my wish to bring it to an end. I may even produce a gentleman friend of my own. It will all be very amicable. Lionel will have to make a suitable settlement on me, of course, the London house, and half his income, and a share of his pension rights, but that can all be arranged by our solicitors. The point is, I won't raise any problems, and it should all go through as quickly as the law will allow. Lionel is going to honour his commitment to you, and quite rightly. And I have to say, my dear, that I hope you will both be very, very happy.'

Louise smiled benignly at them both. Lionel smiled weakly back.

'So it won't be much of a story then, really, will it, as Lionel is offering to marry you? I am afraid they won't pay much for that.'

Amanda Bliss was pink with fury, and her mouth and hands were working impotently.

'You can't do this to me. I – I – I'll make you regret this. I'll make sure this is all over the papers, and I'll make you suffer . . .'

'When you think it over,' said Louise, 'and one should never make important decisions in a hurry, you will realise that in those circumstances we would be bound to go to the police. You see, we would have nothing to lose. I think you will finally decide that it won't be worth a fairly long stint in Holloway. Blackmail is not an attractive crime.'

Amanda was again temporarily speechless.

'You filthy bitch, you could never prove it,' she spat out at last.

'Oh yes, how silly of me. Did I forget to mention this? I have this little tape recorder here.'

Louise stood up and fumbled in the pocket of her cardigan. She brought out a neat black object, and walked round to the back of the armchair she had been sitting on so that it was between her and the angry girl.

'It's quite simple, a Dictaphone, really, but I have tested it and it will have picked up our conversation very nicely.'

She pressed the rewind button for a few seconds, and then played the tape briefly. Amanda's voice was clearly recognisable.

'. . . call to Lionel's stockbroker. It's as simple as that . . .'

Louise nodded and smiled.

'That sounds all right, doesn't it? Just a precaution, in case the police happen to need it.'

She opened her shoulder bag and put the recorder deep inside it as she walked to the door.

'On the whole, Amanda, I think you would be wiser to settle for the wedding bells. I'm sure they would put some lovely photographs in the papers for you then. Come on, Lionel.'

He moved hastily after her.

'You cow, you bloody, bloody cow, you . . . Get out of here, you bastard . . . get out, get out . . . I never want to see you again in my life! I hope you die! I hope you . . .'

The voice had risen to a scream, and with relief they pulled the flat door shut behind them.

Without looking at each other Louise and Lionel

started to walk down the stairs. Near the bottom, Louise said, 'Funny, my legs are shaking.'

They did not speak again until they reached their car. Louise got into the driving seat.

Lionel, sitting beside her, said, 'At one time I really thought she intended to make me marry her.'

'No,' said Louise. 'She never wanted to marry you. But don't worry, you've always got me.'

'Louise, I . . . I . . .' started Lionel.

'No,' said Louise, starting the engine, 'I know everything you are thinking. But I wouldn't say anything at the moment, if I were you.'

Monday evening at Patrick's antique shop in the Pimlico Road, and already after five thirty. Len, who was always so punctual, was late. Remembering the previous occasion when this had happened Patrick's nerve, already at screaming point, was near to breaking.

When the bell above the door tinkled he was almost grateful for the arrival of the moment he had been dreading. His heart thumped and his mouth went dry. Through the glass he saw the studded black leather jacket, the stubble-covered head, the familiar rubicund face, Len's cheerful smile, the Sainsbury's bag, and a wave of relief swept over him. Behave normally, he kept saying to himself.

'You're late,' said Patrick gruffly, as he let him in, moving towards his office.

'Sorry, old cock. 'Ad trouble parkin'.'

'Parking?' said Patrick, taken aback.

'Well, you know these small streets. Not much room for a Roller, and me chauffeur don't like it gettin' scratched. Got yer shoppin', though.'

'Right. You'd better come through. I've been busy. The money's in the office.'

Len shrugged, and following him into the small back room put the bag down on the desk top.

'Quick, then, I 'aven't got all night,' he said, as Patrick fumbled in his breast pocket for his wallet. He seemed to have forgotten which pocket it was in.

'Got a sore 'and, then?' asked Len, grinning.

At that moment the bell tinkled again. They looked at each other.

'Did you lock the door?' snarled Len.

'I think so,' said Patrick.

But the door opened and shut, and footsteps came towards them. Flora's face appeared in the office entrance.

'Hi,' she said.

'Who's this, Patrick?' said Len.

'I'm Patrick's sister,' said Flora, cheerily. 'Who are you?'

'Just a friend,' said Len reluctantly. 'Brought the shoppin'.'

'Oh, I recognise you. I saw you just now. Isn't that your motorbike just down the road, a Honda, registration G 436 LNX? I am afraid I have blocked it with my car. But I won't be long. Is that the shopping? Good. I'll take it, shall I? See you at the flat, Patrick.'

Before either of the men could move, she had lifted the Sainsbury's bag off the desk, and was back in the showroom.

'Oi,' said Len, then, to Patrick, 'Get it!'

Patrick hesitated, and Len made a threatening gesture. Together they went into the showroom. Flora was on the far side of a long dining table, and she already had the top off a large packet of Sainsbury's Non-biological Washing Powder. She had moved fast with a pocketknife. While they watched, transfixed, she pulled out a plastic bag from deep in the powder, scattering white grains across the table. As Len leaped forward, she slashed the top of the bag, and stepped quickly sideways, keeping the table between herself and the angry youth. He growled and lunged across it, but failed to reach her. Smiling at him, she licked her finger and stuck it into the white powder in the bag. She tasted it, and spat it out.

'Just as I thought,' she said, triumphant, and tossed the bag past Len as he came round the table, to Patrick. 'Taste it, Patrick. Go on. What is it?'

Len stopped dead and turned to see Patrick fumbling, sticking his finger in the bag.

'Give me that, you bastard,' he said.

But Patrick's finger was in his mouth. He too spat with disgust on the floor.

'What is it, Patrick?' called Flora again.

'Soap. Detergent,' said Patrick, grimacing.

'So it is,' said Flora. 'What a surprise. A packet of soap powder inside another packet of soap powder.'

Len looked from one to the other, unable to decide how to react.

'Right,' said Flora, 'you nasty little creep. You get back to your boss and tell him he's got nothing on my brother, but we have got your description and bike number and the police will have it in five minutes, too, if they don't get here sooner.'

At that moment they heard the sound of a police siren wailing in the distance.

'That sounds like them now,' said Flora.

Len moved like an eel to the door and out.

'He's gone the wrong way for his bike,' said Flora cheerfully.

'You said you'd blocked it,' gasped Patrick, collapsing into a chair.

'Nope. I came on foot. That was a fib. But I did get its number, just to frighten him.'

'Flora, what am I going to say to the police, for God's sake?'

'The police aren't coming here,' said Flora. 'There's probably a traffic accident somewhere. That siren was just a happy coincidence. We didn't need it, but it helped. Just on cue, wasn't it? He fairly moved!'

'Good God,' said Patrick.

'You realise, you unutterable idiot, that you have been conned? You have paid out heaven knows how much money for bags of soap powder? You have been taken for the most monumental ride of all time. God, you are stupid.'

Flora stood with her hands on her hips, shaking her head in despair at her brother.

'But the bank account, all that?'

'Forgeries, laddie. How much of a look at the papers did you get when your boyfriend – Simon, whatever he's called – when he waved them at you?'

'Not much. He snatched them away.'

Patrick looked dazed. He felt totally limp and exhausted, as if he had undergone a major operation.

'Well, of course he did. The whole story sounded fake. It's got holes right through it, as anybody but you would have seen.'

'Simon . . . he uses the stuff, though. That's how he got it . . . I was bringing it to him.'

Patrick seemed unwilling to believe what she was telling him.

'He may well use heroin,' said Flora, 'but you weren't bringing it to him. If I were you, I would ring him at home now, and tell him the police are on their way round. Tell him you know the whole story. He'll move pretty fast, don't worry. If you like, I'll do it for you.'

'Flora, how the hell did you work all this out?' Patrick stared at his sister, still not moving.

'Just a good hunch,' she said, not looking entirely displeased with herself. 'I counted on your gullibility. And my certain knowledge that what you told me is just not the way the drug scene works. This bunch who have been conning you, they're not the heavy types. They are the small-timers, the cowards who prey on other people like themselves. People like you are fair game.'

'How do you know all this?'

'Patrick, you'd be amazed at what you get to know when you do my work. A lot of different people need counselling. I get ex-addicts, people who are trying to stay off it. I get their relations, too. They all pour it out. I could write a book about it.'

'Did you have to put me through all that business tonight? I was shitting in my pants.'

'I know you were,' said Flora. 'But I had to make sure they knew that you'd seen their story shot to pieces, don't you understand? Once you knew there was no heroin in that bag they had nothing on you.'

'But what if you had been wrong about the whole thing? If it *had* been heroin? If he had been carrying a gun?'

'Oh, it was always on the cards,' she said, shrugging, 'that I could have been wrong. I didn't think it mattered much.'

'You mean that? We could have been killed!'

'So what, Patrick?' Flora looked at him, challenging. 'Would you and I be much loss to the world?'

He thought it better, on the whole, not to reply.

'Right,' she said, picking up the groceries from the table and packing them back into the Sainsbury's bag. 'That's everything. We'll go to your flat now. I think maybe we had better not hang around here too long, just in case. Let's not ring Simon first, after all. I rather like the idea of helping you get rid of that little bastard, if he's still there. But I guess they will have rung him already, I'll bet you, and he will have moved so fast that he may not have bothered to take too many of your goodies with him, if you're lucky. And tomorrow, I will come with you and we will take all that furniture and stuff back to Bloomfield.'

Chapter Fourteen

It was Wednesday morning. Meg and Ruth had agreed to meet at eleven outside the offices of Asprey, Asprey & Walton in Robert Street. Meg was mildly worried as the time went by and there was no sign of Ruth.

When they had parted company the day before at Gatwick, she had felt curiously reluctant to say goodbye to her companion, and had watched her back view with regret as she disappeared towards the London trains. It had surprised Meg that Ruth should head for London. She had expected to go back with her to Bloomfield. But Ruth, with no explanation, had made it clear that she was not coming. She had accepted some money for her fare, saying, 'I'll pay you back tomorrow.'

So Meg headed alone for home and a change of clothing. They were both still dressed in earth-stained jeans and waxed jackets.

It was not the thought of Bloomfield, but the thought of her clothes there that made Meg change her mind. She got as far as the taxi rank, when suddenly she couldn't face the idea of dressing in those familiar clothes in her old bedroom. Putting them on would be like going back to her self of a month ago, and she no longer wanted to be that person. The thought of the wardrobe in her bedroom was infinitely depressing.

A few minutes later she too was on the station

platform. Ruth had gone, but after a quarter of an hour another London-bound train swept in.

Now, after a night in an hotel following a shopping spree that had made her feel both wicked and well dressed, Meg strolled up and down the pavement near the solicitor's office. She had been satisfied with her reflection in a shop window as she had walked up the Strand.

She looked again at her watch. It was ten past eleven. Ruth was probably unfamiliar with London. She had the address, in writing – surely she would come? A pang of anxiety ran through Meg, and the disturbing thought that perhaps Ruth was about to vanish as mysteriously as she had appeared. Then she remembered the promise to 'pay you back tomorrow' and knew that Ruth would not break her word. She decided to wait no longer.

Upstairs the secretary at the desk greeted her.

'I am a few minutes late, I am afraid,' said Meg.

The girl smiled.

'Please don't worry, Mrs Rokeby-Jones. Mr Asprey said to show you in as soon as you arrived.'

She led the way to his office and opened the door. Smiling, Wilfred Asprey lifted his tall, spare figure from his chair and walked forward, both hands outstretched.

'Meg, how lovely to see you. My goodness! You look – well – wonderful!'

'Dear Will, I feel wonderful. But I am so sorry. I didn't mean to be late. I know how busy you are, and it is awful to keep you waiting.'

'On the contrary, I haven't been waiting. I had another appointment relating to you, at half past ten. She's still here. I think you know my niece, Teresa.'

He gestured past her to a figure sitting in a leather-covered chair near the fireplace. Meg took in the elegant short skirt and blazer, the slim crossed legs and fashionable shoes, almost before she looked into the smiling face. Ruth got to her feet.

'Forgive me,' she said.

'Am I going mad?' said Meg, turning to the solicitor. 'Your niece? Ruth?'

She looked back at her travelling companion.

'What is going on?' she said. 'Is this a joke of some kind?'

'Meg, my dear,' said Wilfred Asprey, 'come and sit down. It was rather cruel, but, childishly, we couldn't resist it. Don't hold it against us.'

He took her hand and led her to a chair.

'I don't know what to think. I didn't recognise you for a minute,' said Meg to Ruth.

'I hardly recognised you, either. You look extremely elegant. I love the trouser suit,' said Ruth, smiling.

'How are you suddenly called Teresa? How do you know each other? How is she your niece?' Meg looked from one to the other.

'Teresa is the daughter of my sister Janet, who married Jamie Ruth. Don't you remember him? We were at university together.'

'I do remember him,' said Meg, still bemused. 'Ruth. I thought it was your Christian name.'

'Well, it did well enough, didn't it?'

'Look,' said Meg, 'it seems to me that there is a lot of explaining to be done before I tell you, Will, why I am here.'

'All right,' he said. 'Shall I kick off, Terry, or will you?'

'You do. It was all your idea, after all.'

Four hours later Meg and Will Asprey were sitting in a quiet corner of a particularly good restaurant just off

Jermyn Street. Their wine glasses were nearly empty, and the coffee was tepid.

'Give me your hand,' said Will, extending his own, palm upward across the table, 'and tell me you forgive me?'

'I can't forgive you, but I do thank you from the bottom of my heart, Will. I feel like a sleeper awoken.'

'I always thought of you as a chrysalis. When you were young, you were a quite enchanting caterpillar, but with that appalling marriage you grew brown and hard, and somehow the butterfly never got out. But here you are now, flapping your wings like mad, and looking dazzling.'

'All these things are relative, Will,' said Meg, laughing. 'Don't overdo it.'

'Meg, you remind me so much of yourself as a girl. No, don't stop me. Of course you don't look quite the same, and God knows I don't, but you have the same vibes, as they say now. And you produce all the same feelings in me.'

'Will,' said Meg, 'be your age. We have both had too much to drink. It makes one too free with one's thoughts, I find.'

'Yes, Terry told me,' said Will.

'How dare she? When?'

'Oh, she used to ring me up every now and then.'

'Yes, she did tend to disappear occasionally,' said Meg. 'If I had known what was going on . . .'

'Thank God you didn't,' said Will soberly. 'I may joke now, but it was deadly serious. It was my last throw, Meg. If Terry couldn't get through to you, I felt there would never be any hope. I had tried to crack that impenetrable carapace of yours too often. It was Terry's idea to make you dig yourself out from the inside.'

'Why did you tell her about me in the first place? You said she is a professional actress.'

'Yes, of course. Resting, as they say. But she is a wise girl. Woman. We have always been quite close, since she was a little girl. She's my goddaughter, you know? I often discuss things with her, and she has known about you for a long time. She read psychology at university, which might have some bearing.'

'A strange way to practise, in buses and bars all over Britain,' said Meg, smiling.

'It was the only way we could think of to hide you from your family, by keeping you on the move,' said Will. 'The problem was to get you out of that bloody house. She had all sorts of contingency plans, but it seems she did it by sheer personality.'

'I wonder if my family looked for me.'

An expression of disdain came over Asprey's face.

'They looked for you, all right. They had a private detective searching for you.'

'I don't believe it! A detective? On my trail? How amazing. I didn't think any of them cared enough,' said Meg. 'Perhaps I have misjudged them. Oh dear.'

'I sincerely doubt it. Their motives are entirely suspect. There's just one, though, that I wonder about. She is an oddity, Flora, isn't she? She rang me yesterday and said a rather strange thing. She said that if I had any idea where you were, or if you got in touch with me, I was not to let her or any of the others know. It was the very opposite of what the rest of them had been saying.'

'I wonder why she said that?' said Meg, wrinkling her brow. 'It is always hard to know what Flora is really thinking. I would not exactly call her "still waters", but she does run deep. I think I may have to get in touch with Flora. But I don't really want to face the others yet.'

'After tomorrow, Meg. We'll go down first to Bloomfield

and check that everything is all right there. After that you can think about Flora and the others.'

The following day they sped towards Sussex in Will Asprey's car, talking as they went.

'Did Ruth – Terry – tell you everything I said?' said Meg apprehensively.

'You mean yesterday? Hardly everything. We only had a little over half an hour together. You and she had over a month. She told me enough, though, to help me understand a lot of what you have been through. She said she thought you would probably tell me the rest, some day.'

'Yes, perhaps, Will. Some day. And I would rather you heard it from me than from Ruth, I think.'

'Did you ever tell her about me, Meg?'

'About you?' Meg hesitated. 'I . . . I referred to my solicitor at some point, yes.'

'No, I don't mean me, your solicitor,' said Will. 'I mean me a long time ago, when we first knew each other.'

Meg paused again.

'I may have, talking about my early life. But not by name. I had no idea, anyway, that she might know your name.'

'She would have been very surprised if you had said my name,' said Will. 'I have never suggested to her that you had been anything but a dear friend.'

'I was not a good friend to you, Will, in those days. I find it all hard to look back on now. Talking to Ruth – oh dear – I can't stop calling her Ruth. Talking to her, telling her things about those days, I was reminded of how I behaved then, and of how you were treated. It was so shameful.'

'No, you didn't treat me badly, Meg. You were firm, and clear. That letter you sent, after I had . . . had told you how I felt about you, do you remember, after that party, that dance in that big house near Steyning? You do remember. I remember every minute of that evening, Meg. The nursery upstairs and the window seat, looking out at the moonlight.'

An unfamiliar heat rose in Meg's face, and she looked away, out of the car window. Surely, she thought, people don't blush, at my age? How very odd.

'I telephoned next day, and they said you weren't in,' Will went on. 'And in the evening, and the next morning. And then the letter came. You could not have made yourself more clear. It was cruel, Meg, but it was not shameful. You were more cruel afterwards, though, when you never answered my letters, even when I was abroad. I only wanted you to write, just newsy letters. The army was not much fun in those days, and it would have been a distraction, at least. I should not be saying all this, dear Meg. I forgave you so long ago.'

Meg could not bring herself to reply for some minutes, and Will did not seem disposed to go on. Eventually she said:

'Thank you for that. That forgiveness, I mean. In fact there was both more and less to forgive than you know. The almost unforgivable thing is that that letter – that awful letter – was not mine. My mother made me write it. She guessed, I suppose, about you. She questioned me, that awful morning, and I told her . . . that I was . . . fond of you. But she made me tell her what we had . . . talked about.'

'You mean, you told her we were engaged?' His voice carried little expression, and he did not look at her.

'I told her. How can I explain it, now, Will? She was so strong, and I . . .' Meg paused again, to recover herself. 'And then, she made me write the letter. She told me what to say, and then she read it and posted it. I have no excuses, I can hardly believe it happened, I only know it did.'

'Are you saying that what that letter said was not what you felt?' Will's voice shook slightly.

'Will you believe me, if I do?' She was pleading for his understanding.

'My God.'

Now it was Will's turn to be silent. And then, 'But my letters from France? You could have answered them, surely?'

'Will, I never saw those letters, not one,' said Meg. 'You must believe me. She got them all. I swear that if you had come, or if I had known you were writing, I would have run away and joined you. I thought of it, but I had no idea where I would go. I had no idea where you were. I thought you had just given up and forgotten me.'

'How do you know then, Meg, about my letters?' It was not said accusingly, but curiously, and partly to hide some emotion.

'My father. You remember my father. He told me, not long before he died. He said he had always been worried about the letters, and he blamed himself for not standing up to my mother about it. I understood – I knew what she was like, and look what she had made me do! I didn't tell Father what he had done, by not helping me. I couldn't do that to him. You see, it was already much too late. It was about two months before Louise was born.'

Will Asprey's speed had slowly dwindled to well below motorway requirement. The hooting of a car behind them in the slow lane reminded him of where they were going, and he speeded up. After a bit, he spoke again.

'The whole story is like a Victorian novel. It doesn't seem credible.'

'No,' said Meg, 'but it happened, and there is no undoing it. But in the end, Will, you were all right, weren't you?'

'Of course. More than all right. Jeannie and I were very happy, and I am sure, at least I think I am, that she never knew that she only had half of me.'

'You mean I still had the other half, after the way I treated you?' Meg was incredulous.

'Of course that's what I mean,' said Will. 'And after Jeannie died, there was more available. Only there was no getting through to you. You had shut all the doors and battened down the hatches. I was just your solicitor, and lucky to have that contact, I suppose.'

'You have been wonderful as my solicitor, Will. Such a relief to have an adult human being to talk to occasionally. And I am so glad you are going to help me over Bloomfield.'

'Meg,' said Will gently, but not taking his eyes off the road, 'don't change the subject. I said you have always had half of me, but you can still have it all, for what it's worth, if you want it. It's a bit creased, now, and part worn, and some of it is obsolete, but it is still prepared to be totally devoted to you.'

'Will,' said Meg, 'you are the most amazing man. I don't know if I am understanding what you are saying.'

Spotting a slip-road not far ahead, Will pulled off the motorway and parked under a tree on a grass verge. He then spent some little time explaining more precisely what he had been saying. As a solicitor, he believed in clarity.

They drove on southwards towards the coast.

Will Asprey became aware that Meg was less comfortable as they neared the South Downs. She was silent and thoughtful.

241

'Dearest Meg, something's worrying you, isn't it?' he said, placing his hand over hers as it lay on her knee.

'It's the thought of everything that has to be faced,' she said.

'Meg, there is nothing to be faced at the moment. I will be with you at Bloomfield. We collect your suitcase, anything you need, and then away. I am making arrangements for the house, so you don't have to worry about that.'

'Don't take over, Will,' said Meg emphatically. Then, more gently, 'I have allowed other people to run my life for too long. I know you mean it kindly, but I must act for myself now. I mustn't fall into the same trap again, even with you.'

'All right. Forgive me,' said Will. 'I do understand. But share your worries, won't you? That's something else you have to learn. After all, I am your solicitor.'

'Sharing,' said Meg, 'is something I am only slowly getting used to. But since you ask, I am not looking forward to getting back to Bloomfield, for fear of – I hardly know how to put it – for fear of being infected by it, I think. To use your butterfly analogy, I don't think my new wings are quite dry yet – not strong enough to carry me away from it all. And I am dreading contacting the family, because of, well, memories of what they can do to me. Families have a strange hold. Call it nature, whatever you like, but it is hard just to turn your back on them, even when they are more than grown-up. At the moment, I still feel clear and free. You know, Will, when we were in Shetland, in Lerwick, we saw some men by the waterfront, working on an upturned fishing boat. Careening, isn't that what it's called? They were scrubbing and scraping the hull, getting off all the barnacles and seaweed growing on the wood. We talked to one of them, and he said it all accumulated over years, and it slowed the boat, and made it more and more incapable of manoeuvring in the water. It has to be cleaned off so that the boat can move freely again.

'Well, that's what has happened to me, Will: I've been careened, and given a new coat of paint. I am now scared of going back into the water. I know those barnacles are waiting to attach themselves again, because that is what happens. And bit by bit they could get me back into the state I was in before.'

'One moment a butterfly, next moment a boat,' said Will, laughing. 'Guess who's in a muddle. Listen, Meg, it needn't happen. I've told you what you can do to stop it.'

'Yes, I know, dear Will. I am not going to let it happen. I have the strength, now, for that. But I have to face up to the fact that I cannot totally run away from my old life. Perhaps my sense of impotent subjection has gone, but even you wouldn't totally remove any sense of duty.'

'Who do you owe any duty to, for goodness' sake?' The indignation was plain in Will's voice.

'And to think you used to correct *my* grammar. You're slipping, Will Asprey. Well, for instance, to Flora. I don't feel responsible for what the others have managed to become, but I do feel guilty about Flora. I owe her a debt. She is the only one who ever tried to save me, to show me what was happening to me, and I shut the door in her face.'

'I am afraid this is something I am not going to be able to help you with.'

'No, not really. But you do help, Will, so much, just by being there.'

They drove slowly on to the gravel in front of Bloomfield, and sat in the car looking up at the house.

'I never liked it much,' said Will, 'even in the early days.'

'Well, that's a relief,' said Meg, 'because neither did I. It was my mother who persuaded my father to buy it. Her status symbol, I suppose. He used to take me walking on the Downs, and I always felt his spirits rise as he got further from the house. We would walk for miles. All day, sometimes.'

'Should we go in, and get it over?'

Meg found her key, and they went into the hall.

'What a strange smell. Do you smell it?' she said. And then, 'There's someone here.'

'Are you sure?' said Will.

'Hush. Listen.'

There was no sound, at first. Then they heard a creak from above. They looked up the staircase, and saw Flora standing at the top of the second flight, staring down at them.

'I thought you were burglars,' she said, not moving.

'We thought *you* were burglars,' said Meg, waiting. 'Hello.'

'Hello,' said Flora. She did not look at Will, only at her mother.

She walked slowly down the stairs and stood facing Meg.

'You remember Will Asprey?'

'Yes,' said Flora. 'Why are you here, Mother? I hoped you wouldn't come back.'

'You hoped . . .?' said Meg, unsure of herself.

'I hoped you had got away.'

Meg stared at her for a moment.

'I have got away,' she said. 'I am not coming back. I am selling Bloomfield.'

Flora turned abruptly. She stood for a moment with her back to them, and then walked out of the front door.

'Wait there, Will. Don't come,' said Meg quietly.

She followed her daughter down the overgrown gravel path through the garden, and joined her as she stood by the stream, gazing into the water. Despite the sunlight a fringe of ice still hung on the weeds in the shade at the far side.

'That's where Sherry went in,' said Meg. 'It seems such a long time ago.'

'A long time ago . . .' echoed Flora.

'Why are you here, Flora?'

'A lot of things have happened, since you left. Things that probably would not have happened if you had been here.'

'To you? Happened to you?'

'To the others, mostly,' said Flora, 'But we all affect each other. There is a sort of web that holds us all together. It has been a strange time. In the end, I had to come down, to see if I could face myself here. I hate this place so much.'

'I know.'

Flora glanced at her, and then away again.

'I thought I could, you know, exorcise it, if I stayed here for a night or two. At least I might find out if it was the house, or you, or Father, or just myself that I hate.'

'Have you?'

'Well, it's not you,' said Flora.

'I'm glad.'

They walked along in silence for some moments.

'You know I tried to burn it down?'

'Bloomfield? When?'

'While you were away. Last weekend.'

'That smell,' said Meg, nodding. 'And your hands. I noticed.'

'They're all right.'

'Perhaps you should have tried harder.'

Flora stopped, and turned to Meg, looking her straight in the eyes, in a way, Meg realised, that she had not done for years. Suddenly Flora smiled.

'What has happened to you, Mother? For a start, you look completely different.'

Meg put her hand to her head.

'No,' said Flora, 'not just the hair, everything about you. You look years younger. And you talk differently.'

'Do I? I know I have changed, or reverted, perhaps. But I didn't know it was quite so obvious.'

'Mother. Have you really got away?'

Her mother nodded.

'I really think I have.'

She walked on, and Flora stayed by her side.

'I thought you might. It was that woman, wasn't it?'

Meg nodded again.

'She's not at all what you think, Flora, not at all.'

'I wondered,' said Flora.

'In some ways,' said Meg, 'she is not unlike you, and I think you would like her. I owe her a great deal. There's too much to go into, Flora, and it's all too soon. Some day, perhaps.'

'I don't need to know. Just to see you clear of all this is enough for the moment.'

'You rang Will and told him not to let you all know if I turned up. You were trying to help me, Flora, weren't you?'

Flora nodded.

'In a way. But it was self-interest as well. I had suddenly begun to realise what you were doing, and it could all come to nothing if they found you. You're the key, you see. Perhaps if you can get free of it all, I can too. You are selling the house?'

She looked at her mother, who smiled back at her.
'As soon as I can.'

'We don't need any money.' There was a note of anxiety in Flora's voice. 'The others and me. Please don't give any of us any money.'

'I wasn't planning to; not at the moment.'

'Good,' said Flora, with audible relief. 'That is the only way you can help us. And we all need help, God knows. But not that kind of help, and not from you.'

'I know.' Meg sighed, her breath hanging in the frosty air. 'Flora, I'm sorry.'

'For what?'

'For everything that happened.' She knew she did not need to be specific.

'Then, you mean?' asked Flora

'Oh, yes. Then. Perhaps if we had been able to talk, then . . . I wouldn't feel so guilty now.'

'I don't know if we could have talked, not the way I was then. Not the way you were. Perhaps. But I don't think so. I couldn't forgive you for being the victim. And I have never been able to forgive myself for deserting you. I have thought so much about it since I have been here.'

'We will talk, some day,' said Meg, with one awkward hand on her daughter's shoulder. 'When we are more used to each other.'

Reaching the end of the path, they turned and looked at the house. It seemed curiously harmless in the distance. They walked back towards it as a pair, both feeling a new sense of assurance.

'Will you come and meet Will properly?' said Meg. 'You really don't know him. He told me about your visit.'

'He looks different today. Is he different?'

'Come and meet him and find out for yourself.'

Will Asprey was sitting in the kitchen. He looked up, and pushed away the glass of wine he had been drinking.

'I raided your drinks cupboard,' he said.

'What a good idea,' said Meg. 'Will you pour some for Flora and me, too?'

Will looked relieved.

'All right?' he said.

Meg nodded and smiled at him.

Handing Flora her glass, he said:

'I am sorry I was rather obstructive last time we met.'

'Obstructive?' said Flora. 'You were like a character actor in a play.'

'Well, it was a bit of an act,' Will said. 'I thought I was quite good.'

'You were amazing,' said Flora, smiling at him for the first time. 'I am glad that's not what you are really like. I don't think I could take it for long.'

'Flora, my dear,' said Meg, 'I am so very glad you were here, and for more reasons than one. May I use you? Will you do something for me?'

Flora nodded.

'I am going to write to all the others, and tell them I am back. But will you explain to them that the furniture is going into storage for the time being, and that I am putting the house on the market? It will be in the hands of Will's firm, so there will be nothing for any of you to do. I will tell them in my letters that Will and I are going away for a while.'

'You and Mr Asprey?' Flora looked from one to the other.

Meg looked down.

'Your mother,' said Will, trying not to smile, and failing, 'has agreed to continue with an arrangement

248

that we made a very long time ago . . .'

'Not immediately, Will,' interrupted Meg, laughing.

'No, all right, not at once,' said Will. 'We are going on a long holiday together first, to see how it feels. Your mother appears to want to go virtually round the world. She has developed a wanderlust.'

'Muckle Flugga to you, Will Asprey,' said Meg.

Flora was looking from one to the other, in smiling disbelief.

'She deserves it,' she said. 'And I really mean this, I hope it feels absolutely wonderful.'

'Terry? We're at the airport. We just wanted to say good-bye. We've only got ten pence, so it's a quick one.'

'Nice of you, Will. Have a great time!'

'And thank you. We both want to say thank you, just once more.'

'As long as you understand that I am responsible for nothing that happens from now on. I wash my hands of you both.'

'I don't blame you. What are you going to do?'

'Me?' said Terry. 'Well, after what you have told me, and as I've still got some time on my hands, I thought I might go and see Flora . . .'

And she was cut short as the money ran out.

A selection of quality fiction from Headline

THE POSSESSION OF DELIA SUTHERLAND	Barbara Neil	£5.99 ☐
MANROOT	A N Steinberg	£5.99 ☐
CARRY ME LIKE WATER	Benjamin Alire Sáenz	£6.99 ☐
KEEPING UP WITH MAGDA	Isla Dewar	£5.99 ☐
AN IMPERFECT MARRIAGE	Tim Waterstone	£5.99 ☐
NEVER FAR FROM NOWHERE	Andrea Levy	£5.99 ☐
SEASON OF INNOCENTS	Carolyn Haines	£5.99 ☐
OTHER WOMEN	Margaret Bacon	£5.99 ☐
THE JOURNEY IN	Joss Kingsnorth	£5.99 ☐
FIFTY WAYS OF SAYING FABULOUS	Graeme Aitken	£5.99 ☐

All Headline books are available at your local bookshop or newsagent, or can be ordered direct from the publisher. Just tick the titles you want and fill in the form below. Prices and availability subject to change without notice.

Headline Book Publishing, Cash Sales Department, Bookpoint, 39 Milton Park, Abingdon, OXON, OX14 4TD, UK. If you have a credit card you may order by telephone – 01235 400400.

Please enclose a cheque or postal order made payable to Bookpoint Ltd to the value of the cover price and allow the following for postage and packing:

UK & BFPO: £1.00 for the first book, 50p for the second book and 30p for each additional book ordered up to a maximum charge of £3.00.
OVERSEAS & EIRE: £2.00 for the first book, £1.00 for the second book and 50p for each additional book.

Name ....

Address ....

....

....

If you would prefer to pay by credit card, please complete:
Please debit my Visa/Access/Diner's Card/American Express (delete as applicable) card no:

Signature .... Expiry Date ....